DEAD IN THE DOG

DEAD IN THE DOG

Bernard Knight

severn
House

This first world edition published 2012
in Great Britain and in the USA by
SEVERN HOUSE PUBLISHERS LTD of
9–15 High Street, Sutton, Surrey, England, SM1 1DF.
Trade paperback edition first published
in Great Britain and the USA 2012 by
SEVERN HOUSE PUBLISHERS LTD

British Library Cataloguing in Publication Data

Knight, Bernard.
  Dead in the dog.
  1. Pathologists–Fiction. 2. Singapore–Social
  conditions–20th century–Fiction. 3. Detective and
  mystery stories.
  I. Title
  823.9'14-dc23

ISBN-13: 978-0-7278-8161-8 (cased)
ISBN-13: 978-1-84751-424-0 (trade paper)

All Severn House titles are printed on acid-free paper.

Severn House Publishers support the Forest Stewardship Council [FSC], the
leading international forest certification organisation. All our titles that are printed
on Greenpeace-approved FSC-certified paper carry the FSC logo.

MIX
Paper from
responsible sources
FSC
www.fsc.org   FSC® C018575

Typeset by Palimpsest Book Production Ltd.,
Falkirk, Stirlingshire, Scotland.
Printed and bound in Great Britain by
MPG Books Ltd., Bodmin, Cornwall.

AUTHOR'S NOTE

None of the characters portrayed existed in real life and every effort has been made to avoid suggesting the identity of people who were in North Malaya in the nineteen-fifties. In particular, the portrayal of characters in the Armed Forces, especially the Royal Army Medical Corps and Queen Alexandra's Royal Army Nursing Corps, is utterly fictitious. The three years the author spent there as an Army doctor were the most interesting of his whole career, but none of the events in this novel actually took place. However, he hopes that he has captured some of the ambience of the last years of the British military presence in that fascinating country.

The campaign against the Communist Chinese insurgents led by Chin Peng, in which 519 British and over 1,300 Malayan troops and police lost their lives, was one of the longest on record, lasting from 1948 until 1960. It was also the only successful one, thanks to the painstaking efforts of British and Commonwealth forces in fighting the terrorists virtually hand-to-hand in the jungle. Yet in spite of more than a decade of strife, few now remember this vicious 'Forgotten War', without which modern Malaysia would not exist.

The Federation of Malaya was not known as 'Malaysia' until 1963 and place names are given here as they were in the nineteen fifties – 'Melaka' was 'Malacca', 'Pulau Pinang' was 'Penang' and so on.

PROLOGUE

T he shoe flew across the room, its high heel catching
James hard on the side of his neck, leaving a red mark
on the skin.

'You bitch, what d'you think you're doing!'

With a roar he launched himself at his wife and caught
her a resounding smack across the face that made her teeth
rattle. James was a big, powerful man and the imprint of
his fingers immediately began to appear across her cheek.
But Diane was a woman of spirit and instead of collapsing
into a sobbing heap on the rattan settee, she hopped on her
one bare foot, trying to pull off the other shoe to throw
at him.

'Bastard! You dirty, rotten bastard!' she screamed. 'I'll tell
Douglas! I will, this time!'

To avoid more shoe-throwing, he grabbed her bodily and
threw her down on to the cushions.

'Look, cut it out, you silly fool! I doubt it'll be any surprise
to Douglas, so you can save your breath.'

Suddenly aware that she had no chance against his physical
strength, Diane began to cry, though they were more sobs of
frustrated rage than real distress. She held a hand to her face,
which was stinging from his blow.

'I'll have a bruise there now, you swine!' she blubbered.
'Everyone at The Dog will know that you've been knocking
me about again.'

'Then put some more Max Factor over it, you daft cow!
You wear so much, a bit more won't be noticed!'

He turned and stalked out of the lounge on to the verandah
of the bungalow, then clattered down the steps outside. She
heard a car door slam, then the Buick started up and with

an angry roar, accelerated away with a crunching of gravel. The blonde rocked back and forth on the settee, hissing through the fingers that were held across her aching cheek.

'You bastard, one of these days, I'll kill you!'

ONE

He was hot, tired and slightly bewildered. His fibre suitcase, lashed with a strap that had once been his father's belt, was in the back of the Land Rover. Alongside it was the new holdall that he had bought in Singapore to carry the overflow of his belongings. They said that the cabin-trunk he had packed so carefully in Gateshead wouldn't arrive for another six weeks.

Tom had come by air-trooping, four days' flight from Stansted Airport, cooped up in a Handley-Page Hermes that seemed only slightly faster than the Wright Flyer. His heavy baggage was allegedly on its way by sea, but as he slumped in the passenger seat of the olive-green vehicle, he had his doubts whether he'd ever see the trunk again.

Tom Howden was a pessimist by nature, as he had learned that it was the best way to avoid disappointment. Still, as he was going to be stuck out here for years, he supposed he had to make the best of it. He wondered for the hundredth time, what temporary insanity had led him to sign on for three years, when he could have got away with two as a National Serviceman? Was an extra pip on the shoulder, better pay and the promise of a three hundred quid gratuity at the end, worth another twelve months in this saturated sweat-box?

With a resigned grunt, he shook off the mood of near desperation and forced himself to look at the scenery – though already he had decided that one Malayan road looked much the same as the next. All bloody trees, thatched huts, scruffy shophouses and fields that looked like rectangular swamps.

The driver was a skinny lance corporal in a faded jungle-green uniform that looked as if it had been tailored for a Sumo wrestler. He took a covert look at the officer alongside and with the smug euphoria of someone who was only three weeks away from his 'RHE' – *Return Home Establishment* – date, he diagnosed a new recruit to Her Majesty's Far East Land Forces. He saw a sturdy, almost squat young man with a round, plain face sporting a few old acne scars. It was a face that seemed to glare out at the world as if defying it to do its worst, with a downturned mouth and a brow too furrowed for someone in his mid-twenties. The corporal, a philosophical Cockney with an abiding curiosity about his fellow men, reckoned that this officer was a 'prole' like himself, different from the usual toffee-nosed, chinless wonders from the Garrison. But then, he wasn't a proper officer, was he? He was an MO, according to the brass RAMC tabs on his shoulders.

'Train a bit late, sir? They're usually pretty good out here.'

The doctor jerked himself out of his weary reverie.

'On time leaving Kuala Lumpur. Then one of those tortoise things broke down and delayed us.'

The driver nodded sagely. Those 'tortoise things' were armoured railcars that ran ahead of the trains, escorting them through the Black Areas on the long run up from Singapore.

'They've been very quiet lately, the CTs,' chirped the soldier.

'The what?' grunted the new arrival.

Gord, a right one here! thought the driver. Needs to get his knees brown pretty quick.

'CTs, sir,' he said aloud. 'The communist terrorists. That's why we're all out here, innit?'

He stole another look at his passenger, taking in the new green bush jacket and shorts, tailored in one day in Singapore. Though they were all issued with ill-fitting rags at their Depot near Aldershot, he knew that officers were supposed to look smart and had to cough up for tailor-mades at their own expense.

'How much further is it?' grunted Howden, lifting his new cap to rub off the sweat that had gathered under the leather hatband. The Londoner managed to decipher the marked Geordie accent.

'Another six miles, sir. It's a twelve-mile run from Sungei Siput railway station to the gates of Brigade – and BMH is slap next door.'

Howden was beginning to accept that the Army ran on acronyms and 'BMH' now held no mystery for him, though he thought it could just as well stand for 'Bloody Miserably Hot' as for 'British Military Hospital'.

The road began to climb gently from the flat plain that stretched for many miles back to the sea and the new doctor began to take more interest as the hills and high mountains of Perak State rose in front of them. The road this far had been fairly straight, running on causeways built a few feet above padi fields and banana plantations, but now it started to curve in repetitive bends as it passed between low hills. Regimented rows of rubber trees lined the road, all decorated with parallel diagonal scars running down to little pots to catch the latex. As he passed, Howden could see the rows were ruler-straight, millions of the slim trunks marching away from the road to cover thousands of acres, providing the world with the rubber for everything from bus tyres to condoms. Small houses roofed with *attap*, a palm-leaf thatch, or with red-painted corrugated iron, were scattered alongside the road, with grinning urchins, some stark naked, playing in the muddy water in the ditches outside. To someone brought up in the terraces and council estates of Tyneside, it was still as strange as the planet Mars, even though Tom had spent three days on Singapore Island and travelled almost the whole length of the Malayan Peninsula to get here.

'First time in the East, sir?' persisted the corporal.

'First time out of bloody England,' growled Howden. He preferred to forget the trip to Lille with the Newcastle Medicals' rugby team in 'forty-nine, when they were beaten thirty-six to five.

There was silence for another mile and the doctor felt he should say something to avoid being thought snooty.

'You from the hospital as well?'

'Nossir, I'm Service Corps, from the Transport Pool in the garrison. Don't do no soldiering, thank Christ! Not like them poor sods in the battalions.'

Tom Howden thought it was an opportunity to find out more about the place that was to be his home for most of the next three years – unless the mysterious ways of the Royal Army

Medical Corps found somewhere even more obscure to send him. His knowledge of the military machine was rudimentary, as six weeks' basic training in Britain had only taught him how to march badly, miss every target with a revolver and learn a little about intestinal parasites and numerous types of tropical lurgy.

'What's this Brigade you talk about, then?'

The driver sighed under his breath. They shouldn't let virgins like this out alone, he thought.

'You're part of it now, sir!' He squinted at the pristine green oblong sewn on to his passenger's sleeve, portraying a yellow lion alongside a palm tree.

'That dog-and-lampost flash'll have to come off pretty quick, sir. Your CO will spit tacks if he sees it. That's Singapore Base District, but we're Twenty-First Commonwealth Independent Infantry Brigade. Different flash altogether – you need one like mine.'

Tom looked at the dhobi-faded patch on the corporal's uniform – a blue shield and crossed red swords below the figures '21'.

'Is the hospital part of that, then?' he asked dubiously.

'Well, you've got your own CO, a half-colonel. Queer bugger, he is too . . . oh, sorry sir!' The driver had the grace to look sheepish at his gaffe. 'But the big chief is the Brigadier, runs the whole outfit.'

The explanation was cut short as the Land Rover rounded a bend and came into a village, where they were forced to crawl along behind an ox-cart heaped with dried palm fronds for roofing. The driver swerved to avoid mangy pi-dogs, men on high bicycles, wandering chickens and assorted children scattered across the road. Ramshackle stalls selling fruit and Coca-Cola stood on the beaten earth in front of a few two-storied shophouses, from which taped Chinese pop songs blared out at ear-splitting volume. Malay girls in *sarong-kerbayahs*, colourful tunics over long skirts, swayed gracefully through the hubbub, resisting the raucous invitations of the shopkeepers to buy tin alarm clocks, dried fish or plastic toys. A dilapidated bus was coming the other way and they were forced to stop for a moment behind a grimy truck, from which several emaciated men were unloading heavy sacks of rice. Across the tailboard large Chinese characters were painted and underneath, Tom read a presumed translation in Roman lettering proclaiming the owner to be *'Wun Fat Tit'*, which left him wondering if it could possibly be true or was just some oriental leg-pull.

As the bus passed, blaring its horn raucously and belching black diesel smoke, the Land Rover pulled out, but almost immediately, the driver had to brake to avoid a Chinese woman wearing a *samfu*, a kind of floral pyjamas, leading a skinny cow on a length of rope.

'This is Kampong Kerdah, sir, the last village before our place. Tanah Timah is a proper town, not like this 'ere dump,' said the soldier, with an almost proprietorial air.

As Howden was thinking that most places in Malaya seemed to have alliterative names, the driver twisted the wheel again and squeezed past the ox cart and accelerated out of the village on to more curves between more rubber estates.

'Where's this road go to?' he asked.

'It forks at Tanah Timah – or 'TT' as everyone calls it. Straight on it goes up a few miles to Kampong Jalong, then fizzles out against the mountains. Big buggers they are, some go up to six thousand feet. The other track just goes through the rubber up past Gunong Besar, with a village at the end called Kampong Kerbau. Damn-all beyond that for 'undreds of miles across the jungle and mountains, until you hit the China Sea. All Black Area that, real bandit country, very nasty!'

He said this with morbid glee, as if he had daily experience of hunting terrorists, though in fact he had never heard a single shot fired in anger during his two years up at this 'sharp end' of the campaign.

'Is this a Black Area?' Howden looked uneasily at the deserted plantations, where the rubber trees stood in endless ranks, reminding him of the war graves he had seen on his rugby trip to Flanders.

'Nossir, but this White Area stops just beyond TT. If it was Black here, we wouldn't be allowed out without an escort – and have to carry a weapon.'

He bent his head towards the officer as if to impart some great secret.

'Best not to carry a pistol, sir. You only get a ticking off for not having one, but if you lose the bloody thing, it's a court martial.'

Tom had no intention of carrying anything more lethal than a syringe, especially as Aldershot had proved that he could barely hit a house at ten paces. The vehicle suddenly slowed to a stop and he looked around in alarm.

'Just thought you'd like to see the view, sir,' reassured the corporal. He leaned on his steering wheel and pointed through the windscreen.

'That's TT down there, you can see the garrison and BMH next to it.'

Howden saw that they had stopped at the crest of a hill and were looking down on a bowl-shaped area a couple of miles across. It was open on the left where a broad valley went back towards the railway and the far distant sea. On the right, above the rubber estates, green jungle-covered hills climbed towards remote blue mountains, their tops wreathed in clouds. Below, the road snaked down for another mile to a small town, little more than a main street with a few parallel lanes of buildings. A little further on, there was a large rectangular complex of huts and other buildings, with many vehicles parked in rows, the sun glistening on their windscreens. Next to it was a smaller compound with more regular lines of low buildings, which the doctor took to be the hospital.

'Dead flat down there, sir. It used to be a tin mine, before the Army bulldozed it to build the garrison.'

It was almost like an aerial view or a map and Tom was intrigued by the geography of what was to be his home for the foreseeable future. He saw that the road that passed through Tanah Timah forked at the further end of the main street. The left branch crossed a small bridge over a brown river that ran behind the little town, then climbed a rise on the other side of the valley before vanishing into the ubiquitous rubber. Just beyond the bridge was a large bungalow-style building, perched on a grassy mound. It had a wide green-painted tin roof and there was a tennis-court and a small swimming pool behind it.

'What's that place – the school?'

'Nah, that's 'The Dog', sir. It's the posh club, white planters and officers only. They don't let no wogs in there – nor ORs like me.'

Howden's meagre stock of Army lore told him that ORs were 'Other Ranks', but 'The Dog' was beyond him. He asked his driver, but the corporal shrugged.

'Search me, sir! I think the proper name's the Sussex Club.' He pointed again, this time slightly to the left.

'Alongside them big hills in the distance, there's another valley, see? It's all Black country, goes up to Chenderoh Dam and a lake. The road goes all the way to Grik and the Siamese border, they say, but it's bloody dangerous up there. Chin Peng himself hangs out in that area.'

Tom twisted further to his left, looking at more mountains on the other side of the flat plain below. 'What's over there, then?'

'That's Maxwell Hill, above Taiping. Decent town, is that. Another hospital there, BMH Kamunting, bigger than this one here. I drives a truck up there now and then, for stores and stuff.'

He decided that sightseeing was over and coasted down the long hill towards TT, his passenger looking sideways at the changing vegetation as the rubber gave way to oil palm and then bananas, before the rice padi appeared again on the flat land at the bottom. Black water buffalo trudged through the mud pulling crude ploughs, thin farmers urging them on from behind. Women in colourful sarongs and head cloths stood up to their knees in water, planting rice seedlings. As the Land Rover passed, they giggled and quickly turned their faces away in case a camera should appear.

As they came downhill, a long convoy of green military vehicles passed them in the opposite direction, three-tonners and Land Rovers grinding up the slope, shepherded by armoured cars in front and behind. As they passed, Tom saw scores of soldiers sitting in the trucks, some wearing bush hats with one side of the brim turned up.

'What's all that about?'

The driver shrugged nonchalantly. 'Going off on a sweep

of the "ulu" to chase out some of the little yellow sods. Some of those in the TCVs were Aussies.'

The Tynesider knew what Aussies were, but it was another day or so before he added 'Troop Carrying Vehicle' to his list of acronyms. 'God knows what "ulu" might be,' he muttered to himself.

As they approached some buildings, the corporal pointed ahead.

'Here's the town, sir. Don't blink or you'll miss it!'

Tanah Timah was about four hundred yards long, a straight wide road lined on each side by 'shophouses', two-storied terraces of sun-bleached cement. The upper floors overhung a continuous arcade supported by pillars, known as the 'five-foot way' behind which were a multitude of colourful shops, selling everything from refrigerators to Nescafé, from paraffin stoves to rolls of silk brocade. Some were work-shops and the glare of welding and the hammering of bicycle repairs spilled out into the arcades and across the ramps that crossed the deep monsoon drains that fronted the buildings.

There were people everywhere – old ladies squatting behind piles of fruit for sale, men chopping firewood, girls selling fried rice from huge woks, cobblers sitting cross-legged at their lasts and shoppers and loungers wandering across the road, oblivious of the traffic. Bicycle trishaws carried gaily dressed Malay women holding up paper umbrellas against the sun and barefoot labourers pushed bikes piled high with green fodder or crates of live ducks. Ungainly local trucks belched fumes, competing in noise and pollution with the battered bus that came up from Sungei Siput three times a day. An occasional green Army vehicle passed through, but the town seemed to be ignoring the fact that they were on the edge of a vicious terrorist war that had been going on for years.

As his driver had warned, they passed through the town in less than two minutes and as the shops ended, the new arrival saw the side turning off to the left, leading towards the bridge and the mysterious 'Dog'. Facing the road junction was a solid-looking building, freshly painted in white, with radio aerials on the roof. It was set in a compound behind a high perimeter wall topped by a barbed-wire fence. A barrier at the entrance was guarded by a Malay in a smart khaki uniform, with a black peaked cap and a pistol holstered on his belt.

'That's the Police Circle HQ – dunno why they call it a Circle, but they always do,' volunteered his oracle.

Another half mile along the dead flat road brought them alongside what seemed to be a huge Mississippi riverboat made from rusted corrugated iron. It was sitting forlornly in a few feet of dirty water, which appeared to be the remnants of a dried-up lake.

'What the hell's that?' asked Howden.

'The old tin dredge, that is. Abandoned after the Japs came. Like I said, the garrison and hospital are built on the old tin tailings. And here we are, sir.'

Not far beyond the dredge, on the left side of the dead straight road, Tom saw the corner of a formidable fence. A double line of ten-foot high chain-link formed two barriers, with coiled barbed wire in the space between. A large square of about fifty acres was filled with barrack huts, low brick buildings, workshops, vehicle shelters and at the back, some houses and a few bungalows. As they drove along the front, separated from the road only by a deep monsoon drain, they passed the main gate, made of steel bars. It was open, but a counter-weighted pole barred the entrance, outside a fortified guardroom where two red-capped Military Police stood scowling at the world.

'Bastards, they are!' muttered the corporal under his breath, obviously giving vent to some private hatred. Things were much more relaxed at the next gate, another three hundred yards down the road. The double fence continued around the smaller hospital compound and a similar gate stood open in the centre, also with a striped pole across the entrance. A lance corporal in a navy-blue beret and white-Blancoed belt stood outside a small guardroom, a rifle clutched in one hand, the stock resting on his boot. Tom half-expected a challenge, with a 'Halt, who goes there?' and a demand for their identity cards. Instead, the sentinel leaned on the counterweight, lifted the pole and as the Land Rover passed, raised a derisory two fingers at the driver.

'Up yours, Fred!' yelled the cockney and accelerated into the front vehicle park, turned right in front of the Admin huts and then sharp left on to the perimeter road that ran all around the hospital compound. The new doctor had a blurred view of a series of long huts that seemed to come off a central open corridor, like ribs from a spine. On the other side of the road, next to the outer fence, was a barrack block, then a series of smaller buildings before an open space appeared where a camouflaged Whirlwind helicopter was waiting. Some distance beyond this, standing lonely and isolated in the furthest corner of the compound, were two parallel asbestos-roofed huts, joined at the near end by a short open corridor, forming a 'U'. Wide eaves projected from each building, supported on wooden pillars to form austere verandahs. A series of louvred doors down the sides of the huts had been painted green, now bleached by the sun. Some sparse grass formed a central lawn between the two buildings and, around the entrance, some scraggy flowering plants tried to survive amongst the gravel of the tin tailings. A short path led from the road to the concrete strip beneath the cross-corridor and alongside it was a faded wooden sign bearing the legend 'RAMC OFFICERS' MESS' in the Corps colours of blue, yellow and cherry red.

The Land Rover jerked to a stop.

'Here we are, sir. Home sweet home!' sang out the driver.

He hopped around to the back and took out the officer's two bags which he dumped on the concrete. Tom Howden climbed out more slowly and looked with dismay at his new domicile. It looked more like a chicken farm set down in a desert, than the residence of holders of the Queen's Commission. As the corporal passed him on the path, he gave a salute worthy of the Grenadier Guards.

'Best of luck, sir!'

As the doctor hesitantly touched his cap in return, he was conscious of the sweat-blackened areas of fabric under his arms and over the whole of his back. He heard the vehicle roar away behind him, but kept his eyes fixed on the deserted huts, a feeling of almost desperate loneliness engulfing him.

As Tom Howden was staring despondently at his new home, Diane Robertson sat alone in hers, the late afternoon sun striking through the open doors. The silence was broken only by her sniffs of petulant self-pity, until a small voice asked, 'Mem want anything now?'

The face of her *amah*, Lee Mei Mei, appeared timorously around the door to the dining room, half scared, half intrigued by the domestic dramas that were becoming more frequent in the Robertson household. Mei was a slight, fragile Chinese girl of twenty, with an elfin face that always looked slightly startled. Her glossy black hair was pulled back into a ponytail held with a rubber band, the end hanging down the back of her blue floral pyjama suit.

'Yes, May. Tell Siva to bring me a stinger, will you? A large one.'

Diane sat alone in the wide, lofty room, the big brass fan whirling slowly over her head, trying to waft the cloying air into a draught. She thought of Norfolk now, at the beginning of December, cold and perhaps wet, but not with the all-pervading dampness they had here, where there was an electric light bulb in every wardrobe to keep the mould off the shoes and where the camera had to be kept in a sealed biscuit tin with a bag of silica gel.

She wished to God she had stayed in England and not been seduced by both James's body and his glowing descriptions of life on a Malayan rubber estate. Twenty-six years old, she was the third daughter of a minor squire from Norfolk, rejoicing in the name of Henry Blessington-Luke. After an expensive and largely wasted education at Cheltenham, she had done little but ride, party and hunt for both foxes and a husband. Three years earlier, at a Hunt Ball near Newmarket, she had met James Robertson, home on leave – and three months later, had married him in the cathedral in Singapore.

The bastard! She gingerly touched her face again and

wondered how well she could cover up any marks by tomorrow night, when there was the weekly dance at The Dog.

A slim Tamil came in through the dining room, carrying a tray bearing a bottle of Johnnie Walker, a tumbler and a jug of iced water.

'A big one, Siva,' she murmured, still shielding one side of her face with a scarlet-nailed hand, though the *amah* had already given him a blow-by-blow account of the fracas. He poured a liberal shot of whisky into the glass and added an equal amount of water – the famous 'stinger' was a corruption of the Malay '*stengah*', meaning 'half'.

He lowered the tray for her to take the glass, but she gestured to a small table at the end of the settee. 'Leave it, Siva. I may want another.'

He put the tray down and stepped back.

'Mem want anything else? Sandwich, curry puff?'

She shook her head, managing to give him a wan smile. He was a good-looking fellow of about her own age – but of course, he was Indian. Not that that seemed to bother her bloody husband!

The cook-cum-butler padded silently to the door but stopped there to throw a look back at the woman sipping her drink. Though he considered her no more attractive than most of the sleek girls of his own race, the contrast between their dark beauty and her startling blondeness always intrigued him. Slim but full-breasted, her long pale neck was framed by the silky swathe of hair the colour of light honey that came down to her shoulders. He knew that some English women got their colour from a bottle, but this was surely natural. With a little sigh at such forbidden fruit, he padded off to his kitchen hut behind the house, to sit over a cup of tea with the *amah* and gossip about the latest domestic developments at Gunong Besar Estate.

On the settee, the blonde drank her first stinger quickly and poured herself a stronger one. She lifted her shapely legs up on to the cushions and leaned back against one of the padded arms, cradling the drink in her hands. Her temper had cooled, but it was replaced by a steely determination to do the swine down as effectively as she could.

'Two can play at that game,' she whispered to herself, then smiled into her whisky. The game had already started, though James didn't know it. She didn't care if he did, she thought with uncertain bravado. But there were problems – she was still his wife and though she had a small allowance of her own from Daddy, this damned plantation was their livelihood. If she blew the whistle on him with Douglas Mackay, what would happen to the place? James was too dependent on his manager to survive on his own and even if their marriage was becoming decidedly rocky, she didn't want to divorce a bankrupt and have to go home penniless. And she certainly didn't want to be divorced by him and go home both penniless and with her tail between her legs, so she had to watch her mouth and her step.

Diane mixed a third drink, resolutely deciding that it would be her last before dinner. There were magazines on the little table, but after riffling through the curled pages of a six-month-old *Vogue*, she threw it petulantly on to the polished floor and stared aimlessly around the room, which took up the full width of the bungalow. It was large and bare by British standards, the walls lined with darkly varnished planks that carried a few conical Malay straw hats and a set of framed hunting prints. There was no ceiling, the inside of the high peaked roof being wood-lined like the walls. The furniture was equally sombre, a locally made wicker suite with a large settee and four armchairs.

A ponderous teak sideboard, an old-fashioned piano left from the twenties, and a sandalwood chest on which sat a radiogram, completed the decor.

'God, what a dump!' she murmured, self-pity washing over her. After a moment, she rose restlessly to her feet and took her glass across to the verandah. The front wall of the lounge had three pairs of slatted doors designed to let in air, but keep out the sun. The centre ones were open and Diane walked out on to the wide verandah which extended the full width of the big bungalow, furnished with some rattan chairs and a couple of small tables beneath the overhang of the tin roof. It was railed in by a varnished fence, except at the centre, where wide wooden steps went down some eight feet to the ground, the whole building being raised high on brick piles. Her Austin Ten was sheltered underneath, alongside the mud-spattered Land Rover that James used around the estate, though he rarely bothered to park his old armoured Buick under there.

She leaned on the rail, with her glass gripped in both hands, as she had done hundreds of times before and looked out over the estate. Though Norfolk became increasingly desirable with every passing month, she had to admit that the view from here was spectacular. The bungalow was built on a small knoll above the dirt road that led down on the left to Tanah Timah, three miles away. It was at the foot of an isolated hill about a thousand feet high, hence the name *Gunong Besar* – 'big mountain' – though it was a mere hillock compared to the peaks ten miles behind them, on the border between Perak and Pahang States. The bungalow faced west and looked over their acres of rubber down into the distant valley. On rare clear days, they could see as far as the towns of Sungei Siput and Kuala Kangsar and even imagine that they could see the Malacca Straits on the far horizon, over which there were often fantastic sunsets.

She dropped her eyes to the road at the bottom of the knoll fifty yards away, made of the red laterite soil that was dust when it was dry, but usually was a tenacious mud that stuck to wheels and bodywork. There was very little traffic on it, as only one small village, Kampong Kerbau, lay a few miles up to the right. Police patrols and a few military vehicles were the main users, apart from a couple of Chinese trucks and the twice-daily bus to the village.

The whisky was getting warm and Diane tossed down half of it and walked to the right-hand end of the verandah to lean on the side rail. Here her elegant features, with the cornflower blue eyes and enviable bone structure, seemed to darken as she stared past the flowers of a large Flame-of-the-Forest tree down towards another bungalow a few hundred yards away. Built nearer the foot of the knoll, it was smaller than theirs, but of the same general appearance, though all she could see through the trees was the red tin roof and the end of their verandah.

As she watched, trying to project hatred across the space, a battered pre-war Plymouth pick-up came from the latex-processing sheds on the other side of the road and crossed into the drive to the next-door bungalow. The trees obstructed most of her view, but she could just see the driver get out and run up the verandah steps. After spending most of his life in the East, Douglas Mackay seemed impervious to the heat, which made most Europeans slow-moving. She had no quarrel with Douglas, more a mild pity for his weakness in dealing with his domestic life – though she was in no position to criticize in that direction, she thought cynically.

As she leaned on the varnished rail, one of her fingers found a deep scar in the tropical hardwood. It had recently been painted over, but her gaze automatically moved up the planked wall of the bungalow at the end of the verandah. Here were a row of similar marks and she knew that Douglas's bungalow had even more. They were bullet holes, a legacy of the last terrorist attack on Gunong Besar, earlier that year. Thank God she had been away on a shopping trip in Singapore – at least, that's what she had told James.

If she had been here and survived, nothing would have stopped her from getting the next Blue Funnel boat home from Penang. As it was, her dear husband had had a tough job persuading her to stay, even though no one had been hurt – apart from a couple of rubber-tappers being killed down in the worker's lines across the road. A pity that bitch next door hadn't stopped a bullet, she thought vindictively. If the CTs hadn't been disturbed by the chance arrival of an armoured patrol on night exercises from Brigade, maybe she would have been. So might James and Douglas, she supposed, but somehow that possibility didn't tug too much at her heart strings.

As it was, the attackers must have been a pretty small bunch, as they scarpered as soon as the Aussies poured out of their Saracens – she had thanked the good-looking captain personally a week later, in the back of his car behind the club. The two planters had blasted off a few rounds into the darkness just before the troops arrived and certainly James had basked for weeks afterwards in The Dog, as the hero of Gunong Besar – fighting off the Communist hordes like some gunslinger in a Western film. Secretly, when her initial terror had subsided, she rather admired him for a while, until she saw the extra attention that his fame gained him from the women in the club, which soured her back to her normal dislike of her husband.

Downing the last of her tepid drink, she walked barefoot back into the lounge to retrieve her shoes, one from under the settee, the other from near the unused piano, where it had come to rest after bouncing off her husband's neck.

Going through another door at the rear of the lounge, Diane went into a corridor which led to the dining room, guest bathroom and two spare bedrooms. She turned left to reach their own at the farther end. Like the rest of the rooms, it had no ceiling, the partition walls stopping eight feet up. The high, raftered roof was common to all the rooms, to allow as much circulation of air as possible – though privacy was a problem on the rare occasions when they had visitors staying, especially ones who became vocally amorous in bed.

She dropped her shoes on the floor and walked past the white tent of their mosquito-netted bed to reach the bathroom at the back. Inside there was a white-tiled floor and a wash-basin against one wall. Opposite were three doors, one to a toilet, the other to a cubicle with a chipped cast-iron bath and the third a shower. Anxiously, Diane went to the damp-spotted mirror over the basin and stared at her face while she fingered her cheek. No doubt about it, there was faint blue bruising within the reddening – she could even make out two lines where the swine's fingers had struck her. As the sarcastic bastard had suggested, tomorrow would require some careful adjustment of her make-up, before she went to the club that evening.

With a sigh, she stripped off her dress of cream raw silk and dropped it into the straw laundry basket, along with her white bra and pants, ready for the *dhobi-amah* to collect. Going to the shower door, she opened it cautiously and stared at the bare cement floor, which sloped down to a drain pipe in the centre, emptying on to the ground beneath the house. Once she had been confronted by a snake which had crawled up the pipe – her screams had brought Siva running, who had been greatly impressed by her nudity, especially the blonde pubic hair, which he could hardly believe. As she dived for a towel to cover herself, the Tamil had calmly picked up the serpent and thrown it through the window.

'Only wolf snake, Mem. Not poisonous,' he had said, but ever since she had peered suspiciously around the door before venturing in to stand under the lukewarm spray that came from a tank of rainwater behind the roof.

When she had finished, Diane put on a light dressing gown from one of the wardrobes and went to get another drink. She flopped back on to the settee to sulk and wonder if that bastard would come home in time for dinner that evening.

Sometime after six o'clock, that particular bastard was sitting on a bar stool in the Sussex Club, drinking his fourth Tiger beer and reading yesterday's *Straits Times*. He concentrated on the rubber prices and the reports of CT activity, topics which were studied here as seriously as the football results and weather forecast were in Britain. Turning back a page from the commercial news, he read that two days ago there had been an abortive attack on a train down south in Johore which had been fought off by the escorts, but thankfully there had been no incidents up here in Perak for over a week. Maybe Chin Peng was getting the message, thought James, as the supply lines of the terrorist chief were being progressively strangled by General Sir Gerald Templer's policy of fencing-in all the villages in the Black Areas, depriving the CTs of food and local aid.

James Robertson folded his paper and stared at his tall glass, the condensation running down the sides on to the polished teak of the bar. He was trying to decide whether or not to stay here all evening and get blind drunk – or to go home and read the Riot Act to that stupid bitch of a wife. Just because she suspected him of getting his leg over another woman, gave her no right to throw things at him – even if her suspicions were correct.

James was not a very intelligent man, using bluster and his powerful physical presence to swagger his way through life.

He depended heavily on his manager, Douglas Mackay, to keep the business solvent. After four Tigers, he was feeling rather sorry for himself and the nagging suspicion that Diane was also playing away did nothing to put him in the mood for reconciliation.

He gulped down the ice-cold lager and slid the glass across the wide bar, rapping with his knuckles for service. A short, chubby Eurasian hurried over, wearing a black bow tie on his white shirt.

'Another beer, Daniel,' demanded James. 'Where's your barman tonight?'

'His day off, Mister Robertson. The other silly fellow, who should stand in, fell off his bicycle today, so I have to be bloody barman.'

The manager of the Sussex Club was the son of an Indian mother and a British sergeant, who had been posted home in 1922 and had not been heard of since. Though he had mid-brown hair and fairly pale skin, he had been brought up by his mother and had the sing-song accent of that side of the family. He had worked in a large hotel in Penang for some years and had landed the job of running The Dog when it reopened after the war.

After getting his new beer, James swivelled round on the high stool to look around the club. It was early and almost deserted. A fat Education Corps captain was fast asleep in one of the big armchairs that were dotted around the large room like islands in a lake. The doors to the terrace were open and under a Coca-Cola umbrella at one of the white tables outside, a young man was almost nose to nose with a pretty girl. James recognized her as one of the sisters from the military hospital. The only other patrons were a bridge four, playing with grim determination in a distant corner.

'Damned quiet in here tonight,' complained the planter, as if it was a personal insult to him not to have company in his hour of need.

'Thursday always quiet, Mister Robertson. But later, we get more from garrison, after the officers have eaten their *makan*.'

Daniel spoke good English, but had the habit of throwing in words of Malay, Hindi and even Hakka or Cantonese, which annoyed James – though almost everything annoyed James, apart from alcohol and an attractive woman.

He began to wonder how long he would stick it out here in Malaya. Though in some ways he enjoyed himself, with this superficially superior lifestyle that suited his snobbish upbringing, the place was beginning to pall, especially since his three-year-old marriage was beginning to crumble. He ate well enough, drank plenty and enjoyed a succession of sexual adventures – but he was beginning to miss English county society, with its pubs and golf and upper-class gossip.

James had actually been born near Cork into a Protestant 'planter' family. His father had been an Anglicized gentleman farmer and horse-breeder, but dislike of the founding of the Irish Free State had made him move in 1923 to Norfolk, where he established a successful stud farm. James was sent off to a minor public school in Cambridgeshire, then to agricultural college, where he finished in 1937 at the age of twenty-one. He worked for his father for a year, but they failed to get along and he began looking for a farm manager's post. However, with war imminent, James volunteered for the navy in '39, spent a year at sea, then was posted to Ceylon and spent the rest of the war as an undistinguished lieutenant at HQ Trincomalee. Demobbed in 1946, he got a job as an estate under-manager in Gloucestershire, but became restless and wanted to emigrate and set up on his own somewhere. His father had died a couple of years earlier and when his mother sold up the stud farm, she funded his purchase of Gunong Besar. Though he would have preferred going back to Ceylon, the place was cheap, having been run down during the war and in 1948 he moved in. Advertising for a manager, he was lucky enough to have got Douglas Mackay up from Johore, who had long experience of the rubber trade, of which James knew little apart from what he had picked up in Ceylon.

Now he sat turning his beer glass around in his fingers, ruminating about the future and wondering if he should pack up and go back to Britain or try Kenya or New Zealand – but whether with or without Diane was the question?

It was beginning to get dusk outside and the manager

switched on the lights in the club-room – large, rather dim glass globes hanging from the beams high up in the ceiling, from which also dangled the half-dozen big fans that turned endlessly above them. The nearness of the equator, just south of Singapore, meant that it got dark at about seven o'clock all year round – just as there were no noticeable seasons, as the long, thin peninsula got monsoons from both sides, so it rained at some time on almost every day of the year.

As the lights came on and the darkness deepened outside, so members began to drift into the club, chattering in a variety of accents, from a Home Counties drawl to the abrasive rasp of Alice Springs. Soon the line of stools filled up and Daniel was scurrying back and forth with gin and tonics, *stengahs* and the ubiquitous Tiger and Anchor beers. Robertson's mood lightened, as he knew almost everyone and nodded and exchanged greetings in his usual loud and hearty style, concealing his aggrieved chagrin beneath his habitual bonhomie.

Les Arnold, an Australian planter from the next estate beyond Gunong Besar, plumped himself down on one side, giving James a playful punch on the arm in greeting, as he yelled for his beer. A lean, wiry fellow, he was unmarried, as far as anyone knew, and was the ultimate extrovert. Sometimes the suspicious James wondered if his habitual flirting with Diane was a cover for more serious lechery with her, but Les behaved like that with everything in a skirt.

On the other side, an older man with a toothbrush moustache and a bald patch sat himself down more decorously. Alfred Morris, a major in the Medical Corps, was the Administrative Officer from BMH. He was a trim, erect man, who had come up through the ranks and been commissioned from Warrant Officer during the war. A popular figure in TT, he seemed like everyone's uncle, with his calm, amiable manner and his ability to pour oil on the frequently troubled waters in both the hospital and the club. James knew that this was his last tour before retiring to grow roses at his cottage in Kent. After making signs to the harassed manager for beer, Alfred turned to Robertson.

'James, let me introduce you to a prospective new member. Just out from home, only arrived today.'

He leaned back to reveal Tom Howden on the next stool
and allow the ritual of exchanging of names and handshakes.
However surly and objectionable Robertson could be to his
family and employees, his public school education and snobbish upbringing had given him an almost exaggerated sense
of good manners where new acquaintances of an acceptable
social standing were concerned and he greeted the medical
man almost effusively.

'Tom's our new pathologist,' explained Alfred Morris.
'About time, too, as Dickie Freeman was RHE a month ago.
Went home on the *Empire Fowey*.'

Although technically a guest of Major Morris, Tom's appli-
cation to join was a formality, the club committee accepting
any officer on the nod. A few others gathered around with
their drinks to inspect the new member. Though officers came
and went fairly frequently, it was always a novelty to meet
someone new, especially one fresh from home, who may have
actually seen a recent International or who had perhaps been
to the races at Kempton Park. Tom could oblige them on the
first count, as he was a keen rugby fan, though he had never
seen a horse race in his life.

He felt much better this evening, as his earlier bout of
acute homesickness had passed. Standing here with a glass
of beer amid convivial company in this bizarre kind of pub,
he decided that he was going to enjoy his time in Malaya.
An ardent devotee of Somerset Maugham, he felt as if he
was reliving some of his favourite stories. At the moment,
it was an all-male gathering at the bar. Although everyone
was in civilian clothes, they were in virtually another kind
of uniform. All stood in trousers and white shirts and all
wore ties, as it was a club regulation that no shorts were
allowed after six o'clock and that ties would be displayed.
In fact, Daniel kept a few spares behind the bar for members
who turned up without one. Long-sleeved shirts were required
– the Army demanded this everywhere after seven o'clock,
the rationale being to reduce the area available for malarious
mosquitoes to feed on! The only exception to these rules was
on Sundays and when there was a fancy-dress dance. Who
had made these peculiar demands, no one remembered, just

as the origin of the Sussex Club's nickname was shrouded in mystery. Tom raised this question after a few more beers and James, whose browbeating personality usually monopolized the conversation, delivered his opinion in his loud, plummy voice.

'Damned club's been here since the 'twenties! Started by a few chaps most of whom happened to come from Sussex.'

'But why "The Dog"?' asked the doctor.

'I think a couple of the fellows came up from KL and had been members of the Selangor Club on the *padang* there. Everyone in the bloody world knows that that's nicknamed "The Dog", so they borrowed the name to make them feel more at home in this God-forsaken hole.'

No one volunteered any reason why the Kuala Lumpur club should have carried the odd name, but the conversation careered off in a different direction and Tom went with it, enjoying himself more with every glass of cold lager. He was introduced to a dozen more people and promptly forgot every name, though there seemed to be twice as many military as civilians.

The faces along the bar came and went, as some left for their evening meal at home or in the various messes in the Garrison – and others arrived to eat in the club dining room, which lay through a door at the end of the room. At seven thirty, Major Morris tapped his arm and pointed to the big clock above the bar.

'Time to get back to the Mess, lad. Number One will give us the evil eye if we're late for his soup.'

Tom had learned a lot in his first few hours at BMH Tanah Timah. 'Number One' was the title of the Officers' Mess Steward – an emaciated Chinese of indeterminate age whose real name was Lim Ah Sok, and who ruled the inmates with a rod of iron concealed behind a deferential manner. He was assisted by his ferocious, if diminutive wife Meng, who wielded her iron rod without any pretence of deference.

The two officers climbed into Morris's 1939 Hillman Minx and drove the mile back to the hospital. As they crossed the little bridge and came to the junction with the main road, Tom asked about drinking and driving regulations.

'Good God, lad, the way the locals drive here, the coppers could never spot a drunk driver, unless they noticed he was doing better than the others!'

As the old car ground its way past the ghostly bulk of the old tin dredge, the major offered some further advice.

'When you get a car – and you can't get anywhere without one – take my tip. If you hit anyone, for God's sake don't stop or the locals will beat you half to death! Just drive like hell to the next village with a police station and report it.'

As Tom silently digested this new variation on the Highway Code, the Hillman turned in through the gates of BMH, the driver getting a ragged salute from the sentry, who sprang erect from his habitual slouch when he saw his Admin Officer behind the wheel.

They drew up outside the Mess and as he walked in, the new doctor had another look at the place in the light of the bare bulbs hanging under the verandahs. The left-hand hut was given over to the dining room and beyond it the lounge, rather grandly called the 'anteroom'. The kitchen was this side of the dining room and the ablutions were at the far end. The other hut opposite contained about ten small rooms for the resident officers, their row of slatted doors reminding Tom of the changing cubicles in a swimming pool. His room was near the middle, a plywood cell with a single bed inside a sagging mosquito net, a clothes locker, a washbasin, a desk and a 'chair, easy, officers for the use of, one', as it was described in the inventory.

For fear of incurring the steward's displeasure, they went straight to the dining room and sat at the long table just as Number One came in from a door at the other end, where the cooking was being done by his tiny wife. He bore a tureen of soup which he put down between the place settings, then padded out, his flip-flops slapping on the linoleum.

'Bit thin on the ground tonight, aren't we?' said Alf Morris, looking across at the other pair of diners. One of them was Percy Loosemore, a major who specialized in skin and venereal diseases. He was a bony man of about forty, with sparse fair hair, a long nose and a waspish nature.

'Some panic in theatre, apparently. The sawbones and the

gasman are dealing with some MT accident – a REME squaddie who stuck his hand in the fan of a Saracen's engine.' He ladled some tomato soup into a bowl and slid the tureen towards Alfred.

Tom's vocabulary of acronyms was already wide enough to gather that some accident had occurred to a private in the Royal Electrical and Mechanical Engineers from the Motor Transport section. What a 'Saracen' was, he had no idea.

The younger man was Alec Watson, a fresh-faced, gingery Scot only eighteen months out of medical school, who added his two-pennyworth to the conversation.

'They say that an alternative cap badge for REME should be a crown surmounting a crossed screwdriver and a condom, with the motto *"If you can't fix it, f— it!"'*

Major Morris grinned, but then wagged a finger at the lad.

'That'll cost you a dollar in the box, laddie. You know the rules.'

Their Commanding Officer had instituted a strict no-swearing regime in the Mess, the penalty being putting a Straits dollar in the swear-box for the Red Cross. There was even a faded list of words pinned on the anteroom wall, listing the proscribed oaths. There was also a 'no-treating' rule, which meant that though a member could invite another to have a drink, each had to sign a chit to go on their own mess bill.

Alec Watson grinned ruefully and promised to fork out later. He was a mere GDMO – a General Duties Medical Officer – which meant that he was too junior to have a speciality and was a medical dogsbody in the hospital. He ran the Casualty Station during the day, as well as the Families Clinic, though there were relatively few of those, apart from the dependants of the Malay-enlisted Other Ranks and some Gurkhas.

They ploughed through the soup course, which came straight out of Campbell's tins, then a tough piece of local chicken that the sardonic Percy claimed must have died of senility. The best part was the dessert, which was a fruit salad of fresh mango, papaya and pineapple, the first two being a totally new experience for Tom Howden.

After the meal, they went through the door at the other end into the anteroom, which like the dining room, was across the width of the long narrow hut, louvred doors running down each side. Most of these were open, letting in the heavy scent of the tropical night, along with the incessant twitter of the cicadas and monotonous burp of a bullfrog lurking in a nearby monsoon drain.

Number One glided in with a tray of coffee which he put on one of the low tables within the rectangle of easy chairs that filled the centre of the room. Another table at one side carried outdated magazines, the *Lancet, British Medical Journal* and a few copies of the airmail edition of the *Daily Telegraph*, as well as the *Straits Times*. Apart from a faded picture of the Queen on one wall, a clock and a shelf of books abandoned by former residents on the other, the room was bare. All the furniture was uniform Barrack Store issue, plain no-nonsense wood with anaemic fabric on the foam cushions.

There was a sleepy silence while they all sipped their coffee, which was blatantly Nescafé with a dash of Carnation tinned milk. When they had finished, Number One came to collect the tray and take orders for drinks. They all ordered a beer, except for Alec Watson who regretfully shook his head.

'Sorry, I'm OMO tonight, Number One.'

Two days ago, Tom might have thought that the young Scot was confessing to being queer, but now he knew that it stood for 'Orderly Medical Officer', the doctor permanently on duty overnight – which explained why he was the only one in uniform.

Alec must have read his thoughts.

'Soon be your turn, Tom! Everyone under field rank has to go on the rota. As there's only five of us lieutenants or captains, it comes round more than once a week.'

Howden grinned. 'Don't know that I'll be of much use. I haven't seen a live patient for over a year.' After qualifying, he had been able to delay his call-up for National Service by getting deferment for another twelve months. This allowed him to get a pathology training post in Newcastle's Royal Victoria Infirmary and come into the Army as a junior specialist on a Short Service Regular Commission.

When the Tigers arrived, there was another long silence. Percy Loosemore, the wiry Essex man with the long, leathery face, studied the Appointments Vacant section of the *Lancet*, while Alfred Morris dozed in his chair with a handkerchief spread over his upturned face.

The young Scot, who to Tom looked about sixteen, sat immobile, staring out through an open door into the velvet darkness, listening to the cicadas and thinking inscrutable thoughts. The new arrival began to think that the main danger of Active Service was not being shot by terrorists, but dying of boredom. It was hardly eight thirty, but everyone seemed ready for bed. The only socializing influence in TT seemed to be The Dog and in an effort to break the ennui, Tom brought up the subject.

'Who exactly can be members?' he asked. 'That chap with the loud voice said it had been there since the nineteen-twenties.'

Alf Morris, who was not asleep after all, gave a snort of amusement.

'That was James Robertson – self-appointed squire of Tanah Timah! Though at least he's a planter and it was that lot who started the club. But if it wasn't for the Army, it wouldn't have had all those facilities like a swimming pool and squash court. It's only our membership fees that keep it afloat.'

'And the bar profits!' said Percy. 'Very exclusive, The Dog – only officers and white men, very pukka!' Tom wondered if dealing every day with scores of men with the clap had made him cynical about human nature.

'What about women?'

The magic word brought Alec out of his trance. 'Women? Well, the QA sisters are officers, so they qualify, but not their Other Ranks, of course. The only others are the wives of the members, though there's a civilian English teacher seconded to the Garrison who they let in as a special favour.'

Tom thought that the GDMO had picked up a lot of local gossip in the few months that he had been here – though he supposed there was little else to do except absorb all the tittle-tattle.

'That James Robertson – he seems a pretty forceful chap.'

'He's full of bullshit!' snapped Alec. 'And that's not on the swear-word list, Alf, so don't look at me like that!'

'A colourful character, James,' mused Percy Loosemore. 'We could tell you a lot about him.'

Alf Morris pulled off his handkerchief and sat up.

'Now watch what you say, Percy, especially around here.'

Intrigued, Tom's jug-handle ears almost wagged in anticipation.

'Tom should know the basics of the situation, Alf,' said Percy. 'It might stop him innocently putting his foot in it.'

'And now's as good a time as any, when the other fellows aren't here,' suggested Alec Watson. With Morris still looking uneasy, Percy, the venereologist, launched into a tutorial on the local scandals.

'The plain fact is that our beloved senior surgeon, Peter Bright, has had a bit of a thing going with Robertson's wife. A real cracker, is Diane, a blonde gorgeous enough to make your eyes water! Everyone seems to know about it except the damned husband.'

'I'm not so sure about that, Percy,' grunted Alf Morris. 'So don't go mouthing it about or there'll be hell to pay.'

Alec Watson seemed to be looking forward to some High Noon drama in TT.

'If Jimmy Robertson does find out, there'll be a shoot-out. Plenty of guns up at Gunong Besar, I'll bet!'

'There'll be a shoot-out if he hears you calling him "Jimmy", my lad,' snapped Alfred. 'Our James is very touchy on that point – even "Jim" isn't posh enough for him.'

There was a pause while Percy rang a small brass bell that stood on the table. Number One padded in to take orders for more beer, offering his pad of chits and a pen for the drinkers to sign their pay away. As they waited, Tom recalled the object of the gossip, whom he had met briefly over a cup of tea that afternoon. Peter Bright was a Major, the senior of the two surgeons at BMH. A tall, good-looking man in his mid-thirties, Tom felt he was the sort of man that appeared on the covers of Mills & Boon hospital romances. Swept-back fair hair, blue eyes and an aristocratic nose gave him a head start in the lady-chasing stakes, to say nothing of his Oxbridge accent.

After the drinks had materialized, Percy Loosemore was off
again.

'Our Peter got divorced a couple of years ago, when his
missus did a runner with some German chap at BMH Munster,
so now he's casting around for a new wife. And as the
Robertsons are having a stormy passage these days, maybe
he'll get lucky.'

The Administrative Officer clucked under his breath. 'You
really are a proper old washerwoman when it comes to gossip,
Percy!'

'Well, the new lad here needs to know what subjects to
avoid in the club – and in the Mess here. It could be
embarrassing.'

'Not only Pete and Diane,' cut in Alec. 'Best not to mention
Lena Franklin and James Robertson in the same breath, if our
gasman is within earshot!'

The new pathologist's brow wrinkled as he tried to keep
track of who they were talking about. A 'gasman' was an
anaesthetist, so that must be David Meredith, a Short-Service
captain like himself. He was a dark, intense Welshman, to
whom Tom had also spoken briefly at teatime. Percy continued
to develop the theme.

'Lena's one of the juiciest QA sisters, if you like the arty,
passionate type. Dave Meredith is ass-over-head in love with
her and was working himself up to pop the question, but then
last month, it suddenly cooled off. The clever money is on
James as the cause, so Dave is seriously pissed off!'

He leered at Morris.

'And that's not on the list, either, Alf!'

At midnight, the Buick roared up the road to Gunong Besar,
its headlights cutting a bright tunnel through the darkness. The
pale trunks of young rubber trees flicked reflected light as it
passed, until they gave way to elephant grass and crumbling
red rock at a cutting where the track sliced between high banks
on either side.

The heavy American sedan was even heavier than when it
was made in Detroit in 1942, as steel plates had been welded
inside all the doors. A metal flap was hinged over the

windscreen, a lever inside enabling it to be lowered in an emergency. The glass of the side windows had been replaced by heavy-gauge steel sheets with just a small slot cut in the panes, so that the driver could see a little to the side. The rear window was similarly blanked off, so that the mirrors perched on the fronts of the wings provided the only view backwards. James Robertson had acquired the car seven years ago, as part of the deal when he bought Gunong Besar. The previous owner had had the armour fitted and James thought it added glamour to his image, especially since the attack on the estate a few months back. The police and army patrols along the road had been increased since then and there was little danger during daylight. However, James continued to parade up and down from The Dog in a two-ton saloon that guzzled petrol, as he was loath to give up his pose as the fearless planter, careless of any danger.

The old car seemed to know its own way, helped by the grooves cut by traffic in the soft laterite of the single track road. With a good many beers and whisky chasers inside him, James was sleepy rather than drunk and took little notice of the three miles of gritty track. He certainly had no way of noticing the figure crouching on top of the right-hand side of the cutting, a rifle trailing from one hand, staring intently down at the lone car passing below him.

Half a mile further on, James turned into the short side track leading to his bungalow and noisily revved the engine to climb the slope up the side of the knoll. He swung on to the flat area in front of the verandah in a spray of gravel and hoisted himself unsteadily out of the driving seat. Slamming the car door, he tramped up the steps and clumped across the hollow boards, careless of disturbing anyone. Marching through the bedroom, he jerked open the bathroom door and switched on the light. After tearing off his clothes and throwing them vaguely in the direction of the dhobi basket, he got rid of some of his beer in the toilet, then sluiced cold water over his face at the basin.

Stumping back across the echoing boards of the bedroom floor, he hauled out his side of the mosquito net from under the mattress and crashed naked on to his side of the bed, ignoring the slim figure under the single sheet. Within minutes, he was snoring, but on the other edge of the bed, Diane lay with her eyes open, weighing up the pros and cons of the men currently in her life.

Not far away, the figure with the rifle had come down from the cutting and was loping through the rubber by the light of a pale half moon.

TWO

'The old man wants to see you before Daily Orders,' announced Alf Morris, as Tom Howden appeared in the dining room. 'The colonel's back from his leave in the Cameron Highlands, so it's business as usual. Get to his office at eight sharp, OK?'

It was seven fifteen on Friday morning, the new boy's first full day at BMH. Six other officers were at the table and nodded a greeting, though this early in the day, no one was in much of a mood for conversation. They were all in newly laundered jungle greens in various stages of fading, depending on how long they had been out from home. Some wore a tailored shirt and shorts, others the longer bush jacket and trousers, but all had brass or dark red pips or crowns on their shoulders and the regulation cherry red lanyard around the left armpit. All had the green and purple ribbon of the '*General Service Medal with clasp Malaya*' on their breasts, though some like Alf Morris, had a few more campaign markers alongside. Even Tom had his GSM ribbon, as they were issued within two days of arrival in FARELF. It was claimed that some chaps in Hong Kong had the Malaya Medal, because their troop plane had been delayed in Singapore by engine trouble for twenty-four hours, which qualified them for being on active service!

Morris filled a bowl with cereal at a side table and went to sit down with the others. As Tom followed his example and spooned up some limp cornflakes, the swing door from the kitchen crashed open and a small tornado emerged, carrying two plates of fry-up which she banged on the table in front of Percy and Alec. On the way back, she planted herself in front of the pathologist and scowled at him ferociously. He looked down at the small, squat Chinese woman, who had a frizz of jet black hair above her round face.

'You wan' egg?' she demanded loudly.

'Please – and bacon and beans.'

'OK, I bring! Now siddown!' She jabbed a finger at the table and marched back to the kitchen, her morning ritual accomplished.

Tom took his bowl and sat opposite Alf Morris, who grinned.

'I see you've made a hit with Meng. She's as good as gold, really.'

'What's this about seeing the colonel? What do I have to do?'

Morris poured more diluted Carnation on to his cornflakes.

'March smartly into his office and stand in front of his desk. Give him a salute, then stick your hat under your left armpit and stand at attention.'

Tom stopped his spoon halfway to his mouth. 'Bloody hell! I thought the medics were a bit more relaxed than that?'

'Dollar in the box, lad,' said Alf automatically. 'No, our CO is a bit of a stickler for the traditions, I'm afraid.'

'Colonel O'Neill thinks he should have been in the Household Cavalry, not the RAMC, old chap.'

Peter Bright, the subject of last night's gossip, spoke for the first time. Again Tom noticed his aristocratic profile and the immaculate uniform. He never seemed to sweat like the rest of them.

'Should have been in the Waffen SS, not the Household Cavalry,' muttered the man next to him, a thin, beetle-browed Welshman. He was so dark that he always looked as if needed a shave, but David Meredith was handsome in a melancholy sort of way.

Tom was rapidly getting the impression that their Commanding Officer was not the flavour of the month in the Mess. As the colonel had been on leave for a few days, the new arrival had not yet met him and looked forward to the event with some unease.

'What's wrong with him, then?'

The loyal Administrative Officer, with twenty-six years of unswerving deference to rank behind him, jumped in ahead of any other replies.

'Nothing's wrong with him. He's just a rather strict disciplinarian.'

There were derisory snorts from around the table, but no one ventured to enlarge on the subject, though one or two looked rather uneasily over their shoulders.

Meng smacked a plate in front of him and the others peered at it.

'Fried bread and a tomato as well, eh?' observed Percy. 'She's taken a real shine to you, Tom.'

At ten to eight, he was out on the road from the Mess to the hospital. It ran all around the site, parallel to the chain-link perimeter, the wards being inside it. Various other buildings such as the two Officers' Messes, the ORs' barracks, Casualty, Sergeants' Mess, Quartermaster's stores, mortuary, dental unit and armoury, all lay between it and the boundary fence. The inner square was bisected by the main corridor that ran up from opposite the front gate to the little armoury that lay at the back, between the RAMC Officers' Mess and that of the Queen Alexandra's Royal Army Nursing Corps. Cynics had long claimed that they needed the guns to keep the two sexes apart.

Tom Howden walked in the already-warm morning as far as this armoury, watching the steam rise off the wet ground as the sun began to make itself felt. When he looked beyond the hospital fence to the edge of the valley, he could see the jungle-covered hills less than a mile away, wraiths of mist winding through the tops of the trees. The air smelled so different from Tyneside, a cloying mixture of flowers, humid vegetation and stagnant water.

He turned sharp left into the long corridor that was the main artery of the hospital, a place where sometime during the day you could meet every inhabitant of the place. It was a concrete strip edged with deep monsoon drains, each side completely open, with a gabled asbestos roof supported on green-painted posts all the way down to the front of the hospital. On each side, every twenty yards or so, were double doors to the wards, which stuck out like ribs from a spine. They were long green-painted huts, similar to those of the Mess, with slatted doors down most of their length on each side. Just inside the front doors were the sisters' and doctors' offices and at the far end, the sluice-rooms.

Halfway down the corridor, he saw that one of the buildings was different. It was shorter, built of concrete and had a few glass windows, which had several air conditioning units sticking out. This was the operating theatre, the domain of the amorous pair, Peter Bright and David Meredith. On the other side of the corridor was the X-ray Unit and further down the corridor was his own bailiwick, the pathology laboratory, opposite the dispensary.

Beyond these, he had to dodge a group of barefoot Tamil labourers, who were energetically scrubbing the concrete with brooms, slopping soapy water from buckets carried on a trolley. Just past them, he came to the end of the corridor, where the first two ribs on the spine were offices, fronting the car park and entrance gate with its guardroom. On the right were the RSM's cubbyhole and the general office, where several Indian and Chinese clerks filed records and banged away on old typewriters. To the left were the rooms of the QA Matron and the Admin Officer, with the Holy of Holies on the far end – the CO's office.

Feeling like a fourth-former going to see the headmaster, Tom pulled up his long khaki socks with the red garter tabs, adjusted the lanyard around his shoulder and straightened his cap. Striding to the middle door, he tapped and waited.

A harsh voice commanded him to 'Come!'

Inside, he found himself in a bare office with a dozen hard chairs lined up against two walls, like a vet's waiting room. Opposite the door, was a large empty desk, on which were a cap and a bamboo swagger stick, lined up with meticulous accuracy to face the entrance. Behind the desk was Lieutenant Colonel Desmond O'Neill, Commanding Officer of BMH Tanah Timah.

Tom marched across the wide empty space to stand in front of the desk, gave his best salute and whipped off his hat.

'Captain Thomas Howden reporting for duty, sir.' He thought this sounded about right for the occasion.

The colonel looked up at him impassively. He was a trim,

stiff-backed man of average height with dark short-cropped hair, greying at the temples. His face was thin, the skin stretched tightly over his high cheekbones. Darkly handsome in a horrible sort of way, thought Tom. As a keen cinema-goer at home, he immediately compared the CO with either Stewart Granger or Michael Rennie, the sardonic heroes of many an adventure film. But it was the eyes that made him uneasy, piercing pale globes that never seemed to blink, the kind that inept police artists drew on wanted axe murderers. The colonel now covered them with a pair of steel-rimmed glasses to stare at his new officer.

'Pathologist, is that what you claim to be, Howden?'

The harsh voice had a strong Ulster accent.

'Yessir, one year's experience as a Senior House Officer in Newcastle.'

Tom had hoped for some kind of welcome to the new unit, but it seemed that O'Neill was above such pleasantries.

'Well, you'll have other duties here as well – take your turn as Orderly Officer, act as the Hygiene Officer and run the blood transfusion service. That means you also have to act as the medical officer to the MCE next door, that's where you get your blood.'

This was one acronym he'd not come across yet and he had no idea where he was to get his blood, but had the sense not to query it from this peculiar man.

'Yessir, of course, sir.'

O'Neill continued to glare at him, his narrow lips compressed into a thin line. Then he spoke again, the Belfast accent strange to Tom's Geordie-tuned ears.

'Short-Service man, aren't you? Well, you'll have to be a good example for these National Service fellows! Smartly-dressed, strict discipline, understand? Then you'll not fall foul of me too often.'

He sat with his hands on his empty desk, fingers flat on the wood, with an immobility that reminded Tom of a snake, ready to strike. The new arrival stood stiffly, unsure whether to make any response, but the decision was made for him.

'Right, Howden, dismiss. Daily Orders at eight fifteen, every day except Sunday.'

The skull-like face gave a jerky nod of dismissal and Tom managed one of his salutes again, which he had been practising before the mirror in the washroom – 'hand furthest way up, shortest way down', as they had been instructed in the Depot at Crookham.

He swivelled to his left and marched out, closing the door behind him. Outside, he sagged against the adjacent wall and took off his cap to wipe the sweat from his brow, generated both by the heat and the stress of meeting the man who theoretically had the power of life and death over him for the next few years.

'Good morning, captain, are you our new pathologist?'

A gentle voice came from behind him and he turned to find that he had been leaning against the edge of the open window of the next office.

Inside, standing against a table on which she was arranging bright tropical flowers in a vase, was a large woman dressed in grey-blue QARANC uniform with a triangular headdress of starched white linen hanging down her back. Her scarlet shoulder tabs carried a Major's crown, so this must be the Matron, he thought. Uncertain of protocol, he slapped on his cap and gave her a salute, but she smiled benignly.

'Only need do that when he's around,' she hissed in a stage whisper, jerking her head towards the office he had just left. Coming to the low window sill, she offered her hand.

'Welcome to the madhouse. Hope you'll be happy here. Keep your sense of humour and you'll survive.'

He shook her hand and introduced himself, glad to find someone who made him feel welcome. She was almost motherly in her manner and Tom felt a sudden pang of homesickness again, as she was almost as old as his mother. Large and rather ungainly, she had a big, placid face and a ready smile. Her upper lip carried a faint moustache and he suspected that this was her last tour before retirement.

'Are you married, captain?' she asked, unashamedly gathering essential gossip to carry back to the Sisters' Mess.

Tom grinned and shook his head. 'Got a girl or two back home, but nothing serious yet.' He thought he'd better keep his options open for a bit.

After a little more chit-chat, he wandered away to wait for this mysterious Daily Orders. His wristwatch told him there were a few minutes left and he stood at the bottom of the main corridor, watching hospital life pass by. Vehicles came and went through the gate. A Bedford ambulance lumbered up to Casualty, which was a large hut over on the right-hand side of the parking lot. The driver and an orderly from Casualty went to the back door and helped out a dishevelled trooper in high jungle boots, one arm in a bloodstained sling.

Next was a ramshackle Chinese truck delivering to the Quartermaster's Stores further up the perimeter road. A Land Rover with the flash of a New Zealand battalion sped out after delivering patients to the STD, the 'Special Treatment Department' which was a euphemism for Percy Loosemore's 'clap and pox' clinic, housed in a large khaki tent on the open area beyond the ward blocks. Next to this was a small shed-like structure with another mysterious acronym painted above the door – PAC. Later Tom learned that this was the unit's Personal Ablutions Centre, where squaddies going out for a night on the town could obtain a free condom and a tiny tube of mercuric chloride; if they had signed the record book to prove their attendance, then they escaped being disciplined for 'self-injury' if they later reported sick with 'a dose of the clap'.

From the other side of the hospital frontage, the RSM appeared, a burly red-faced man, who seemed all chest and boots. His Warrant-Officer's badge of rank was on a leather wristlet, the same hand holding a cane with which he approached the quaking private on gate duty outside the guard-room. Tom couldn't catch what the problem was, but the private seemed to shrink at the same rate as the RSM appeared to get larger.

At that moment, a clutch of medical officers appeared at the end of the corridor and swept up Tom on their way to the colonel's office, Alf Morris joining them from his own room. There were several that Tom had never seen before and headed by Peter Bright, they all filed into the CO's room. After saluting, each went to stand by one of the chairs against the side walls. Tom followed suit and at a barked command from Desmond O'Neill, they all sat down, with their caps on their knees, peak facing forwards.

'Orderly Medical Officer's report!' snapped the colonel, his cold eye fixing on Alec Watson. The youngest officer shot to his feet and consulted a piece of paper, on which were recorded his activities during his twenty-four hour shift.

'Two patients on the SIL, sir, no change in their condition. No one on the DIL. Three minor injuries treated in Casualty, nothing else to report, sir.'

O'Neill continued to fix him with his cobra-like stare. 'What are these men on the SIL, Watson?'

'One leptospirosis, one malaria, sir. The malaria came off the DIL on Tuesday.' Tom was to discover later that these new initials meant 'Dangerously and Seriously Ill Lists.'

The colonel swivelled his eyes to an older man whom Tom had never seen before. 'Major Martin, what about these patients?' he snapped.

Martin rose to his feet. He was a big man with a bright pink complexion and a fair bushy moustache. Tom assumed he was the senior physician, the medical equivalent of surgeon Peter Bright. As he had never appeared in the Mess, he presumably lived in the Married Quarters in the Garrison compound. He explained in a deep voice how the malaria victim was from 22 SAS in Sungei Siput and the leptospirosis or Weil's disease sufferer was from a jungle patrol of the West Berkshires who had had to sleep in rat-infested swamp water.

'Both are improving, they should pull through well enough,' he ended.

This is how the meeting went for the next fifteen minutes, with the gimlet eyes of the colonel transfixing each officer in turn, demanding to know what he had been up to during the last day. He left the pathologist until last.

'Well, Howden, any problems in the laboratory?'

'Nossir, just settling in,' answered Tom cautiously, as in fact he had yet to set foot in the place.

'Better be up to speed by tomorrow, you've had almost a day here already!'

He stood up suddenly, the signal for everyone to lumber to their feet, put on their caps and salute, before filing out in silence.

As the door closed behind them, Tom heard Major Martin comment to Peter Bright. 'The old man was very benign this morning, his few days' leave must have mellowed him.'

Bloody hell, thought the new boy, what's he like when he's in a bad mood?

It was past noon before the news first reached the Officers' Mess. Most of the residents had drifted back there for their pre-lunch drink and even some of the married officers had forsaken their domestic gin and tonics for a gossip with their colleagues. The table just inside the open doors of the ante-room was scattered with caps and webbing belts, as mess rules demanded that they were not worn inside. Most of the chairs were occupied and Number One was padding about with beers and fresh lime drinks, the drinking of hard liquor being frowned upon in the middle of the day. A couple of doctors were hidden behind newspapers or magazines, but most were lying back, letting the ceiling fans blow some of the sweat off them.

'The damned Engineers in Garrison have installed air conditioning in their mess,' complained Eddie Rosen, another Short-Service captain who worked in the surgical wards under Peter Bright. A small Jewish doctor from London, he had done a year's 'midder and gynae', so was the nearest they had to a woman's specialist, though a senior gynaecologist could be flown in at short notice from BMH Kinrara, near Kuala Lumpur.

'Well they would, wouldn't they,' drawled Clarence Bottomley, a National Service lieutenant, known to all as 'Montmorency' for some obscure reason. He was a rather posh young man who, when in civvies, always wore a Marlborough tie and let everyone know that he was a Cambridge graduate.

Though he seemed an amiable enough chap, Tom classed him amongst the 'chinless wonders' and the garrulous Percy had already reported that Montmorency was only marking time in BMH, until he was posted out to one of the more elite Guards' battalions as a Regimental Medical Officer. He said they always wanted doctors who knew which fish knives to use at Mess Dinners and the correct direction in which to pass the port.

Before the ventilation iniquities of the Garrison Mess could be debated further, there was an interruption from near the door. Alfred Morris had arrived and after dropping his cap on to the table, rapped on it with his short swagger stick.

'Chaps, listen a moment, please!'

The blunt authority of his voice was a reminder that he had once been a Regimental Sergeant Major. 'The Commanding Officer wants me to tell you that more vigilance is required regarding security, especially outside the camp.'

There was a silence, as this was a new one, even given the eccentricities of their colonel.

'What's all this about, Alf?' demanded the physician, John Martin.

'Looks as if the lull in CT activity around these parts may be over,' replied Morris. 'There was an attack on one of the estates last night, only a few miles from here.'

A buzz of interest and concern went around the anteroom. If the area was returned to being a Black Area, it would interfere with their travelling, which meant problems with golf and weekend trips, to say nothing of the possibility of being shot. There was a clamour for more details as the members got up and advanced on the Admin Officer, who held up his hands for some quiet.

'It seems that in the early hours of this morning, shots were fired at both bungalows and the workers' lines at Gunong Besar. No one was hurt, but they drilled a few holes in the walls again, smashed the windscreen of Diane Robertson's car and scared the shit out of some of the Indian labourers.'

Alf forgot his own swear-box penalty in the babble that followed his announcement.

'Is that all that happened?' demanded Percy Loosemore, who had been in TT the longest and remembered the previous more serious terrorist attacks.

'Seems to be! Couple of dozen shots fired, then they melted away into the *ulu*.' Tom had already gathered that this was the common name for the dense secondary vegetation around the edge of the jungle.

'James Robertson and Douglas Mackay rolled out of their beds and grabbed their guns, but it was all over by then.'

'The state James was in, in The Dog last night, it's a wonder he even woke up at a mere few dozen gunshots!' observed Peter Bright, sarcastically.

'Where were you in the early hours, Pete?' asked Percy provocatively, but no one laughed.

'Did our lot find the bandits?' asked David Meredith, his dark eyes brooding over the rim of his tankard.

'Not a sign of anyone by the time the police got there, just ahead of a squad from the garrison. Douglas rang them and they were there within twenty minutes.'

'Odd, that!' ruminated Percy Loosemore. 'The CTs usually cut the phone wires before they go on the rampage. They did last time they hit Gunong Besar, about six months ago.'

Peter Bright looked desperately worried. 'Alf, are you sure no one was hurt?'

'The lovely Diane must be OK, or we've had heard,' said Percy, with a look of innocence, as he slipped in what all the others were thinking. With her husband at home, poor Peter would be unable to ring up the estate to see how his beloved was bearing up. The way Diane had reacted after the last attack, when she had been miles away in Singapore, suggested that she would be frantic now that she had actually been on the wrong end of gunfire.

The Admin Officer slumped into the last vacant chair and signalled to Number One for a beer, as the others settled back to listen and debate.

'We'll hear all about it endlessly tonight at The Dog,' he said. 'No doubt James Robertson will be there, playing the hero.'

*   *   *

In spite of the heat, the atmosphere in the Robertsons' lounge that afternoon was decidedly frosty. The ice was provided in full measure by the two women present, the wives of the owner and his manager.

Rosa Mackay sat stiffly on the edge of one of the rattan easy chairs, with Diane slumped on the settee as far away as possible on the other side of the room. Douglas Mackay hovered uneasily in front of one of the verandah doors, while James stood with his back to the rear wall, his hands clasped behind him. The third man in the room thought whimsically that if the climate had allowed for a large fireplace, James Robertson would have stood like this in front of it, to emphasize his dominance as squire of the household.

Steven Blackwell was the Superintendent of Police, based at Tanah Timah, but responsible for a huge tract of country, much of it uninhabited. He was a burly, short-necked man of forty-five, almost completely bald above a rim of iron-grey hair running horizontally around the back of his head. Steven suffered severely from the sun, his face, head and neck always bright pink above his crisply starched khaki uniform. He wore shirt and shorts, with long black socks, black shoes and black peaked cap, which now lay on the piano, along with his leather-covered stick. A black 'Sam Brown' belt and diagonal cross-strap supported a holstered revolver.

'I don't know what to make of this, James,' he was saying with a worried frown. He had a deep, pleasant voice, still with a trace of a Midlands accent. 'It's not like the last time they had a go at you. That was a much more determined effort.'

'Well, eight bullet holes in my wall is hardly a Christmas greeting, Steven!' retorted Robertson. 'We had two fellows killed six months ago. It only takes one bullet to kill me, determined or not!'

He sounded aggrieved that any doubt should be cast on his heroic role as the besieged planter. Blackwell held up a conciliatory hand.

'Good God, James, I'm not trying to play down what

happened! But it's so out of character for the bastards to turn up, fire a few shots and then slope off! Last time, we were all very lucky that a patrol happened to catch them in the act. We even managed to shoot one of the sods that time.'

Douglas Mackay spoke for the first time. He was a thin, stringy man in his late forties, a widow's peak on his forehead where his sparse fair hair had receded at the temples. Douglas seemed all arms and legs in his shorts and bush shirt, the exposed skin still showing a slightly yellowish tinge from his years as a prisoner of the Japanese. His soft Scottish voice was a contrast to Robertson's usual bluster.

'D'you not think it could have been one or two of Chin Peng's boys doing a bit of freelance work – or even a couple of local guys with Commie sympathies, maybe from one of the kampongs?'

James made derogatory noises under his breath at this attempt to downgrade his ordeal, but Blackwell thoughtfully rubbed his pink jowls.

'It's a possibility, though I don't know where anyone outside the CT organization would have got weapons. We've clamped down so hard on the villagers now.'

'They make their own bloody guns,' objected James. 'A piece of water-pipe, a handful of rusty nails and they're in business!'

The police superintendent shook his head,

'Not this time. These were no country guns. Inspector Tan has dug a few bullets out of the woodwork for me. They're all three-oh-threes, good military hardware.'

Robertson had an answer for everything. 'The CT's have stacks of those. We Brits supplied them with thousands of the things when we wanted them to kill Japs with them a few years ago.'

Steven Blackwell nodded. 'Sure, but the local loonies don't have them. It has to be a CT unit – yet why should they bother to make such a feeble attempt? I don't get it.'

'It didn't sound damned feeble to me in the middle of the

night!' snapped Diane, tremulously indignant. 'I was terrified, I felt sure I was going to die!'

She had been all for driving to Penang that morning to stay in the Eastern and Oriental Hotel, until she could get a passage back to Britain on one of the regular Alfred Holt passenger ships, but her husband had persuaded her to stay. He was in something of a cleft stick, as even though things were deteriorating between them, his pride didn't want her to go, leaving him with the ignominy of being branded as a dumped husband. Yet to play down the incident to reassure her, would devalue his own Errol Flynn image amongst his male cronies and female admirers.

As usual, he solved his dilemma by calling for drinks. Yelling for Siva, he got Blackwell and Mackay to sit down while gin, whisky and orange juice were dispensed, the policeman and his manager refusing anything alcoholic.

'Let's go through this once again, though I know Inspector Tan has taken it all down earlier,' said the superintendent.

He looked across first at the manager's wife, Rosa, who had sat silently on her chair. She was a small but beautiful woman, as dark as Diane was fair. Black glossy hair was cut in a rather severe pageboy, with a fringe across her forehead. Large brown eyes looked out rather fearfully from a smooth oval face, with full lips that needed far less cosmetics than Diane's. Though she looked European, with the complexion of an Italian or Spaniard, Blackwell knew that she was Eurasian, though she would have passed for any nationality around the Mediterranean. She was not the daughter of an Asian and a European, but the daughter of two other Eurasians. Her father came from Goa, the son of a Portuguese merchant and an Indian mother and he had married a woman with similar ancestry. He had emigrated after the war to Malacca, originally a Portuguese settlement in southern Malaya, setting up a furniture and curio business. His daughter Rosa, now twenty-six, had been educated in a Catholic convent in Goa and after coming to Malacca, worked as a receptionist in a beach hotel. Here she had met Douglas Mackay on a weekend leave from his plantation job in Johore. When James offered him the post of manager in Gunong

Besar, he had married Rosa and brought her up to Perak. Now the superintendent turned to her to get her account of last night's drama.

'I know nothing more than I told the inspector, Steven,' she said in her low, soft voice, keeping her eyes well away from the glowering Diane. 'I was fast asleep when shots woke me up and I heard splintering of wood when some must have hit the front of the bungalow. Then Douglas dashed in from the lounge and told me to hide low down in the bathroom, while he went out with a gun. I saw nothing, I was too frightened to move until it was all over.'

'Can you remember how many shots you heard?

'Not exactly, but there must have been at least a dozen, I think. They became quite distant after the first few.'

Blackwell turned to Robertson's wife.

'What about you, Diane? Does much the same apply?'

She glared first at Rosa, then turned to the policeman.

'The shots woke me too, but the distant ones were first, then they came nearer. I had to wake him up, he was out for the count. Too much beer at The Dog.'

James scowled at this slur on his heroics. 'Come on, Diane, I was out of bed like a shot!'

'Well, anyway, eventually he staggered up after I'd started screaming, and told me to lie on the floor next to the bed.'

'To be furthest away from the walls – bullets can knock holes right through that old woodwork,' grunted her husband.

'Then he went out – to get his gun, I suppose. But then it all went quiet. That's all I can tell you.'

'Except that you were wailing like a bloody banshee for ages!' muttered James. 'It took three stengahs and a gin and tonic to calm you down.'

'D'you blame me, after that!' she flared. 'Why the hell did I let myself come to a place like this, where I might get raped and shot and God knows what?!'

The policeman hastily turned to the estate manager to dampen a return of Diane's hysteria.

'Douglas, you were the first to get outside, according to what you told Tan?'

The calm voice of the manager was in counterpoint to the woman's panic.

'Yes, I was working late on the accounts when it started. From the sound of the shots, they attacked our bungalow first, then went down to the worker's lines, before coming up to James's place here. I grabbed my pistol and rifle and went down the servant's steps at the back, as I didn't want to risk the front porch. There were more shots, well ahead of me, then silence! I kept hopping from tree to tree and worked my way around to the front of James's bungalow, but there was no one to be seen. By then James had come out, so I went back to phone your police station and the guardroom at the Garrison.'

'And you saw nothing at all?'

'Not a thing. If it hadn't been for the others hearing it – and the holes in the woodwork – I might have dreamt it all!'

Steve Blackwell sipped his orange juice as he turned to Robertson.

'What about you, James? Anything to add?'

'I've told you all this before – and your inspector chap. Like Douglas, I grabbed my rifle, then crouched down on the verandah, peering through the struts. Couldn't see a thing, all the shots had been fired before that. I went down the steps and hid behind a bush, then hollered for Douglas. He shouted back that he was going to phone for help, so I went around the whole place to see what the hell was going on. By that time, the servants and the tappers had crawled out of their holes and were jabbering fit to burst, so I had to calm them down. By that time, your boys and the army had arrived.'

'Have they found anything?' demanded Diane, pouring herself another gin, without offering one to anyone else.

'Not so far, but they're widening out into the rubber and the *ulu* on both sides of the road.'

A platoon of the Royal West Berkshires were at that moment tramping through the estate behind the scatter of buildings that lay beyond the bungalows and across the road, where the tappers and labourers were housed. The house servants lived in huts immediately behind the two dwellings, already the subject of intensive searching by half a dozen constables under Inspector Tan and his Malay sergeant.

'We've found fifteen spent cartridge cases, all standard three-oh-three calibre, no surprises there,' added the superintendent.

'What about footprints?' asked Douglas Mackay.

Blackwell shrugged dismissively. 'Pretty hopeless, it rained like hell early this morning. Plenty of smeared prints about, but they could be anyone's. I doubt if even the Rangers could make anything of them.'

He was referring to the Sarawak Rangers, Ibans similar to Dyaks, recruited from Borneo as trackers. Heavily tattooed all over below the neck, these little men were superb at following terrorist trails in the jungle.

'So what happens next?' demanded James Robertson.

'I've got men turning over every house up the road as far as Kampong Kerbau and the army is searching each side of the road all the way from there back to TT. Then I'm going back to see the Director of Operations in Brigade to decide if we need to widen out the search into the hills. I haven't got enough men for that, it's up to the Brigadier to decide if he wants to turn this into a major operation.'

'And what happens if those bastards come back tonight – or tomorrow?' snapped Diane, with nervous anger.

'We're running a permanent patrol after dark, up and down between TT and Kampong Kerbau,' reassured the superintendent. 'The police will use an armoured Land Rover and there's a scout car coming from the Garrison.'

He drained his orange juice and picked up his hat and stick.

'I wouldn't worry too much, I've got a gut feeling that this was some spur-of-the-moment shoot-up by some crazy devil. Go down to the dance at The Dog tonight and take your mind off it.'

'I'll use the Buick, at least that's got some protection,' glowered James.

'More than my poor Austin,' snapped his wife. 'I'll have to send Siva to Ipoh tomorrow, to get a new windscreen fitted.'

As Steven Blackwell turned to leave, Douglas rose to follow him, Rosa almost scurrying to his side to take his arm. The

Robertsons offered a surly farewell to the trio and as the manager and his wife walked away across the coarse grass of the knoll towards their own bungalow, Diane went out on to her verandah to glower after them, reserving a specially poisonous glare for the trim figure of Rosa Mackay.

THREE

Although the Friday night function at the Sussex Club was nominally a dance, the majority of the members never set foot on the floor, which was a small area of the big lounge cleared of tables and chairs. The occasion was hallowed by tradition at The Dog, being the main social function of the week, where people came to meet their friends and catch up on the week's gossip. They came to see and be seen, the men to ogle the younger women in their posh frocks and the older women to indulge in some righteous envy and to complain about their husbands.

In such an isolated community as Tanah Timah, the club provided virtually the only social diversion for the wives, who had not even the workplace or the Mess to relieve the boredom. There were not many Army wives there, as the place was still on the fringe of a brutal war, but as the terrorist threat had receded somewhat in this part of Perak, more of the senior officers' wives were coming out from home. The planters' wives had little choice but to stay, though some took extended leave back in Britain, often with the excuse that they had to see their children settled in boarding schools or colleges.

The younger women were almost all commissioned QA sisters from the hospital and being by definition unmarried, were the target of every military bachelor in the Brigade, as well as a few unaccompanied husbands and unmarried planters. Tonight, it was these ladies who monopolized the dance floor, being badgered by subalterns, lieutenants, captains and even the odd major, to gyrate with them on the polished boards, which a houseboy ritually lubricated with French chalk every Friday afternoon.

Tom Howden arrived at about eight fifteen, driven up by Alec Watson in his battered and rusty Morgan sports car. Dinner in the Mess was always brought forward on a Friday, so that they could get to the club reasonably early – a practice almost universal throughout the garrison. At about ten o'clock, the record player was switched off so that the assembled members could adjourn to the dining room, where Daniel always laid out a light buffet to keep them going until midnight, when the revellers drifted back to their mosquito nets.

Alec parked on the tarmac in front of the club, finding a space between the Austins, the Morris's, the MG's, the Land Rovers and a few big American gas-guzzlers, several of them armour-plated like the Robertsons'. Inside, there was already hardly an inch left free at the long bar, which ran across the full width of the lounge. A score of low tables fringed the dance floor, each with its circle of cane chairs. They were filled with people and the Indian servants were performing miracles of gymnastics with trays loaded with glasses and bottles, as they threaded their way through the obstructions. Half a dozen couples were swaying to a smoochy Sinatra number, generated by a Decca radiogram in the corner, operated by a fat Tamil houseboy who was worriedly studying a list of records supplied by Daniel, but constantly amended by the demands of the dancers.

The music was almost drowned by the buzz of chatter, which tonight was a good few decibels louder than usual. The inevitable topic was the new attack on Gunong Besar and as soon as Tom came in, he could see that the focus of attention was on James Robertson. He was perched on a stool at the centre of the bar, holding court amongst a cluster of acquaintances, all of whom had their own pet theory of what had happened. As Alec pushed his way to the bar for a couple of Tigers, Tom moved further along to be in earshot of the James's clique.

'Bloody bullets were coming like hailstones,' brayed the planter, waving his gin like a flag. 'Pushed the memsahib on to the floor out of the way, then took off over the verandah with my shooter!' He stopped for a gulp of Gordon's, then carried on with his elaborated saga.

'But it was too late, the sods had all vanished. They'd shot up Douglas's place first, then had a pop at the natives around the back.'

'Sounds a bloody queer attack to me, Jimmy,' drawled Les Arnold, the Aussie from the next estate beyond Gunong Besar. He was not actually part of the inquisitive circle around James, he had been sitting at the bar before they descended on his neighbour and had been enveloped by them.

'What's queer about being shot at, Les?' demanded a captain from the West Berkshires, rather indignantly.

'Not like the CTs to fire off a few rounds, then bugger off!' objected the Australian. 'Even in Jimmy's last attack they killed a couple of blokes.'

Robertson flushed, both at being repeatedly called 'Jimmy' and at the insinuation that his latest moment of glory had not been all that glorious.

'An attack's an attack, Les!' he snapped petulantly. 'What d'you think all those holes are in the walls – giant termites?'

There was a guffaw from the group at this witticism, but Arnold just grinned.

'Good on you, mate! I'm glad they didn't call on me, just up the road from you. I need my beauty sleep every night.'

Alec came back with the beers and he and Tom leaned against one of the pillars that supported the high roof while they looked around at the talent in the room. The disc jockey had found one of the request records and now Tony Bennett was crooning about a 'Stranger in Paradise', giving the swaying couples the excuse to cling together as if they had been welded front-to-front, their feet hardly moving.

'Some nice-looking birds here, Alec,' murmured the pathologist. Stuck in his laboratory all that first day, he had so far hardly laid eyes on a QA, apart from their motherly Matron, Doris Hawkins. 'Who's the dark-haired one, in the slinky blue dress?'

Watson grinned. 'You got it in one, Tom! Everyone notices her first. That's our in-house *femme fatale*, Lena Franklin.'

Howden looked across to the centre of the dance floor and saw a slim, sexy-looking woman in her late twenties, with dark hair in what he called a Gina Lollobrigida style. Her eyes were enhanced catlike with make-up and her glossed lips were in a slight pout as she rested her chin on her partner's shoulder. Her dress was a westernized version of the Chinese *cheongsam*, a skin-hugging sheath of blue silk with a high collar and a slit up each side to the thigh. Tom could almost see the disapproval coming off some of the older wives, like a black cloud

ascending to the fans overhead. Lena was certainly a dish-
and-a-half, he thought. No wonder David Meredith was brassed
off at the prospect of losing her to someone else.

'Who's the guy she's with? That her new bloke?'

'Nay, he's some prat one-pipper from the Hussars. Looks
as if she's using him to fire up our master gasman – to say
nothing of Jimmy Robertson.'

Looking around the crowded room, they found their anaesthetist standing with Peter Bright against the opposite wall, an
untouched beer in his hand, scowling at the pair on the dance
floor. As they watched, a handsome redhead in a white dress
rose from a nearby table where she was sitting with several
more nurses and a couple of young men. Going up to Peter
Bright, she said something, but he smiled and shook his head.

'That's another factor in the equation, Tom,' said Alec, who
seemed to be a mine of information on the scandals and
intrigues of Tanah Timah.

'Who's she?' Tom asked, as he watched the auburn-haired
girl talk animatedly to the surgeon.

'That's our Joanie . . . Joan Parnell, QA sister on Medical
One. She's like a rash!'

'What d'you mean – like a rash?'

'She's all over you! Especially if you're Peter Bright, she's
got the hots for him even though everyone knows he's after
Diane Robertson.'

Joan had now wrestled the glass from Peter's hand and
putting it down on a shelf, was dragging him to the dance
floor, leaving David Meredith alone and even more darkly
morose.

'I'm getting confused over all this,' muttered the pathologist.
'It's like one of these Whitehall farces, with people popping
in and out of bedroom doors.'

'You won't get that, at least not on hospital premises,' said
young Watson. 'Both the Matron and our Old Man keep their
beady eyes firmly on the bedroom doors in BMH.'

Just then, Alec spotted a couple of members leaving the bar
and they quickly slid on to their vacated stools. 'That's better,
we can see the action in comfort now,' he said smugly.

The nubile Joan Parnell was wrapping herself enthusiastically around their surgeon on the dance floor and Peter Bright, though enjoying the feel of a lithe body in his arms, was casting wary glances around the room as they revolved slowly to the music.

'Pete's on the lookout for the evil eye from Memsahib Robertson,' explained Watson, his boyish face alive with interest at the goings-on around him. 'Though I haven't seen her here yet, maybe the shooting has given her the vapours.'

Tom was still doggedly working out the romantic permutations. 'Her husband's here, anyway. You reckon he's having a fling with this Lena woman, the one that our gasman is keen on?'

'That's it – and rumour has it that for years he's been playing away with Rosa, until just recently.'

'Who the hell's Rosa?'

'The wife of his manager, Douglas Mackay. They're here somewhere, I've seen them.'

'Bloody hell, this is like something out of Somerset Maugham!'

Tom buried his face in his Tiger while he sorted out the machinations in his mind. 'Any more shenanigans I should know about, while you're at it?' he asked, when he surfaced.

'Not that I know of,' admitted Alec regretfully. Then he brightened a little, 'Apart from our dear Commanding Officer, of course!'

'Jesus, don't say he's been rogering someone too? I thought he was married?'

'He is – that's the point! His missus was out here with him until two months ago, then she suddenly ups and goes home to UK. She was a right old battleaxe and the whisper is that she got fed up with him. But no one knows why?'

'Where does he live, then?'

'He's still in his married quarter in Garrison, thank God. By rights, he should quit and come to live in the Mess, now that he's on his own. That would be bloody awful, having the old bastard amongst us, but I think he's got some pull with the Brigadier, who's letting him stay on in his house. He's only got three months to go before RHE, so perhaps we'll escape a fate worse than death!'

Howden looked along the bar to where James Robertson was regaling another relay of listeners with his tale of derring-do.

'Doesn't he know his wife's having it away with Peter Bright?' he murmured.

Watson shrugged. 'Dunno – but it's difficult to keep any secrets in an incestuous place like TT. If the padre farts, everyone knows within ten minutes, so even though Jimmy Robertson is as thick as two short planks, he must surely have his suspicions.'

'Maybe he doesn't want to know, especially if he's at it himself.'

Alec nodded over his glass. 'Quite possible – he's had plenty of practice, I hear. The delicious Diane is said to have been putting it about for years. Not much else to do around here,' he added cynically.

Their scandalmongering was interrupted when a beckoning hand waved at them from one of the tables. It was Major Hawkins, the Matron, resplendent in a pink dress that looked like a floral bell-tent. She was sitting with four other girls who Tom assumed were QAs.

'Come and meet some of the staff, doctor,' she said kindly. Tom was warmed by her words, as he hadn't been called 'doctor' since he left Tyneside – it was either 'Captain' or 'Howden'. The two men perched on the arms of the girl's chairs and Alec helped the Matron to introduce them. Tom caught a couple of names, but remembered only one afterwards as Lynette, a slightly chubby brunette with a pretty round face and a Yorkshire accent.

They all launched into the usual polite babble of 'Where do you come from . . . was it cold at home when you left . . . d'you play tennis . . . what d'you think of it so far,' until Tom was in a haze of pleasant disorientation, but temporarily cured of his homesickness.

Of course, Alec knew them all – and probably all their business – and after a while, went off to dance with one, so Tom recklessly asked Lynette if she would like to take the floor. He was an indifferent dancer, but in the confines of the tiny space, now filled with shuffling couples, there was little harm that he could do to her feet. He acquitted himself fairly well and thoroughly enjoyed it.

The ice broken, he danced with a couple of the others and even offered himself to Doris Hawkins, who tactfully declined on the grounds that she had a bunion. At that moment, a gong was hammered by one of the club servants to announce that the buffet was served and everyone began streaming towards the dining room next door. Standing back to let the ladies through first, Tom found Alfred Morris behind him.

'Fast workers, you Geordies!' he chaffed. 'A nice little girl, that Lynette.'

'I suppose I'll be the target for gossip tomorrow,' grinned Tom.

'Tomorrow? It'll already have started, lad.' The Admin Officer suddenly stopped and Tom noticed his head jerk round, then swing back.

'We've got company, son.' As they shuffled towards the dining room, they were overtaken by a lean figure shepherding a spectacular blonde. The men stood aside to let Diane Robertson through, Desmond O'Neill following closely behind, a fixed grin on his saturnine face.

'Where the hell did he find her?' muttered Alec Watson.

'Maybe that's why his wife went home in a huff!' hazarded Tom.

The young Scot glared at him pityingly. 'Come off it, he's old enough to be her father. Even the fabulous Diane wouldn't touch old Death's Head.'

When they got inside the other room, they saw that their Commanding Officer had ushered the blonde over to her husband, who was vigorously attacking the sandwiches, chicken thighs and curry puffs. James did not seem to be particularly excited at the delivery, giving his dearly beloved a grunt as he handed her an empty plate and serviette.

'Does the colonel come here a lot?' Tom asked Alf Morris, who he found alongside him as their turn came to pile their plates with food.

'Plays bridge quite a bit and uses the pool, but he only started coming to the dance night since his wife went home.'

The pathologist looked across at where their lord and master was picking at his food. Though almost all the other men just wore shirt and tie, O'Neill had a rather old-fashioned cream linen jacket over his, contrasting strongly with the wide red, blue and gold stripes of the Medical Corps tie that hung down from his collar. It reminded Tom of his grandad, who used to wear a similar jacket with a straw hat when he went to play bowls in Gateshead Park.

After they had all eaten, the music began again, but to Tom's disappointment, the depth of which surprised him, Lynette had been commandeered by a lanky officer from the Gurkhas. The bar was less crowded now, as James had vanished and his audience had dispersed.

Tom got himself another beer and signed his chit, wondering what sort of a hole his bar bill would make in his pay at the end of the month, both here and in the Mess. By the sound of it, pretty soon he would have to scrape together enough for a second-hand car – especially if he was to fully enter into the social life, for which a wide back seat seemed to be essential.

The heat seemed to hit him again, the air being an almost palpable mixture of damp, perfume and curry fumes, so he ambled with his glass out through the open doors on to the terrace above the swimming pool, which was a large concrete-walled tank with a sloping floor.

The tables just outside the lounge were occupied with couples gazing into each other's eyes, so he walked to the far end, overlooking a badminton court. As the club was built on the slope of a hill, the court was set a dozen feet lower than the terrace. Normally it was lit at night by fluorescent tubes, but on dance nights, it was dark and deserted. At least, no one was playing badminton there, but as he stood quietly with his beer listening to the still-novel sounds of insects chirruping and frogs burping, he could see two shadowy figures and hear their voices. The figures came closer together in the gloom – very close indeed, until he could see only one larger shape in the dim light from the open doors of the lounge.

'When can you get away, say for two days? I've got to go to KL, to see about some machinery . . .'

Suddenly feeling guilty at eavesdropping, Tom moved away, back towards the doors, but his guilt somehow evaporated sufficiently for him to sink into a vacant chair just inside and accidentally still be there when Lena Franklin walked in, still spectacular in her slinky blue dress. She gave him a glowing smile as she passed on towards the Ladies' Room near the entrance. A moment later, James Robertson stalked in and plumped himself down at the bar, no doubt determined to enlarge once again on the story of his escapade the previous night.

The anxious disc jockey came to the end of his rumba and was being importuned by one of the nursing sisters, who was grasping Montmorency by the hand as if saving him from drowning. As they negotiated with the Tamil for a cha-cha, Alec Watson was abandoned by the girl he had been dancing with and he came across to collapse into the chair next to Tom.

'Too bloody hot for these energetic sports!' His shirt had arcs of dark sweat beneath each armpit.

'Was that one of the QAs you were with?' He had been dancing with a very thin girl, who looked no more than seventeen.

'No, that was one of the daughters of the Commandant of the MCE.'

The pathologist frowned at yet another set of initials.

'That's this mysterious place I've got to go to on Monday morning, where I get my blood from, apparently. What the hell is it?'

'Military Corrective Establishment – the chokey, the hoosegow, the jail!' explained Alec. 'The RMO of the West Berkshires has been filling in since your predecessor went home last month, but it's traditional that the pathologist does the sick parades over there, as that's where you get your blood donors.'

He explained that the prisoners were only too willing to exchange a pint of their blood for a bottle of Tiger – in fact, they fell over themselves to offer and their donations had to be strictly rationed, for fear of them exsanguinating themselves in return for a few beers. Light dawned upon Tom, as this explained why he hadn't seen a Blood Bank refrigerator when he walked around his lab for the first time that day.

'I see, so the blood is kept "on the hoof", so to speak?'

'Sure, it's kept sterile and at body temperature – and it never gets out of date!'

Their haematological discussion faded as they watched Diane Robertson come in from the dining room and join a group of men at the bar, Peter Bright amongst them. She was worth watching, thought Tom, her shoulder-length fair hair contrasting with a low-cut dress of black Chinese brocade. Diane seemed to have got over her terror at the previous night's shooting and was laughing and flirting with her attentive escorts, one of whom was Les Arnold, though her husband pointedly ignored her.

'How the devil did she manage to arrive here with O'Neill?' he asked Watson, who Tom now looked on as the fount of all knowledge.

'Percy Loosemore said he arrived in the car park just before them. Apparently she turned up in a taxi, as it doesn't look as if she's speaking to her husband and her own car has been shot up. The CO arrived at the same time in his Armstrong Siddeley and gallantly shepherded her inside.'

Tom didn't know that TT had any taxis, but learned later that there were two battered Wolseley 6-80s and a Ford Consul run by a Chinese garage owner behind Main Street.

'The colonel looked as if they had just got engaged, not just walking her in off the car park!' he grunted. 'Think he's got a crush on her?'

'God knows what goes on in that twisted mind of his!' grumbled the Scot. 'He's certainly loosened up since his missus went home. She kept him on a pretty short leash, that's why he took it out on everybody at BMH, we reckon.'

The beers had loosened Tom's tongue a little beyond the point of discretion and he told his friend about the assignation he had seen between Diane's husband and Lena Franklin. 'Sounded as if he was trying to fix up a dirty weekend, the lucky devil!'

Alec nodded. 'Good job it was you that heard them and not Dave Meredith. There'd have been blood on the badminton court if he had!'

He leaned a little closer with a conspiratorial air. 'It was my turn last Friday to overhear Jimmy Robertson. I was in the Gents, standing at attention below that high-up window. He was outside, getting a right earful from his wife, something about her finding a hotel bill. I couldn't hear the rest, as they moved away, but from the tone of her voice, if she'd had a knife, she'd have stuck him there and then!'

Tom shook his head in wonderment as he reached forward for his tall glass of Anchor. 'We don't need a war out here, there's enough "aggro" going on between the residents!'

He looked across the room to where Rosa Mackay was sitting bolt upright, looking very Latin in a lacy white blouse and a black skirt. She was holding a glass of Pimm's and though exotically immaculate, looked very unhappy. Her scrawny husband, looking old enough to be her father, sat alongside her, both of them silent and withdrawn.

'How the devil did those two get together?' asked Tom. 'They seem totally unsuited to each other.'

As usual, Alec Watson had the answers – the pathologist decided that the Army would have been better off drafting him into the Intelligence Corps, rather than the RAMC.

'I heard that he was working on an estate down in Johore before the war. He was interned in Singapore by the Japs and apparently had a hard time in Changi Prison. His first wife died of dysentery in an internment camp in Sumatra. Douglas met Rosa in a hotel in Malacca, where she was the receptionist. It seems that the manager was pestering her and Douglas's interest was a means of escape.'

'He's not exactly love's young dream, is he? Not for a cracking-looking woman like her?' objected Tom.

Watson shrugged. 'What! A Eurasian with no better prospects than slaving in a fleapit beach hotel with the manager trying to pinch her bum all the time? A European husband, her own bungalow far away – not a bad catch. And he's Scots,' added Alec with a grin.

Looking across the room at the smooth-faced woman from Gunong Besar, Tom had his doubts about her contentment, which the ruthless Watson soon confirmed.

'Of course, they say that Jimmy Robertson has been servicing her for years, probably ever since the Mackays came up here in 1950.'

The pathologist's eyebrows rose on the part of his face still visible above his glass. 'You really are a wicked young gossip,' he grated, when he came up for air. 'I don't know how much of your slander is true and how much you invent!'

The young doctor, who looked almost angelic in spite of his genius for trading scandal, shrugged off the criticism. 'I just keep my ears open, that's all. And I've got a good memory!'

He finished his drink and stood up. 'I'm off for a pee, then a couple of turns around the floor again, before heading for bed.'

'And no listening at the bog windows tonight, Alec!' chastised Tom, as he looked around to see if Lynette was available now.

FOUR

Next morning, Steven Blackwell sat alongside his Malay driver as the dark blue police Land Rover turned into the gates of the garrison. The barrier went up and the superintendent raised his stick to return the stiff salutes of the two red-capped MPs outside the guardroom. Unlike the hospital compound, the much larger enclave of the Twenty-First Commonwealth Independent Infantry Brigade had a central road passing straight up from the main gate, with a number of side lanes reaching across to the perimeter track that ran round inside the wire. The Headquarters was near the centre, an untidy collection of brick, concrete and wooden buildings set around a parade ground, where the Union Jack and the blue flags of Australia and New Zealand hung limply from a tall flagpole.

The driver, wearing his *songkok*, a black boat-shaped cap, pulled up at the side of a flat-roofed two-storey brick building, which should have been the despair of any self-respecting architect. Telling him in Malay to wait in the car park along the road, the police officer climbed a metal staircase to the upper floor and went into a short corridor. Familiar with the place from many previous visits, he tapped on the second door and went in unbidden. It was an outer office, with some spartan desks behind which a couple of corporals were working. A staff sergeant in the far corner turned from a filing cabinet.

'Colonel Flynn's expecting you, sir.'

He tapped on an inner door and stood aside to let Blackwell enter. The inner office was almost as dreary, but large maps pinned to the walls brightened it up a little.

Three men were sitting around the solitary desk and rose as he came in. He knew them all well and after a handshake and a few pleasantries, they all sat down again, with the colonel in his own chair behind the desk. The Director of

Operations was a tall, lean man with slight stoop, a pair of intelligent eyes peering out from beneath bushy fair eyebrows. Each shoulder carried the crown and pip of his rank and he wore the flash of the Airborne regiment from which he had been seconded. He was a military planner, who with the more senior brass in the Brigade, coordinated the campaign against the terrorists in that area, subject to the directions – or what he often felt was the interference – of Command Headquarters down south in Seremban, and their bosses at GHQ FARELF in Singapore.

The other two soldiers were a rather plump captain from the Intelligence Corps and a burly SIB staff sergeant from Ipoh, who looked every inch the Coventry detective he had been before joining the Special Investigation Branch of the Military Police. Though a non-commissioned officer, he had a ponderous presence that made him seem a peer of the senior men. The office sergeant brought in mugs of tea and when he had left, they got down to business.

'We have to decide what this damned affair at Gunong Besar was all about,' began Flynn. 'We've got a big operation planned up towards Grik and I don't want it to be sidetracked by a wild goose chase nearer home.'

'Yet we can't shrug it off completely,' said Steven Blackwell. 'The planters are entitled to all the protection we can give them. Someone has to grow the bloody rubber and one of Chin Peng's objectives is to damage the economy in Malaya.'

The colonel nodded abruptly. 'I couldn't agree more! I'm damned if I'd like to sit out in some lonely bungalow with my wife and be shot at by some murderous bastards.'

'But the point is, sir,' growled the SIB man, 'which lot of murderous bastards was it?'

The Intelligence officer, Captain Preston, wiped some sweat from his pink forehead with a khaki handkerchief.

'That's what we must try to decide, isn't it? Was this a CT escapade – or some local Johnny banging away with a three-oh-three?'

'So you tell us, Willy,' retorted the colonel, rather shortly.

'There's nothing to indicate that any of the known Commie

cells is active around here at the moment, though of course, that can change overnight. The sods can trek through the hills and appear next day twenty miles away from where we last spotted them.'

The police superintendent added his own knowledge.

'The last activity I know of through police channels was a fortnight ago near Sauk where they tried to blow up a sub-station on the hydroelectric grid coming down from Chenderoh dam. Otherwise, it's been pretty quiet up here for a couple of months. They seem to be concentrating more down south in Johore and Negri Sembilan.'

'The point is, gentlemen, am I to recommend to the Brigadier that we send patrols out into the hills beyond Gunong Besar? He won't like that, as he wants the West Berkshires and the Gurkhas to get prepared for this push up around Grik. The alternative is to write this off to some local thuggery and let it ride?'

'With some extra protection up around the estates, I would hope,' cut in Blackwell. 'I've increased the police presence along the road, but there's only so much I can offer with the manpower I've got.'

The Director nodded curtly. 'We've promised that already – and we'll certainly keep it in place for a number of weeks. I'll get some of these dozy soldiers off clerking and painting flagpoles and truck 'em up and down to Kampong Kerbau every few hours.'

The raw-boned sergeant joined in, to justify his drive up from Ipoh.

'If it's not the CTs, sir, what's the alternative? Why should any local Malay or Chinese want to shoot up a couple of bungalows?'

'Or an Indian, as it could be a disaffected tapper or latex worker,' Blackwell reminded them. The two policemen began a dialogue, leaving the Army men out of it for the moment.

'There's no suggestion that any of the workers at Gunong Besar have been sacked or victimized lately,' replied Blackwell. 'Though the owner certainly isn't loved by one and all up there, I'll admit.'

'No possibility of any Europeans having it in for him, is there, sir?'

The superintendent smiled rather wryly. 'There might be a few who'd like to take a swing at Jimmy Robertson, but I doubt they would want to shoot him!'

Colonel Flynn's laugh was more like a bark.

'I wouldn't be too sure about that, Steven! But spraying two bungalows and the workers' lines with bullets is hardly an effective way of going about an assassination!'

'What about these bullets, sir?' asked the humourless SIB man, who had a craggy face with a lantern jaw. 'Have they been identified? And what about the cartridge cases?'

They looked at the local police chief for information.

'We've got them all, they were all standard three-oh-three to fit either Lee-Enfields or Brens, but I don't see what they can tell us, with no chance of getting any weapon to test. I've sent some of them, together with bullets that my inspector dug out of the woodwork, down to the Government Chemist's place in Petaling Jaya, just in case.'

This was the nearest they had to a forensic laboratory, in the suburbs of Kuala Lumpur.

'Maybe the Ordnance Corps boffins could tell us when they were manufactured or issued,' suggested the Intelligence Corps officer.

'They'd probably have to send them back to the UK for that, but it's worth trying,' said the sergeant. 'Trouble is, there's so much of that stuff knocking around. The CTs have stolen some and a lot is still left over from when they were fighting the Japs.'

'These were all single shots, according to the witnesses,' continued Blackwell. 'So it's unlikely they were fired from a Bren. Someone had to keep pulling a trigger and working a bolt, which seems a bit odd, with about fifteen shots fired.'

'That's if it was one person, sir,' observed the sergeant, cussedly. 'It could have been twenty persons firing one shot each – though that's bloody unlikely, I know.'

The discussion went on for some time and the eventual conclusion was what the colonel wanted, which was to avoid a major hunt through the many square miles of hills beyond the rubber estates on the Kampong Kerbau road. When they eventually broke up, the SIB man drove his own vehicle over to the police station to collect a couple of the empty shells that Inspector Tan had retrieved, to send to the Army ammunition experts. After he had gone, the superintendent decided to take a trip up to Gunong Besar to reassure the Robertsons about the increased patrols on the road.

As he sat in the Land Rover's passenger seat for the fifteen-minute drive, he absently watched the clean, straight lines of the rubber trees passing by and like so many expatriates and military, wondered what it was like back home now, just before Christmas. He came from Derbyshire and nothing could be more unlike the winter-cold heathland and crags of the Peak District than this steamy, lush land of padi, rubber and jungle-covered mountains. His wife had gone home in October, on a six-month visit to be with their eldest daughter, who was having her first baby in the New Year. Steven Blackwell had been in Malaya since the end of the war, taking the chance of promotion from a sergeant in the Manchester force to Inspector in Malaya, helping to re-establish the police after the Japanese occupation. Now forty-five, his ability and dedication had pushed him up to Superintendent and if he could stay alive for another five years, he would be eligible for a good pension and the chance to start another career back home. Wryly, he thought that though he had been exempt from military service during the war, he was now as much soldier as policeman, a large part of his duties being anti-terrorist, especially this liaison with the military.

As the heavy tyres whined on the hard-packed earth of the track, he wondered what the locals thought of their country being turned into a battlefield for year upon long year, for ideological reasons. Maybe they would have been just as contented – or discontented – under the Communist Party of Malaya as under the imperialist British? He doubted that, as though the Malays were generally a placid people, there was little love lost between them and the Chinese, who held the commercial power in the country. There had already been bad riots and plans for independence were well advanced. Blackwell stole a look sideways at his driver, a smooth-faced, amiable Malay and suspected that he was not too bothered about who ruled in Kuala Lumpur. He had regular pay, his family was housed in two rooms in the police compound, he had a nice uniform and he could drive around all day – the acme of ambition for many Malays being a job as a *syce*, a chauffeur.

Steven sighed, maybe all the Europeans should just bugger off home and leave the natives to get on with it – what business was it of ours, anyway? Another disastrous war had not long finished in Korea, but there was little sign of Chin Peng giving up here, though he was slowly being forced back by measures introduced by the stern genius of General Sir Gerald Templer, who had recently returned to Britain to become Chief of the Imperial General Staff.

Blackwell threw off his attack of introspection as they were coming through the cutting on the last lap before Gunong Besar. These moods must be from living alone since Margaret went home, he thought irritably. As they came in sight of the knoll on the right, his driver pulled over to let a Ferret armoured car pass them in the opposite direction, one of the frequent patrols that the Army had promised. With a wave to the driver just visible behind his protective flap, his driver turned up the slope and climbed to the flat area in front of the larger bungalow. As he climbed out, he could see Diane come to the rail of the verandah above, attracted by the sound of their vehicle.

He touched the peak of his cap in greeting. 'Hello there! Is James about?'

The blonde waved a glass and Steven realized that he had rarely seen her without a drink in her hand.

'He's around somewhere. Come up and have a stinger.'

Though he rarely took a drink in the daytime, it was approaching lunchtime, so he climbed the steps and accepted a small gin and tonic, which Siva brought, along with another larger one for the 'Mem'. She was looking as desirable as usual in a slim green linen dress and the police officer had no difficulty in appreciating why she caused so much man-trouble in the area.

'Siva will go out and look for his lordship,' she said with scarcely veiled sarcasm. 'He's probably down in the sheds with Douglas, doing whatever they do with that stuff.'

Her dismissive description covered what Steve knew to be a complex process that needed large open sheds for coagulating the raw latex with formic acid, then rolling it into sheets before drying in the smoke sheds, ready for export. However snooty she might be about it, it kept her if not in actual luxury, at least in new dresses, shoes and gin.

'Did you see the new patrol go by just now?' he said encouragingly. 'They're using an armoured car now, as well as the usual Land Rovers.'

'Great! I wish they'd park one right outside. What happens in the hours between patrols? We could be shot dead five minutes after they've passed!'

The superintendent sipped at his gin, which was still stronger than he wanted at this time of day. 'I don't think you need worry too much, Diane. I've just come from a meeting in Brigade with Army Intelligence and the SIB. We've come to the conclusion that it wasn't any organized CT gang. The best money is on it being someone with a grudge against the estate. That's why I've come to have a word with James.'

'There's quite a few people with a grudge against my dear husband, some not very far from here. In fact, I'm one of them, but I didn't shoot the swine, much as I might like to sometimes.'

Blackwell couldn't think of a suitable response to this, but thankfully he was spared the task, as the crunch of tyres outside heralded James's arrival in the mud-encrusted Series One Land Rover that he used around the estate.

'Staying for lunch, old chap?' he brayed as he swaggered into the lounge, his big body immediately dominating the room.

'Sorry, have to get back. I just came up to tell you that we've markedly strengthened the patrols up and down the road, as I was just telling Diane.'

He related the gist of the meeting they had at Brigade that

morning and emphasized the theory that the shooting may
have been from a single disgruntled person.

'I asked you before, but can you think of anyone who
might have a serious grudge against you or Douglas
Mackay?'

The heavily handsome planter ran a hand through his thick
wavy hair and pursed his lips as he gave the question some
serious thought.

'Every employer has a natural turnover of workers. Some
get fired, if they're no bloody good – either lazy or thieving
or stirring up trouble with the others. But that's been going
on for years, no more at Gunong Besar than any other estate.
In fact, I know that Les Arnold had an actual punch-up with
one of his truck drivers a few months back.'

'I know, we arrested the fellow – he got a couple of months
in Taiping jail for assault,' replied Steven. 'So you can't think
of anyone who could have done this?'

The estate owner shook his head impatiently. 'No! And I
still think you're wrong. The bandits had a go at this place
six months ago and that was genuine enough, because you
even shot one and he turned out to be a CT. So why the hell
should this be any different?'

Nothing would shift James from his conviction and the
policeman felt that the planter was keen to maintain his status
as valiant hero against the communist hordes. After some more
inconsequential chat, Blackwell took his leave. As the police
vehicle drove down the drive, Diane watched from the verandah,
chewing her lip as she saw the Land Rover turn into the road
and vanish towards Tanah Timah.

That night, in the twilight before dinner, Peter Bright sat
morosely in his room in the Mess, drinking a small whisky
from his toothglass. He was no secret alcoholic, but kept a
bottle of Black Label in his cupboard for the occasions when
he preferred his own company to that of the anteroom across
the way. Tonight he was in one of his antisocial moods and
slumped in his unlovely easy chair after writing his monthly
duty letter to his father, a family doctor in Sussex. His mother
had died some years ago and he faithfully kept in touch with

the old man, though tonight his letter was not up to his usual cheerful standard.

With the whisky getting warm in his hand, he glowered at the wall of the spartan room, his eyes fixed on a garish calendar supplied by the Chinese garage that serviced his MG, though the image of the simpering girl in a cheongsam failed to reach his brain. He was thinking of Diane Robertson and of all the unspeakable things he would like to do to that bastard James to get him out of her life.

As he had done at intervals for the past couple of months, he fantasized about ways of disposing of the husband, from poison to running him down with his car. He had fallen for the blonde very heavily indeed and though their flirting had progressed to energetic consummation, Diane had so far refused to consider a divorce. In fact, she seemed to have cooled off appreciably these past few weeks and the little red devil of jealousy that sat on his shoulder kept whispering that she had found someone else – possibly in the plural.

Peter threw down the rest of the spirit and unusually for him, got up to pour another. As he walked to the wall cupboard, few of his patients would have recognized their senior surgeon. Usually his major's uniform was immaculate, with razor-edged creases down the sleeves and legs of his smartly tailored 'jungle greens'. Tonight, after his shower at the end of the block, he had wrapped a cotton sarong around his waist, a red and white chequered tube that looked like a kitchen tablecloth. With bare chest and feet, he looked like some desert-island castaway, but the waved blond hair and the classical features made him look more like a Hollywood Tarzan than Robinson Crusoe.

He took his drink over to the desk and sat on a hard chair to drum his fingers restlessly on his writing pad. In two months' time, his three-year tour in the Far East would be over and he had been promised a posting to the Royal Army Medical College at Millbank. After ten years in the army and having endured the first half of this tour in Korea, it was likely that after London, he would be promoted to lieutenant colonel and either given a senior post in the surgical hierarchy or even offered command of a hospital.

But two months from now, he would be five thousand miles from Diane and all chance of securing the beautiful and passionate woman for a wife would be lost for ever. He deliberately thrust away any niggling doubt that she might no longer want him for a husband and concentrated on what action he could take.

Throwing down the last of the scotch, he made his decision.

Something drastic must be done or he might regret it for the rest of his life.

As the surgeon was mentally beating his bare breast and cudgelling his brains in the Officers' Mess, his surgical teammate, anaesthetist David Meredith, was sitting in the stifling heat of a cinema in the garrison compound across the fence from the hospital. He was in the inflatable auditorium of the AKC – Army Kinematographic Corporation – which looked like the top half of a silver barrage balloon tethered to the ground.

With no air conditioning, the fug from a hundred sweating bodies, most of them smoking their free-issue ciggies, was almost unbearable, but his discomfort was balanced by the fact that he was holding hands with Lena Franklin in the near darkness. The QA sister had wanted to come to see this particular film, rather than go down to Ipoh where there was one air-conditioned picture house. The attractions of Humphrey Bogart in *Beat the Devil* outweighed the near-asphyxia of the AKC and the dark-haired Lena was gazing with rapt attention at the screen where 'Bogie' was romantically chatting up Gina Lollobrigida, to whom Lena bore more than a passing resemblance. In fact, her absorption in the film worsened David's gnawing concerns about her feelings towards him, as although his moist palm was enfolding her fingers, she made no effort to respond, not even an occasional squeeze. The gasman was almost oblivious of the flickering screen and of the scratchy soundtrack that could just be heard above the chugging of the air-pump that kept the bulbous structure inflated. His mind was on Lena's fading interest in him, at a time when he was becoming so

infatuated with her that he had been getting ready to pop the big-M question to her. A month ago, they had managed a weekend away at a beach hotel in Penang and two nights of passion had convinced him that come hell or high water, she must be his soulmate for the rest of his life. Then the rot seemed to set in and though she was still willing to go out with him now and then, he felt that something had changed. Her eyes roved elsewhere when they were together and his hyper-acute senses, inflamed by jealousy and injured pride, told him that Jimmy-bloody-Robertson was behind it. Ten days ago, he had been desperate enough to follow her in his car, when he saw her setting off in a taxi from the Sisters' Mess. She had been dropped at the further end of Tanah Timah's main street where she made a show of inspecting rolls of silk in one of the Chinese fabric shops. Within minutes, an armoured Buick had rolled up and whisked her off in the direction of Ipoh.

Now he sat in the gloom with her hand in his and a leaden feeling in his chest, as he felt her interest in him melting like snow in the sun. Until that bastard from Gunong Besar had decided to become predatory, life had been wonderful – now it was ashes in his mouth. As he felt the unfamiliar burn of hatred glowing inside him, he knew he must think of some way to sabotage this passing infatuation with that arrogant sod, even if it meant some really drastic action.

Tom Howden missed the dance at The Dog the following Friday evening, as he was doing his first session as Orderly Medical Officer. He should have gone on the rota earlier, but the others thoughtfully gave him a few days to settle down. The OMO spell of duty ran from nine in the morning to the same time next day, though unless there was some emergency, there was little to be done during the daytime, as the regular staff coped with any problems. He spent the day in his laboratory, where he now had had a full week to get the hang of the routine.

After being nothing more than a junior to consultants and registrars on Tyneside, he revelled in his new-found independence. None of the other doctors here knew anything about laboratory practice and he was left to carry on more or less as he wished. True, there were set procedures laid out by the Deputy Assistant Director of Pathology down in BMH Alexandra in Singapore, but that was four hundred miles away and the DADP was said to come up to inspect only once in a blue moon. Tom's real bosses were his four technicians, who knew the business backwards and tactfully allowed their captain to think he was in charge, while they carried on blithely as they had done for the last month, since his predecessor had gone RHE.

There was Sergeant Derek Oates, a smart young Regular soldier with a clipped military moustache, who was a well-qualified medical laboratory technician. The other Brit was Lance Corporal Lewis Cropper, another Regular who had been a full corporal, but had been busted back to private when in Germany and had only recently climbed back to one-stripe. He was an engaging, but rather dodgy character, decided Tom – the type of Cockney from whom you would never buy a used car! He was thin and scraggy, with a lock of mousy hair that fell over his forehead and a uniform that fitted him even worse than most of his comrades. However, he was an excellent worker and prepared the best microscope sections of tissue that Tom had ever seen.

The other two technicians were locally enlisted Malayan Other Ranks – 'MORs', as they were known, both having been trained by the Army in the FARELF lab down in Singapore. It was a close little family and after this first week, Tom was perfectly happy and enjoyed every minute of his working day. He had a small room off the main laboratory, with a desk and a good microscope, a shelf of books and an oscillating fan – what more could a man want, he asked himself! The window looked out towards the main corridor, so he could watch the comings and goings of the whole hospital – within a few days, he could recognize every QA by their ankles without having to look up at the face under the crisp white headdress.

It was also an early-warning system in case the CO took a fancy to call, other than on the official weekly inspection of the whole hospital, which O'Neill did at ten o'clock every

Tuesday morning. Then there was much cleaning and polishing to be done before the procession arrived, protocol demanding that each member entered in strict pecking order. First the RSM would clump in to call the staff to attention, his gleaming nailed boots rattling on the concrete floor. The technicians would stand rigidly alongside their benches, as behind the RSM came the Commanding Officer, stick under arm, followed by Doris Hawkins, the QA matron, blinking benignly at everyone. The Quartermaster was next, an ageing captain with a bulbous nose and a dyspeptic mouth. Though he had a strong Liverpudlian accent, he rejoiced in the name of Robert Burns. Alf Morris, the Administrative Officer, brought up the rear, carrying a clipboard, ready to note down any commands, complaints or pearls of wisdom that might fall from the colonel's lips.

The pathologist was more fortunate than some other sections of the hospital, as the inspection of the laboratory was relatively perfunctory. Tom wondered if this was because O'Neill, who had been a public health specialist, knew absolutely nothing about pathology – or whether he was afraid of catching something nasty if he rubbed his fingers on the furniture and fittings to look for dirt. The first inspection lasted about two minutes, with a rapid perambulation around the central bench and a quick look into Tom's office and the little histology lab where Cropper cut his sections and made the tea. With a few grunts and throat-clearings, the CO ended by demanding to know if Tom had any problems. Then with a curt nod, O'Neill left the new pathologist to breathe a sigh of relief as he saw the cavalcade leave and march into the dispensary opposite to persecute the staff sergeant who ran the pharmacy.

This was now the routine of his new life and he enjoyed every minute of it, with just an occasional pang of homesickness for faraway Tyneside.

The past week had been enlivened by Christmas, treating Tom to another bizarre experience, seeing hospital staff in tropical kit going around with red Santa Claus caps – and in the children's part of the Families Ward, even a few with cotton-wool whiskers. In the sweltering heat, wards were hung with paper chains and cardboard reindeers. Carols and Christmas pop songs blared out from record players in the barrack rooms and messes. Tom volunteered to help with the decorations in Lynette's ward and even joined the carol singers who paraded the corridor on Christmas Eve, belting out 'Good King Wenceslas' in competition with the cicadas and bullfrogs.

A few days after New Year was celebrated, the OMO rota again brought Tom on Friday duty. After dinner that evening, Tom sat in the deserted Mess, quite glad of some peace following a busy day. Almost all the others had gone to The Dog, though Peter Bright had left a note to say that he was in the NAAFI library in the garrison, in case there were any major surgical emergencies that couldn't be handled by Eddie Rosen. As well as the OMO, there was always a rota for a surgeon and anaesthetist, which meant that like the Orderly Officer, they had to remain sober for the night. There was another 'gasman' apart from David Meredith, a Regular captain who lived in married quarters and rarely came to the Mess.

The pathologist lolled in one of the easy chairs, reading yesterday's *Straits Times*, which carried all the British sports news on its back pages, making home seem less far away. As he relaxed, Number One brought him a pint glass of Frazer and Neave's grapefruit soda, a satisfying drink for those temporarily on the wagon. He lay back contentedly to catch up with the recent fortunes of Newcastle United.

When he finally put the paper aside, Tom just sat quietly, listening to the endless chirrup of the crickets outside the open doors and the gentle whirr of the fans overhead. The strangeness of being dumped halfway across the world within a few weeks of leaving a cold, wet England was beginning to fade, though he still had fits of unreality about the whole business. He had rarely before been more than fifty miles from his native Tyneside. During the worst blitzes of the war, his parents had evacuated him to an aunt's farm in rural Northumberland, but apart from rugby trips and some childhood holidays to Scarborough or Whitby, he had been very much a home bird. Even as a medical student in Newcastle, he had stayed in Gateshead, living in the semi-detached with his parents and younger brother. His father was a draughtsman in the huge Swan Hunter shipyard across the Tyne in Wallsend and Mum was a dedicated housewife.

Tom's life had been happy and uneventful until now, the only major excitement being his getting a scholarship grant from the grammar school to go to university, as the family certainly could not have afforded it themselves. His parents were slightly overawed by having a doctor in the house, after generations of unambitious industrial workers in their family. When on his embarkation leave, he dressed up for them in his uniform with his three new pips on each shoulder, they stared at him as if he was a stranger from another planet, unable to recognize their 'wee Tommy' in this alien being.

Some of this went through his head as he sat alone in the cloying heat of a Malayan night. He had already written home a dozen times and this little attack of nostalgia decided him to start another epistle later that evening. He had a pack of flimsy airmail envelopes in his room, all with strips of greaseproof paper under the flaps to stop them sealing themselves up spontaneously in the humidity. It was little things like that which brought home to him how far away from home he was – along with the egg cup full of anti-malaria tablets on the breakfast table each morning and the free issue of a tin of anti-foot-rot powder. There was also a free issue of fifty cigarettes each week, but as he had given up smoking at the age of twelve, he gave them to Ismail, the young Malay mess boy who made his bed, cleaned his room and polished his shoes.

Lim Ah Sok padded in again from his kitchen-cum-bar, to ask if he wanted another drink.

'No thanks, Number One, on duty tonight. Must keep a clear head in case Chin Peng comes!'

He immediately wondered whether he should have make such a feeble joke to another Chinese, but the razor-thin steward merely grinned and made a dismissive gesture with his hand.

'Those devils not come anywhere near here – too many guns in garrison!'

Tom wasn't so confident, as he had heard the tale of BMH
Kinrara, where the terrorists had come up to the perimeter
wire and shot up the Sisters' Mess, fortunately without injuring
anyone. Before he left, Number One bent towards Tom as if
to impart some confidence.

'That trouble at Gunong Besar, that not CTs, sir. No, not
at all!'

He grinned again and tapped a lean forefinger against his
nose in a cryptic gesture, before padding out to share a bottle
of Bulldog stout with his wife. Tom was left suspecting that
the servants, especially the Chinese, knew more about the
local situation than all the Army's intelligence system. They
seemed to have their own Mafia-like organization amongst
the hundreds of civilians who worked for the military, full
of information from all the houseboys, mess servants and
gossip in the central market, shops and eating stalls of Tanah
Timah. Tom's only previous experience of Chinese was
confined to one laundry in Gateshead and films about Fu
Manchu. He had assumed that they all looked the same to
Europeans, but it was patently obvious that there was more
diversity in their features than amongst whites. As for being
inscrutable and impassive, a walk down TT's main street
had soon proved that they could be as garrulous and noisy
as a bunch of drunken Italians. In spite of his sometimes
dictatorial manner, Number One was really a patient and
kindly fellow and had more than once quietly asked Tom if
there was anything he needed to help him settle down so
far from home.

The clock over the Queen's picture showed half past ten
and the pathologist shook himself out of his sleepy reverie to
grope in the pocket of his bush jacket. He pulled out the folded
sheet of paper supplied by Alf Morris. Its poorly duplicated
typing faintly set out the duties of the Orderly Medical Officer
and he studied it once again to remind himself and make sure
that he wouldn't fall foul of the CO at tomorrow's Morning
Prayers.

He had already been to Casualty near the front of the
hospital and checked that there had been no new customers
since Alec Watson had left at six o'clock. The next instruction

was to check with the Duty Sergeant in the RSM's office that
the sentries were in place at the main gate and that the internal
gate between the hospital and garrison compound was locked.
He had to check with Night Sister in the Matron's Office,
then visit each ward and speak to the nurse or orderly in
charge to make sure that all was well. If there were any
patients on the DIL or SIL, they had to be visited and their
status recorded.

Finally, the OMO had to go to the armoury – known to
all as the 'arms kote' – at the back of the compound and
check on the security. Before his first OMO duty, Alf Morris
had impressed on him that the CO was particularly strict
about this and any cock-up would call down the colonel's
wrath upon him. Only after doing this could he go to bed,
prepared to be hauled out at any time if anything untoward
occurred. This was usually someone being brought in as an
emergency to Casualty – or if there was a sudden crisis over
one of the patients.

Tom hauled himself out of his chair and took his hat and
belt from the table, before ambling out into the still night air.
The damp, scented warmth reminded him of the inside of an
orchid house in one of Newcastle's parks, which he had visited
with his parents many years ago – and again he had one of
his periodic attacks of unreality, momentarily refusing to
believe that he was on the other side of the world, within sight
of hundreds of miles of impenetrable jungle, swarming with
oriental terrorists who, given the chance, would be delighted
to kill him.

As he walked down the road towards the end of the main
corridor, the hospital compound looked ethereal in the dim
light from the lamps spaced around the perimeter fence and
under the roof of the corridor, around each of which flitted
swarms of moths and other insects. The brightest spot was
down towards the Other Ranks barrack rooms, where a
badminton court was illuminated by a battery of fluorescent
tubes. Ahead of him in the distance was the closed gate into
the main garrison compound, its lights silhouetting a row
of coconut palms that ran down inside the dividing fence.
On this side of the gate to the right of the road, was the QA

Officers' Mess, as silent as his own quarters on this dance
night at The Dog.

Tom turned into the open corridor and walked down its
length without seeing a soul, a contrast with the daytime,
when it was a bustling thoroughfare. At the front of the
hospital, he turned right and went to the small office
belonging to the RSM, where the night Duty Sergeant
camped out. Tonight it was Staff Sergeant Crosby, a pharmacist from Essex, who occupied the building opposite the
laboratory. He was a neat, dapper young man with spectacles,
a seven-year Regular with 'two to go', working for some
extra qualification that would set him up well in civilian
life. Tom found him busily writing in an exercise book,
copying from a large Pharmacopoeia propped open in front
of him.

'Plenty of time to study, doc!' he announced cheerfully.
'And plenty of experience out here, though I doubt I'll have
to dispense many antimalarials when I get back to Epping
Forest.'

They chatted for a few minutes, the pathologist unconscious of the usual gulf that the Army set between its officers
and 'other ranks'. To him, they were just two disciples of
different branches of medicine. The pharmacist rapidly
confirmed what Tom had already discovered, that the main
trade in BMH was disease, not injury. Though at the RAMC's
Keogh Barracks near Aldershot, the new medical officer
recruits were subjected to grisly displays of battle scenes,
complete with horrific wounds and fake blood, dramatically
enacted amid shouting, screaming, thunderflashes and
smoke-bombs, most of the injuries seen here were from
being run over by Land Rovers or putting fingers into moving
machinery. The vast majority of the work was diagnosing
and treating all manner of infections, from malaria to hookworm, from amoebic dysentery to the sewer-workers' Weil's
disease, leptospirosis, caught from water contaminated by
jungle rats. Sometimes, a whole patrol would have to be
pulled out of the jungle because they had succumbed to one
of the many tropical diseases on offer. Athlete's foot, gonor-
rhoea, glandular fever and appendicitis were all common

grist to the medical mill – even many of the gunshot wounds were from 'friendly fire', a euphemism for careless idiots who should never have been allowed anywhere near a firearm. True, there were frequent real emergencies, when a plane or helicopter crashed or there was a major jungle firefight or an ambush on road or rail, but BMH Tanah Timah had been lucky for several months, in that relatively few casualties from terrorist action had been brought in. As Tom rose to leave the sergeant after this illuminating chat, he fervently hoped that this situation would continue, especially on the nights when he was on duty.

He ambled back up the main corridor, calling into each ward to speak to the nurse or orderly, usually standing with them at the main door to the ward and looking down at the two rows of mosquito-netted beds, each bed set between the open doors on to the narrow verandahs. It reminded him strongly of his house surgeon days in Dryburn Hospital two years ago, before he gave up the wards for the laboratory. The same nocturnal atmosphere of settled calm, with the occasional cough, snore or fart to break the silence – though the muted whirr of the overhead fans and incessant twitter of insects from the grass between the wards reminded him that this was a world away from County Durham!

Halfway up the long corridor, he met the night sister coming the other way, doing her own rounds in the reverse direction. He was delighted to find that it was Lynette Chambers, who he'd not seen to speak to since the previous Friday in The Dog – though he had recognized her ankles several times from his office window. They met as they were both turning into Ward Seven, the one that had the two small air-conditioned rooms for special patients. Feeling easy in each other's company, they sat in the ward office for a few moments, drinking orange squash which the QA corporal fetched from the kitchen fridge. Again, Tom had a *déjà vu* sensation from his days as a house surgeon, drinking coffee in the small hours with a pretty nurse in a Northern hospital.

Lynette was easy to talk to and though their conversation was about nothing in particular, he suddenly felt that he had arrived at some watershed in his life, a peculiar sensation that flooded through him pleasantly, like the effects of a double whisky. After a few minutes, they left rather reluctantly to visit the solitary SIL, who had come off the Danger List the previous week. He was lying awake in one of the cool rooms, a tough trooper from 22 SAS based in Sungei Siput. He replied in broad Brummie accents, when asked how he felt.

'Fine, sir, now that them bloody shaking fits have gone! When can I get out of here?'

The sister explained that he'd be in for a week or two yet, before being sent for convalescence to either the Cameron Highlands or Penang. This brought a wide grin to the man's rugged face. 'Almost worth being bitten by them bloody mozzies, sir!'

Tom wagged an admonitory finger at him. 'I wouldn't try it again, lad, you damned near died, you know. Keep on taking the tablets!'

The pair went out of the little ward and the humid heat instantly wrapped itself around them like a damp blanket.

'Phwah, air conditioning makes it worse when you come out!' grumbled Tom, running a finger around the inside of his collar.

Lynette pointed to the other special room opposite, its humming cool-box sticking out of the wall. 'No one in there tonight. The OMO often sleeps there if it's empty.'

'Maybe I will – if you'll bring me a cup of tea in the morning!'

'Some hope, Captain! I'm off duty at six and straight back to my own bed, thank you.'

There was an undercurrent of playfulness in the innocent exchange and Tom felt an inner warmth steal through him, unrelated to the outside temperature.

'I'll tell the corporal you're staying, so that she can get some sheets put on for you.'

'Thanks – I'll have to go up the rest of the corridor first, then over to the armoury.'

As they parted, they waved at each other, though Tom felt the urge to kiss her, which no doubt would be an offence against Queen's Regulations. He plodded up the corridor, making quick enquiries in each of the remaining wards, where all seemed peaceful enough. At the top of the corridor he crossed the road and went across a wide patch of gravel to the arms kote which was placed between the two Officers' Messes, each a few hundred yards distant. Behind it was the high perimeter fence, lit at intervals with lamps that threw yellow pools of light down on to the gritty ground. Beyond, Tom could just make out a dim glimmer from the scattered Malay huts that lay in the scrub between the hospital and the jungle that clothed the hills that rose half a mile away.

He crunched up to the small building, which was a flat-topped concrete blockhouse with a heavy metal door, like a larger version of the defence pillboxes that had been scattered around Britain during the war.

According to Alec Watson, the place was not a dispensary of weapons to the staff of BMH in the event of a siege, but a temporary repository for the guns of soldiers admitted to hospital. The all-knowing Alec had also repeated Alf's admonition that their Commanding Officer was obsessional about its security and advised Tom to stick to every detail of 'Part Two Orders' concerning the armoury. These mysterious commandments were the Standing Orders for the Unit, as opposed to 'Part One Orders', which were a day-to-day update of tasks and events. From Alec's description, Tom had almost expected them to be carved in tablets of stone set outside the colonel's office, but eventually discovered they were rather dog-eared typed sheets pinned up on a notice board outside the Admin Officer's room.

There was a low-wattage bulb over the door of the armoury and Tom stood under it for a moment to remind himself once again from his sheet of instructions.

'Knock on door,' was the first obvious command and he did so, using a fifty-cent coin on the thick steel panel. There was some shuffling inside and he waited for a 'Who goes there?' in true military style. Instead, a small panel slid aside at eye level and a rather frightened Malay voice quavered, 'Who dat?'

'Orderly Officer. Captain Howden!' he replied, putting

his mouth near the trap, which looked like a small letter box.

There was a silence while the body behind the door digested this. Tom had the suspicion that this was the first time the MOR occupant had been lumbered with this duty; it was certainly not the same chap that was there last time.

'Identity card, sah?' came the voice again, sounding more confident now that it was probably not Chin Peng himself who was standing outside the door.

Tom pulled out his identity document, a celluloid-covered card bearing an almost unrecognizable photograph that had been taken at the Depot in Crookham.

He pushed it through the slot, generating more shuffling and muttering. Then there was much scraping and scratching of bolts being drawn and the massive door slowly swung open enough for him to squeeze through, when it was immediately slammed shut again to keep the bandits out. The pathologist was now in a cell-like room which contained only a small table and one hard chair, apart from the diminutive Malay lance corporal. On the table was a gaudy vacuum flask, a glass half filled with water and a copy of the Koran. The small space was suffocatingly hot, even though there was a fan in the ceiling below some kind of vent through the roof above, but the corporal seemed oblivious of the heat. He handed Tom's card back with a tentative smile on his smooth olive face.

'Everything OK, sir,' he confided, his almond-shaped eyes taking in the shiny new brass of the officer's cap badge and pips.

Tom nodded at him and consulted his creased sheet of paper again.

'I have to look in each of the magazines, corporal. I'm rather new at this business.'

The Malay's face stretched in a conspiratorial grin. 'Me also, sir. I got posted from BMH Kamunting last week. Another fellow from here sent back there – is crazy!' He looked suddenly doleful. 'My wife and my two kid still in Taiping.'

Tom muttered his commiserations at the habitual wayward-
ness of the British Army, but wanted to get out of the stifling
heat as soon as he could.

'I suppose I'd better look in there, corporal.' He waved
his paper at a pair of steel doors, one on each side of
the room. The soldier went to the table and took a
bunch of keys from a drawer, then unlocked the doors and
switched on the interior lights. Tom put his head inside the
first and looked at a motley collection of weapons, some
clipped in wall racks, others on the floor or on top of ammunition boxes. Most had OHMS labels tied to the trigger
guards, with names and numbers written on them. He knew
little about guns, but could recognize Lee-Enfield .303s,
some Stirlings, Stens and a few more modern-looking
weapons which he assumed were the NATO *Fabrique Nationale*
rifles.

In the other room, as well as more rifles, there was a Bren
gun on the floor and a row of grenades and a couple of revolvers
sitting on top of a box. In spite of the CO's alleged mania
about the armoury, the place looked like a second-hand shop,
but presumably Albert Morris or someone knew exactly what
was in here.

'You want to see book, sir?' The MOR scrabbled in the
drawer again and for a moment Tom thought he was going
to pull out a girlie magazine, which seemed an odd companion
for the Koran. But it was a worn red ledger that the corporal
displayed and when Tom opened it, he saw it was a listing
of all the weapons and other armaments that had been left
there, with signed entries for each deposit and withdrawal,
though there were some crossings-out and corrections here
and there.

'God, I hope wasn't supposed to check everything against
this list!' he muttered aghast, urgently consulting his piece
of paper again. But there was nothing there about making
an inventory, only an exhortation to sign alongside the time
and date of the inspection, so with sigh of relief, he scrawled
these in the back of the book and told the corporal to close
up the doors and let him out. After a precautionary peep

through the letter-box, the MOR unlocked the door and creaked it open, to let Tom escape into the comparative coolness of the night.

As it clanged shut behind him, he stepped out in happy anticipation of a good sleep in an air-conditioned room – hopefully the first time for a fortnight that he would stop sweating.

FIVE

C aptain Howden's optimism was premature, as he had hardly slipped under the single sheet of the blessedly cool bed, when he heard the muted ringing of the telephone in the adjacent ward office. A moment later, there was an urgent tapping on the door and the QA corporal put her head in.

'Sir, you're wanted in Casualty straight away. Night Sister says it's very urgent!'

Tom waited until the face vanished before he hopped out of bed, as he was only wearing his underpants. He rapidly threw on his clothes and hurried out, still belting his jacket. Going down the corridor at a trot, he glimpsed figures flitting across the end and when he reached the front, he looked over towards his right and saw the orderly sergeant and the gate guard standing by a large American car, its lights full on and the engine still running. It was on the further side of the vehicle park, outside the Casualty hut and as he jogged across, the dispensary sergeant reached in to turn off the engine.

'What's going on?' puffed Tom, as he passed.

'Don't know, sir, but there's blood on the seats!'

With this cheerful news ringing in his ears, he ran into Casualty and almost knocked over the last person he expected to see there. It was Daniel, the manager of the Sussex Club, whose face was as pale as his Eurasian complexion would allow. Although he looked shocked and agitated, he seemed physically intact as he wordlessly waved a hand towards the other side of the room, where a curtain had been pulled around one of the examination couches. Three pairs of legs were visible beneath it and one pair was instantly recognizable as belonging to the night sister.

Tom pulled the curtain aside and peered in. A still form lay on the couch and a tray of syringes and ampoules rested across his legs. A lanky medical orderly was standing near the man's head, looking as shaken as Daniel. A QA corporal rested a sympathetic hand on his shoulder and Lieutenant Lynette Chambers completed the tableau, as all three were staring down at the patient with expressions best described as impotent sadness.

'There was nothing we could do for him, he was dead before he got here,' intoned the night sister, looking up at Tom with a hint of defiance.

He went to her side and looked down at the body of James Robertson, still wearing the obligatory tie required by The Dog, though the blood-soaked shirt beneath it had been ripped open to expose his chest.

'He's been shot, sir!' muttered the orderly. 'I did a bit of mouth-to-mouth, then I was going to try cardiac massage, but Sister said that with that chest wound, it would do more harm than good.'

'We've given him nikethamide and coramine, just for form's sake,' murmured Lynette. 'But he was gone before he came through the door. No pulse nor heart sounds, no respirations – and his pupils were fixed and dilated.'

The pathologist had not been away from clinical medicine long enough to forget these signs of death – nor to remember that an experienced nursing sister knew more about dire medical emergencies than he did. He bent to peer more closely at the drying blood on the front of Robertson's chest and could see a small circular mark partly obscured by a blood-clot on the left side, just above his nipple.

'Shall I clean it up for you to see, sir?' asked the QA corporal, the first time she had spoken. She was a solid-looking blonde with a square jaw and in spite of the unexpected drama, seemed quite cool and collected.

Tom shook his head urgently. 'No, for God's sake don't touch anything! He's a civilian, this will have to be a police matter from now on.'

He stepped back from the couch and pushed his cap back on his head.

'Do we know what happened?'

'Not really, Captain Howden,' answered the sister, now primly formal in the presence of Other Ranks. 'That car raced up to the gate and Daniel from the club, yelled for it to be opened. I was in Matron's Office and ran across as he drove in. Mr Robertson was slumped in the passenger seat, bleeding. We got him on to a trolley and brought him in, but as I say, he was already dead.'

'Has Daniel told you what happened before that?

Lynette Chambers shook her head. 'It was hardly five or six minutes ago – we've been too busy since then, just in case there was a spark of life left.'

'I'll have a word with him now. Can we get him a cup of tea or something? He looks a bit shocked.'

As the corporal hurried off to the nearest ward for tea, Tom took the tubby manager by the arm and gently sat him in a chair at the duty desk. He perched himself on the top and looked down at Daniel, who looked pathetically incongruous, still wearing his bow tie above a bloodstained white shirt.

'I'm Captain Howden, a new man at the club. Can you tell me what happened?'

The steward passed a hand shakily across his high forehead.

'All members had left, sir, it was just after midnight,' he explained in his sing-song voice. 'The boys were clearing up after the dance and I was totting takings behind bar. Suddenly I heard a car outside and then there was a crash!'

He rolled his eyes dramatically and waved a hand in the air. 'I ran outside and saw Mr Robertson's old Buick had run into the back of the Ford pick-up belonging to the club. Not badly, but enough to have made that noise.'

Tom waited patiently, as Daniel seemed to have run out of emotional steam.

'Then what?' he prompted gently.

'I ran across to car, captain, and saw him slumped across wheel. I thought he had either hit his head in the crash – or was a bit worse the wear for drink.' He lowered his voice at the end, as if embarrassed to mention the possibility of James being 'one over the eight'.

'I called to him. He didn't answer, so I opened the door – and he fell out against me!' These last words came out in a rush, as the mild little man recalled his moment of horror.

'There was blood all over his front – that's when this rubbed off on me.' He picked agitatedly at his own soiled shirt.

'Did you think he was dead then?' asked Lynette, who had come across to stand at Tom's side.

Daniel shrugged and turned up his hands. 'I didn't even think about it, I just wanted to get help. One of the mess boys had come out to see what was going on and between us we pulled Mister Robertson across bench-seat to the passenger side. I jumped in, the engine was still running and I drove as fast as hell down here, five minutes away.'

'Did he move or show any signs of life during the journey?'

Daniel shook his head vehemently. 'Nothing at all, sir, he just lay against the side door, his head on his chest. As I left, I yelled at Nadin, the mess boy, to telephone hospital to say we were coming.'

The QA corporal confirmed that, as she brought mugs of tea.

'The guardroom switchboard put him through here, I took the call. But the car arrived almost as soon as I put the phone down.'

The club manager had nothing more to tell them about the incident and as he gratefully sipped the sweet tea, Tom wondered what to do next – or at least, in which order of priority he should raise the alarm?

'What about his wife? Any idea where she might be?' he asked, thinking that perhaps Diane should be top of the notification list. Daniel looked as abashed as when he ventured the possibility of the dead man being drunk.

'Missus Robertson went home earlier – or at least, she left earlier.' He corrected himself with an almost visible squirm. 'They seemed to be having disagreement in the empty dining room after the buffet. I just happened to walk in, but I left damn quickly when I heard them arguing.'

'What time was that?' As he said it, Tom wondered why he asked such an irrelevant question, but Daniel answered it without hesitation.

'Just before eleven o'clock, sir. Then she went out and they drove off in her Austin. Mr Robertson left a few minutes later.'

'They? Who were "they"?' He seemed stuck in a Sherlock Holmes mode.

The steward gave another embarrassed wriggle. 'An officer

from the garrison, I can't quite recollect his name,' he added evasively.

Tom sensed that the night sister was looking at him rather impatiently and pulled himself together.

'Right, you sit there quietly and have your tea. I'm sure other people will want to talk to you before long. I'd better get on the phone now.'

He backed off and took Lynette's arm to guide her across the room.

'Better not let anyone in here, unless we get another casualty. Keep the curtains drawn around the body and don't let anyone touch him. I'm going over to the guardroom to phone, it's a bit public in here.'

Leaving Casualty in her capable hands, he strode outside and found the orderly sergeant waiting by the armour-plated Buick, both its front doors wide open.

'Best leave one of the chaps here, Sarge. Tell them no one must as much as breathe on it until the police come.'

The pharmacist nodded and yelled for the soldier on sentry duty at the gate to come across. Tom passed him in the other direction and went into the hut alongside the red-and-white striped barrier inside the outer gate. Here he found a corporal sitting behind a bare table, a small switchboard on the wall to one side. The soldier jumped up as he came in.

'You logged the time of that call from the club just now?'

'Yessir . . . twelve-oh-seven, sir.'

The pathologist threw his hat on to the table and mopped his brow with a handkerchief. Of all the bloody nights to be stuck with OMO duty, he thought!

'Right, I've got to make some calls – and quick. I'd better tell the CO first.'

As the corporal swung around to his old-fashioned switchboard, Tom added under his breath, 'I don't want to risk a bollocking from old Death's Head for not telling him first.'

The corporal pulled up a couple of cords and plugged them into the board, then cranked a handle vigorously. Tom waited impatiently, but nothing happened and the soldier wound his bell generator energetically a couple more times, holding one half of a pair of headphones to his ear.

'No reply from the colonel's quarters, sir. Shall I try someone else?'

'Shit! Now what?' muttered the pathologist. Aloud he said 'Ring the Officers' Mess, get whoever answers to call Major Morris and tell him it's vitally urgent to get down to Casualty. Then ring the guardroom in garrison HQ and tell them that I want to speak to the most senior officer who happens to be on duty, OK?'

He was moving back to the door as he spoke, suddenly feeling like a real army officer, confidently giving orders.

'I'll be in the RSM's office, with the orderly sergeant, so put it through there – and don't take any messing from the other end, this is pretty desperate!'

He went off at a trot across the car park, heading for the light streaming from the room where Staff-Sergeant Crosby was lodging. The pharmacist met him at the door, waiting anxiously for orders.

'I've sent for the Admin Officer and I've got a call going through to garrison,' snapped Tom. 'If this is another terrorist shooting, then I expect they'll want to get troops up to Gunong Besar at the double.'

As he spoke, the phone rang on the RSM's desk and he pushed past the sergeant to grab it. On the other end was a captain from the First Battalion Royal Australian Regiment, who was that night's Orderly Officer for the Brigade. In a few words, Tom Howden explained what had happened and with a laconic Aussie acknowledgement, the infantryman rang off, leaving the doctor ticking off his mental list of things to do.

'Will he tell the police, sir?' asked Crosby, as a gentle reminder.

'He didn't say as much, so we'd better make sure.' He rattled the receiver-rest of the heavy black instrument and told the guardroom operator to get through to the Police Circle. 'Get Superintendent Blackwell if you can – if not, the most senior copper.'

As the pair waited for the phone to ring again, there was the sound of a car engine coming fast around the perimeter road and Alf Morris's Hillman pulled up with a jerk. He was wearing a hastily donned plaid shirt and flannel trousers and from the look of his tousled hair, had just got out of bed.

'What's going on? The guardroom made it sound as if Chin Peng was banging on the gate!'

'Not all that far wrong, Major!' Tom rapidly explained what had happened. 'I've tried to get the CO, but there's no answer at his house. I've notified Brigade and I'm just waiting for a call from the police.'

As if on cue, the phone rang again and the Staff Sergeant picked it up and held it towards Tom, who shook his head and motioned it towards Alf Morris.

'I think you should take over now, as senior officer.'

Thankful that he had passed the buck, he left the major talking urgently down the phone and made his way back to Casualty. He wanted to check that James Robertson had not unexpectedly come back to life and to offer any further help to Daniel and the staff – not that the competent Night Sister seemed likely to need any support. All was quiet there and after a quick glance behind the curtain at the still figure lying on the couch, the pathologist turned to the trio sitting around the table on the other side of the room. The QA corporal, a reassuring figure in her no-nonsense blue-grey uniform, was resting her hand solicitously on Daniel's shoulder as he sat hunched in his chair, shivering slightly in spite of the all-pervading heat. The RAMC orderly, a National Service private straight from sixth form, sat in awkward silence, but hopped to his feet as the officer came across. The QA looked up at Tom, her homely face as calm and efficient as that of her nursing officer.

'Sister Chambers has gone up to the Mess to tell the Matron, sir. She thought she ought to know what's going on.'

He nodded and turned to the club manager. 'Sorry to make you hang about like this, Daniel, but the police will be here very soon and they'll need to talk to you. Is there anyone you want to phone to tell them where you are – your wife, maybe?'

The rotund steward shook his head. 'Thank you, sir, but no, I'm not married. I live in club, they know where I am.'

Things began to happen then at an increasing tempo and Tom began to wonder how much of this he'd have to report to the colonel at Morning Prayers. First, Alfred Morris came across and wanted to see the body. Tom had a lurking suspicion that he wanted to make sure that his new Orderly Medical Officer was not having hallucinations or was playing some awful practical joke – but the sight of Robertson's bloody body soon reassured him. Alf was no stranger to blood and mangled bodies, having served in Field Ambulances in both North Africa and Normandy during the war. The oak leaves on one of his medal ribbons showed that he had been mentioned in dispatches, so a single shooting was unlikely to faze him. He went across and sat with the club steward for a few moments, reassuring him in a low, calm voice. They knew each other well, as Alf had been a club member for more than two years. 'The police are on their way, Daniel. Mr Blackwell is coming himself, so you're among friends.'

As he spoke, there were more engine noises outside and when the two officers hurried to the door, they saw a Land Rover and a three-tonner, both with the 21 Brigade insignia, turning in through the main gates, which the sentry had opened for them after hurrying across from where he had been guarding James's car. The newcomers drove across the front of the hospital, homing in on the lights from the Casualty Department. A tall major from the West Berkshires uncoiled himself from the smaller vehicle, followed by a lieutenant wearing an Airborne beret. Two military police, a red-capped Warrant Officer and a corporal, got down from the Bedford truck and four squaddies hopped out of the back.

The major saluted Tom's uniform, not knowing that Morris was senior in rank, but the pathologist rapidly made the introductions and stepped back smartly to let Alf carry on. As Morris explained the situation and took the infantry field officer for a quick look at the deceased, Tom saw that the MPs were looking curiously at the armoured Buick and pointing at the prominent blood staining visible inside by the light of their large torch. The four soldiers were stood at ease in front of their truck, wondering what the hell was going on.

At that moment, the developing jamboree was further enlarged by the arrival of another Land Rover, this time a blue one. It raced up to the now open gate and swerved across the

car park, its daredevil Malay driver squealing to a halt alongside the three-tonner. Steven Blackwell emerged, dressed in
mufti, as he had been at The Dog that evening and unlike Alf
Morris, had not yet gone to bed.

Once again, the RAMC major recounted the little that was
known. As soon as he had finished, his counterpart from the
garrison decided that 'something must be done'.

'Like the last attack on Jimmy Robertson, this sounds bloody
unlikely for a terrorist attack,' growled the officer from the
West Berkshires. 'But we can't ignore the possibility.'

What he really meant was that he had no intention of carrying
the can if the affair went pear-shaped and they missed the
opportunity to nail a few CTs.

'The deceased is a civilian, so investigating it is down to
me,' added the police superintendent. 'But chasing bandits is
both our jobs, so I'd be grateful if you'd kick-start that. We
need to know where this happened and whether Gunong Besar
has been attacked or is under threat.' A new thought dawned
on him.

'And where the hell is Diane Robertson?'

SIX

As the police superintendent was asking the question, Diane was driving fast up the lonely road towards her bungalow. The Austin was going well in the cooler night air and she had her shapely foot flat on the floor, urging every extra bit of speed from the little car. Her face was grim as she peered down the bright cone of her headlights that cut a tunnel through the darkness of the endless trees.

She had drunk quite a lot, but no more than usual on a Friday night and had the usual delusion of drinking drivers that their performance was that much better with a few gins inside them. She threw the small saloon around the bends, veering a little from edge to edge of the rutted red road and within minutes had covered the few miles to Gunong Besar without seeing a single vehicle. At that time of night, it would have been extraordinary if anything else was on that road, apart from the occasional police or military patrol, which as had been promised, were now more frequent.

At the estate, Diane swung up on to the slope of the knoll and drove straight under the house, stopping in an abrupt scuffing of gravel. She slammed the door and ran up the front steps to the verandah. With servants on the premises, the doors to the lounge were never locked and she hurried inside, stepping out of her heels and throwing her evening bag on to the settee as she went straight to the side table to pour herself a large gin and tonic. Her hands were shaking with a variety of emotions and the ice she had spooned out of a vacuum jug rattled against the side of the glass as she raised it to her lips.

After a couple of gulps, she calmed down and walked back out to the verandah, to lean on the rail with her glass cupped in her hands. Ironically, she wondered how many boring hours she had spent in exactly this posture since she came to Malaya. Taking another mouthful, she looked out into the velvety night, seeing only a few distant points of light far away in the valley.

Somehow, she thought, it's going to be Norfolk I'll be looking at before very long. Now down to the bare ice in her glass, she was debating whether to get another, when a sound caught her attention that penetrated the turmoil in her mind. The sound of engines came rapidly closer and even her slightly fuddled senses recognized that more than one vehicle was approaching. Almost at once, headlights flickered through the trees and moments later, a Land Rover tore up the drive, followed by an armoured car and a three-ton truck. The last two were in army drab, but the first was a blue police vehicle. A dozen soldiers in jungle green scrambled from the truck and dispersed themselves and their weapons into the trees on either side of the drive.

Two men cautiously emerged from the Land Rover, one in officer's uniform, the other in civvies. Both held revolvers as they stared up warily at the bungalow. In the light escaping from the lounge, they saw a figure leaning over the verandah – a figure with blonde hair.

'Diane? Are you alright?'

The woman recognized his voice, even though the starlight was too dim to see his face. 'Steven? What the devil are you doing up here at this time of night?'

There was some murmuring down below and the officer peeled off and went back to his men, as the policeman began climbing the steps. As he reached the top, the armoured car revved away and vanished up the road towards Kampong Kerbau. Holstering his pistol, Steven Blackwell walked across towards Diane Robertson, anxious to carry out this unwelcome task as best as he could manage.

'What's going on, for God's sake? Anyway, come in and have a drink!'

Her bright, brittle voice rang out as she went into the big room and he followed her with a heavy heart.

'Diane, forget the drink for a moment. Come and sit down, I have to tell you something.'

Hardened policeman that he was, he had been dreading this moment on the drive up from Tanah Timah, but in the event it was almost an anticlimax.

The new widow heard the news of her husband's death with

what at first seemed incredulity, then amazement tinged with curiosity. Diane neither fainted, nor screamed, nor sobbed. What she did do was go across the room and refill her glass, insisting against Steven's protests that he have a drink as well. She came back to the settee and sat down, looking up at the superintendent. Her face was pale, but otherwise she seemed unmoved.

'I don't understand this, Steve. I have to believe it, if you say so! But I can't understand it.'

He found that he needed the whisky after all and sat down rather heavily opposite the blonde, bemused by her reaction – or the lack of it.

'We don't even know where it happened yet, Diane. He just drove up to The Dog – God knows from where!'

She sipped her own drink, staring at him over the rim.

'So I'm a widow now. I don't even have a suitable black dress.' She looked down at the slinky blue model that she was wearing. It must be shock, he thought. Soon, the facts will sink in and she'll break down.

'You can't stay up here on your own. Is there someone who can stay with you? What about Rosa next door?'

Her eyebrows went up about an inch. 'Rosa! Like hell she will! That bastard was screwing her, didn't you know? Sorry, I suppose I mustn't speak ill of the dead.'

Slightly tipsy now, she jumped up and staggered slightly, then went across to get more gin. She held the bottle up and waggled it at Blackwell, but he shook his head uneasily. He didn't want a drunken witness on his hands, bereaved or not. He stood up and beckoned to her.

'Diane, come back and sit down, please! You do realize what's happened, don't you? James has been killed and we have to find out how and where, urgently.'

She padded over in her bare feet and dropped heavily on to the settee.

'I hear you, Steve, I'm not numbed with shock. You may as well know, I'd decided to leave him anyway. I was planning to go home to England, I'd had enough of his bloody nonsense.'

She took a deep drink, downing almost half the glass. 'So if I'm shocked, it's because of the surprise, not grief. I'm sorry, you're thinking I'm a hard bitch, but that's the way it is. But what the hell am I going to do now, with the bloody estate and all that?'

There's a lot more to be done before those problems need to be faced, he thought grimly, but he kept his mouth shut for the present. He suddenly realized that she had not even asked where James had been killed or who killed him!

Diane suddenly dropped her empty glass to the floor, where it rolled under the settee. She put both hands up to her head and groaned, rocking back and forth. But it was not sudden grief, but frustrated bewilderment.

'This is unbelievable, Steven! I'm suddenly a damned widow, but I couldn't care less about bloody James. I know I'm supposed to and from here on, everyone will call me an unfeeling cow! Yet everything has been turned upside down. I just can't take it in yet, I'm afraid.'

The policeman in him rapidly came back to the surface.

'I know, Diane, and I'm desperately sorry. But before we settle you somewhere, I have to ask a few things. We still don't know if this was another terrorist attack, like the previous two. When did you last see James?'

She smoothed her hair back and consciously pulled herself together, sitting more upright on the cushions.

'Of course you must get on with your job. I'm sorry, Steve.' Groping in the bag that she had thrown down, she found cigarettes and a lighter. Rather shakily, she lit up, then began speaking.

'We went to the club separately tonight. As you've heard, we haven't been on the best of terms lately. I took the Austin down at about eight thirty, James was already there.'

'What time did he go?

'No idea, he went off this afternoon to Taiping, said he had to see about some repairs to the latex machinery, though for all I know he was meeting some woman there. He didn't come back here, so I suppose he went straight to The Dog. He was there when I arrived, anyway.'

'Did he tell you anything about where he had been – or anything else relevant?'

Diane crushed out the almost intact cigarette in an ashtray

with a force that suggested that it could have been her husband's neck.

'I told you, we weren't exactly on gossiping terms these past few days. I got mad at him earlier tonight, as he was dancing with that bitch from the hospital half the evening, deliberately leaving me stuck with a gang of old biddies.'

Blackwell found it hard to say 'Which bitch?' but Diane sensed his problem and added 'That Franklin woman, the nurse he's been having it off with lately.' Her voice was getting slightly slurred.

'So when was the last time you saw him? I need to get some idea of when this might have happened, as well as where.'

She rocked slightly and Blackwell was afraid that she might fall over, but she pulled herself together and steadied herself with a hand on the arm of the settee. 'We had a row later on, after the buffet. When the room was empty, I cornered him and gave him a piece of my mind. Then I walked out and that's the last I saw of him.'

'What time would that be?'

'I told you, after the supper had finished. About half ten or a bit later, I suppose.'

Almost like an automaton, Diane walked over to the sideboard and poured herself yet another drink, before coming back to flop heavily on to the settee. She lifted the glass to her lips, where it rattled momentarily against her teeth as she gulped at the gin. Her lipstick was smudged, half of it on the rim of her glass.

'And when did you leave the club?' asked Steven.

'Soon after that, I'd had enough of his nonsense. I left him picking at what was left of the buffet.'

The superintendent ran a hand nervously over what remained of his hair, as the next questions would have to probe into sensitive territory. He was conscious again of the difficulties of being a policeman in a small European community, where almost everyone he had to interrogate would be a close acquaintance.

'Can you tell me what the row was about, Diane?' he said gently.

He need not have been so worried about embarrassing her, as she merely gave a derisive snort.

'Need you ask, Steve? I've just told you, everyone in TT knows that he has been getting his leg over that bitch from the hospital, but he needn't have flaunted it in The Dog when I was there!' She waved an unsteady hand in the general direction of the next bungalow. 'Though at least he wasn't playing quite so near home as usual.'

'So you don't know what time he left the club?' Blackwell knew from the club steward that Robertson had left soon after eleven, but he always liked to cross-check when he could. She shook her head, the golden hair swirling across her shoulders.

'I wouldn't be surprised if he went off somewhere to roger that bloody woman in the back of his car. The rear seat is the size of a double bed!' she added bitterly, thinking of the cramped space in her own little Austin.

'And did you leave The Dog alone?' asked Steven cautiously, prodding to see if there was any way of confirming her movements. He had no real reason for this, but from his days as a CID man back in England, he still kept the habit of building up a mental picture of where everyone was at what they called the 'material time'.

Diane peered at him over the rim of her glass. For the first time, the brittle nonchalance over her sudden bereavement seemed to falter and she answered rather defensively. 'I gave one of the guys from Garrison a lift back to the gates, as the fellow who had brought him had gone off with some popsy.'

Blackwell nodded encouragingly. 'Who was that, then? Do I know him?'

'Oh, Gerry something-or-other,' she answered evasively. 'One of the West Berkshires, a lieutenant, I think. I hardly know him.' She neglected to mention that the half-mile journey took them almost an hour.

He thought of pushing her harder, then decided it could wait, if it ever needed to be followed up. The fact was that her husband had been shot in circumstances which suggested it was part of the civil insurgence that dominated life in Malaya – and yet, like the attack the week before, it seemed at odds with the usual run of terrorist activity.

He stood up and looked across at the very attractive woman who was hunched over her drink on the settee. 'Diane, I must get back to TT and see if there's any more news. The army's out in strength looking for any CTs in the area and I need to check with them. But what are we going to do with you? You can't stay here on your own!'

She made a visible effort to pull herself together, putting her now empty glass on the table and standing up, brushing back her hair from her forehead.

'I'll be fine, Steven, really I will. I've got my *amah* and Siva at the back of the house – and Douglas is only a few yards away.'

He noted that she pointedly avoided any mention of Douglas's wife.

'I'll have to talk to him first thing in the morning,' she went on. 'About the running of the estate – not that it will make much difference, he did all the real work around here, anyway.'

Reluctantly, the superintendent had to accept her decision. There seemed little alternative to Diane staying in the bungalow that night – there were no decent hotels nearer than Penang and the government rest-houses in the smaller towns were hardly suitable for an unaccompanied young woman. He could not think of any female companion who would be willing to come and stay with the new widow, given her reputation and the remoteness of Gunong Besar. If only his wife had not gone back to England, she could have sorted this out – Margaret was good at mothering people.

Again reassuring Diane that the police and the army were thick on the ground around the estate and promising to come up again first thing in the morning, Steven Blackwell went out to his vehicle, leaving another Land Rover with two armed constables parked ostentatiously outside the bungalow.

By the time Steven Blackwell got back to BMH, the place was buzzing with activity, mostly centred around the Casualty hut at the end of the car park.

Pushing past two red-capped Military Police standing in the doorway, he found that the Matron had joined the throng and was deep in conversation with Alfred Morris and the night sister. Tom Howden was talking in a corner with Peter Bright, who had seen all the activity when he had driven in a few minutes earlier and come to investigate. Although Morris was his equal in rank, Alf was non-medical and in the absence of the Commanding Officer, the surgeon was assumed to be top dog when it came to a medical problem, which apparently included sudden death. It was not a responsibility he welcomed.

'So where the hell is O'Neill?' he demanded irritably, in his cut-glass accent. 'Did you try his quarters again?'

'Three times, but nobody answers the phone,' grunted the pathologist. 'Alf has just sent a runner up there now, to knock on his door.'

He looked curiously at Peter Bright, who seemed to be in a fever of excitement, more than even these unusual circumstances warranted. The surgeon was agitated, running his fingers through his fair, wavy hair and nervously nibbling at his lower lip. Even Tom's superficial knowledge of the intrigues in Tanah Timah was enough to set him wondering if Peter's thoughts were now dominated by the fact that the love of his life had suddenly become a widow.

The major from the garrison was on the telephone, but now slapped it down and came across to the police superintendent. 'We've had patrols up and down that damned road as far as Kampong Kerbau, but there's not a sign of anything out of the ordinary. I just don't understand it, the bandits don't just loose off a single shot, they usually set up an ambush and blast hell out of whatever comes up the road.'

'That's if it did happen on the estate road,' replied Steven. 'At the moment, we haven't a clue where the shooting took place.'

Everyone in the room gravitated towards the speakers, forming a circle around them. The QA corporal, her orderly and the pharmacy staff sergeant stood on the periphery, a captain from the provost marshal's unit pushing in front of them. He was in charge of the military police, though the nearest investigators, the SIB, were in Ipoh. Speaking to Steven, who he knew well both professionally and socially, he voiced what was in most people's minds.

'Why the hell poor old Jimmy? And where did it happen?'

A confused chatter began filling the room and Blackwell saw that the whole affair was in danger of becoming a circus, with so many people milling about, most of whom had no real need to be involved. He held up his hands and called for quiet.

'This is a police matter until we learn otherwise,' he said loudly. 'Mr Robertson was a civilian and he suffered his fatal injuries somewhere out there.' He waved his hand at the rest of Malaya, before turning to Peter Bright and Alf Morris who were now standing together.

'Could I suggest that the body is taken to your mortuary, as we've nowhere else to put him nearer than the ones at the civil hospitals at Ipoh or Taiping. I'll contact the coroner first thing in the morning, but I'm sure he'll want a post-mortem carried out.'

The coroner for this area of Perak was an Indian lawyer in private practice at Kuala Kangsar and Steven knew from experience that he would agree to almost any suggestion made by the police.

'It's almost one thirty,' he continued. 'My men and the army are still combing the area, but there's nothing more we can do here until the morning, so I suggest we all get back to our duties or to our beds.'

There was a general shuffling as people began moving, but they halted abruptly as a harsh voice suddenly barked at them from the doorway.

'What's the meaning of this? Major Bright, what's going on here?'

It was the Commanding Officer, Desmond O'Neill, dressed in a dark blazer and striped tie, with grey flannels above black shoes. His bony face glowered at them, lips compressed into a thin line.

'What are all you people doing in my hospital at this hour of the night?' Even at this tense moment, Tom Howden noticed the colonel's proprietary attitude towards the BMH.

'There's been a tragedy, sir.' Peter Bright chose his words carefully, being well aware of his senior officer's peculiarities. 'James Robertson has been shot dead. Outside somewhere, but he was brought here in case he could be resuscitated.'

'He's a civilian,' snapped O'Neill. 'He should have been taken to a general hospital.'

No one wanted to point out to him that the nearest was

more than twenty miles away but Steven Blackwell was in no mood to be obstructed by some military martinet.

'He wasn't actually certified dead until he was on army premises, colonel – and the death may well be due to enemy action. I'll clear it with the Brigadier in the morning, but I've asked if we could have the use of your mortuary in these urgent circumstances. As you will know, bodies go off rapidly in this climate and we'll need an examination to help our investigation, as this is a murder.'

The cold eyes of the colonel roved aggressively around the room, then his mercurial moods changed into an almost benign state.

'Of course, superintendent, of course!' He turned on his heel like a marionette and glared at Tom.

'Howden, you're supposed to be a pathologist! Get the corpse to the mortuary and perform a post-mortem in the morning.'

He swung back to the others and his ferocity returned. 'This is a Casualty Department, not a peep show. Everyone who has no business here can clear out – now!'

With a last glare at the discomfited faces, he vanished and they heard his car start up and accelerate away.

'Cheeky bugger,' muttered the garrison major to Alf Morris. 'If I had another pip on my shoulder, I'd have told him where to get off!'

The faithful Admin Officer murmured something about O'Neill's bark being worse than his bite, but the major had joined the general exodus and soon only the RAMC staff remained with the policeman.

'In the morning, I'll have to come and take statements from everyone who was in The Dog tonight,' said Blackwell. 'I'll contact the coroner as early as I can and get his authority for you to carry out a post-mortem, Captain Howden.'

Alf Morris gave an indrawn whistling noise to indicate his concern at this.

'You'd better get back to the colonel to get his consent for that, Steven.'

'But the bloody man has just ordered him to do it!' protested the police officer.

'Our beloved leader can be very fickle,' warned Peter Bright. 'What he says tonight, he might flatly deny in the morning.'

Blackwell gave a small sigh of exasperation and after making his farewells, went wearily out to his waiting Land Rover, the surgeon following him to his own sporty MG. By now, the orderly sergeant had got two RAMC privates to bring a trolley from the Families Clinic next door and with the others watching with sombre expressions, they covered James Robertson's body with the sheet from the examination couch and hauled him across on to the trolley. As they pushed the sad burden away to the mortuary, Tom Howden had a sudden thought, as he had inspected the place only a couple of days ago. The morgue was part of his domain as the pathologist, a hut little larger than a garden shed on the edge of the helicopter landing pad, incongruously next to the badminton court.

'There's no refrigeration there. He'll go off pretty fast in this heat,' he said to Alf Morris.

As usual, the imperturbable Admin Officer had the answer. 'That's under control, we get blocks of ice brought in to put all around them. There's a Chinese contractor in the town who supplies it, I'll organize it first thing in the morning.'

With this bizarre image in his mind, Tom went off to scrounge a last cup of tea from the night sister, before going back to his bed in Intensive Care for what remained of the night.

Morning Prayers went off quite mildly, in spite of the fears of several officers that the Old Man would be ranting about their failure to notify him about the shooting, ignoring the fact that he was nowhere to be found. In the event, O'Neill never mentioned it.

As OMO, Tom had to deliver his report, keeping it as low-key as possible. After describing the satisfactory condition of the only patient on the SIL, he gave a sombre account of how Mr James Robertson had been brought in dead, then finished up with the usual. 'The arms kote was inspected at eleven hundred hours and all was found to be in order, sir.'

He sat down, but jumped up again as the CO barked at him. 'I've already heard from the police, Howden. The coroner wants you to carry out a post-mortem this morning.' He glared at the pathologist over his Himmler glasses, which he always wore at these meetings. The skin over his high cheekbones appeared stretched more tightly than usual, giving his face a skull-like appearance.

'Have you ever seen a gunshot wound, captain? I suppose you do know how to perform an autopsy?'

Tom tried to ignore the insulting tone. 'Yes, sir, I've been with my consultant when he dealt with a firearm death. And yes, sir, I've done at least twenty coroner's cases back home.'

With the abrupt changes of mood that seemed characteristic of this strange man, the CO seemed to lose interest and went on to harangue the quartermaster about some delay in delivery of medical stores. The unfortunate Captain Burns offered feeble excuses about inefficiency in the Base Supply Depot down in Singapore. Robbie Burns was another officer who, like Alf Morris, had come up through the ranks and was fervently hoping that he would reach retirement less than a year away, without being court-martialled for strangling the Commanding Officer, who made his life a permanent misery. He was a short, corpulent Scouse, always sweating profusely and incessantly mopping his red face with a handkerchief.

The meeting stumbled through its usual nerve-racking course, with a dozen officers sitting edgily on their chairs, waiting for their colonel to suddenly turn and attack them for some imagined misdeed. Eventually they were released into the mounting heat and went their various ways to heal the sick.

When Tom Howden got back to his laboratory, he found a mug of milky, sweet tea ready on his desk and a solicitous lance corporal hovering around him. Lewis Cropper's long, sallow face regarded him with spaniel-like concern. A Regular soldier, he was the despair of a series of sergeant majors across what remained of the British Empire, having been posted hither and thither merely to get rid of him. In spite of the fact that he was an excellent laboratory technician, his stubborn refusal to conform to authority kept him in almost continual trouble. He was nosy, garrulous, obsequious and generally bloody-minded to all except his pathologists, for whom he always seemed to have an embarrassingly doglike devotion.

'Hear there's to be a pee-em this morning, sir!' he offered, making Tom marvel at the speed and efficiency of the hospital bush-telegraph.

'That's right. Ask Sergeant Oates to come in, will you?'

He sipped at his tea and flinched at the combination of condensed milk and three spoonfuls of sugar. But Cropper made no move to obey.

'Won't do any good, sir,' he answered mournfully. 'Sarge can't stand the morgue. Last time, he threw up, then fainted. Says he's never going to set foot in there again.'

Tom stared at the lance corporal over the rim of his mug. Was he pulling his leg or working up to some scam of his own?

'I'll have a word with him – I have to have some help in there.'

'Well, Derek Oates won't be any use, I can tell you! The last pathologist, Captain Freeman, said the sarge was to be permanently excused on medical grounds, on account of his puking all the time.'

'What about one of the Malays, then?'

Cropper made a derisory noise, suspiciously like a verbal raspberry.

'No chance, cap'n! It's against their religion or some such.'

He leaned over the desk in an attitude of unwelcome familiarity.

'S'alright, sir, I'll help you out. I've already sharpened up the tools.'

Like a conjuror, he produced an old box the size of a small briefcase, made of dark hardwood and with the historic broad arrow of the 'War Department' carved into its varnished lid. Cropper opened it and displayed the contents to Tom with the proud air of a Kleeneze salesman on a housewife's doorstep.

'Pre-war, these are! Don't know which war, but there's a lovely bit of steel in them.'

Inside was a fearsome array of instruments, worthy of the worst excesses of the Spanish Inquisition. Nestled into faded blue velvet slots were several large knives, which would have looked perfectly at home in a slaughterhouse. An amputation saw, a steel mallet and several chisels jostled for space with scissors, forceps and a gadget that consisted of two half-hoops hinged together, like a folding crown.

'What the devil's that?' demanded Tom.

'A coronet, sir. Captain Freeman was very fond of that. You open it out and put it over the skull. Screw those spikes into the bone to hold it firm and you've got a nice straight guide for sawing off the top of the head.'

The pathologist grunted, thinking that he could manage without such medieval devices. The corporal's importuning was interrupted by the telephone and Tom picked it up to hear the police superintendent on the line.

'Would midday suit you for this post-mortem, captain?' asked Steven Blackwell. 'The SIB chap from Ipoh would like to be present as well as the major from the provost marshal's office in the garrison.'

Tom agreed, then asked about identification of the corpse.

'I was much too junior to do any police cases back on Tyneside,' he explained. 'But I know my boss always had to get someone to officially confirm who the body actually was.'

Blackwell said he had this organized and that he would be bringing James's widow to BMH immediately before the examination.

Ringing off, Tom Howden saw with relief that Cropper had taken his box of instruments back into the main lab, perhaps for a final honing of the wicked knives. Sitting behind his desk, staring into space, Tom sipped his sickly tea and pondered at the sudden responsibilities that the Army had thrust upon him. Already he was doing work and offering expert opinions on medical matters that would have been considered far above his status in civilian life. After only one year's apprenticeship in NHS pathology, he was now examining tissues removed by the surgeons and reporting on them, a task which only seniors did back in the UK. It was true that the younger, healthier military patients rarely had the tumours and difficult diagnostic problems seen at home, but there were some gynaecological conditions among the wives which could be potentially serious.

Apart from this histology, the bulk of the work was detecting bacteria and parasites, from malaria to hookworm, from tuberculosis to occasional cases of leprosy, as many of the patients were Malays or Gurkhas, who suffered a different range of diseases from the British troops. The jungle patrols were susceptible to Weil's disease contracted from water contaminated by rats, a dangerous condition which was sometimes fatal. Though Howden's limited civilian experience had hardly prepared him for all this, his technicians gently carried him along and he was learning fast.

But now, he ruminated, he was being pitchforked into a murder investigation and had to make the best of it. Where tumours and complicated medical conditions were concerned, he could always get an expert opinion by sending the material back by air to the Royal Army Medical College in Millbank, but there was nowhere he could get rapid help over a civilian shooting.

Shrugging philosophically, he swallowed the rest of his tea, realizing that he was in danger of becoming used to the taste of the cloying liquid. Glancing at his watch, he saw it was almost time for him to attend to another of his varied duties, this time the sick parade in the military prison next door. Jamming his cap on his head, he went into the main lab to speak to his sergeant. The room occupied most of the building, only Tom's little office and the tissue-cutting lab being partitioned off the back of it.

Wooden benches lined most of three walls, the other wall being filled with a kerosene-powered refrigerator, an incubator and a sterilizer. The entrance was opposite these, directly on to the concrete strip that ran under the overhang of the corrugated asbestos roof. Slatted windows, all wide open, fed as much air as possible to the pair of whirling brass fans in the ceiling, as there was no air conditioning. The centre of the laboratory was occupied with another large island bench, with a central raised shelf covered with a profusion of reagent bottles and odd bits of apparatus. This was the sergeant's province, as he did most of the chemical testing, though like the others, he could turn his hand to anything. Derek Oates was there now and Tom waited whilst he sucked up some blood into a glass pipette and blew it into a tube to carry out an analysis for urea in a patient from the Australian battalion, whose kidneys had been damaged by Weil's disease.

In another corner, Embi bin Sharif, one of the MORs, was quietly chanting some mournful Malay song as he dried thick drops of blood on glass slides to look for malarial parasites under his microscope. Embi was a smooth-faced lad, unfailingly smart and polite, with almond eyes and sleek jet-black hair. He came from even further north in Perlis, the small state next to the border with Thailand.

At the other end of the bench, another private soldier was happily playing 'postman', rhythmically banging a rubber stamp from ink pad to a pile of pathology request forms universally known as 'F-Med Tens'. Aziz Ismael was a fat, cheerful fellow with a mass of curly hair, unusual in a Malay. He was from nearby Kuala Kangsar and he was a fount of local information on almost any subject.

When Derek Oates's mouth was free of his tube, the pathologist broached the subject of the post-mortem.

'I gather you're not too keen on the mortuary, sergeant?'

The trim young man looked somewhat abashed. 'Sorry, sir, I'd be no use to you. I can't understand it, because when I have blood in a tube, I'm fine!'

He gestured towards the bijou bottles and universal containers filled with the red fluid which were arrayed before him on his bench.

'But when I see it on a dead body, I just fall apart. I feel rotten about it, sir, it's something I just can't beat.'

Tom nodded at him, it was something not worth pursuing. Oates was such an excellent worker that he saw no point in making an issue of the fellow's unfortunate phobia. 'Cropper says he'll give a hand, as I gather the other lads are not keen on the job.'

'They won't go near the place, sir. Malays seem to have all sorts of superstitions, especially about the dead. Aziz will probably give you a run-down on that!'

'Right, sarge, I'm off to see the naughty boys in the nick, then I'll be doing this post-mortem at twelve. Everything under control here?'

Oates assured him that there were no problems and Howden set off up the main corridor, conscious again of the sticky heat as the day warmed up. He passed the operating theatre which lay opposite the X-ray Department and the Officers' Ward before coming to another pair which housed the long-term tuberculous patients. These were mostly Gurkhas, who were prone to many infectious diseases, including potentially fatal measles and mumps. Coming from their remote Himalayan fastness in Nepal, they lacked the resistance acquired by most other races.

Beyond the last pair of wards, were two odd structures before the corridor ended opposite the arms kote. On one side was a large khaki tent, which was Percy Loosemore's stamping-ground, the 'STD' or Special Treatment Department, a euphemism for the VD clinic. Across the corridor was another part of Tom's domain, the blood transfusion 'basha', an open-sided shed with a large *attap* roof, made of neatly laid palm branches. This was where blood donors gave their contributions when needed, though so far he had not been called upon to officiate there. The hospital had no 'blood bank' – at least not in refrigerated bottles – as the precious fluid was kept 'on the hoof' inside the donors until needed.

Tom reached the perimeter road and turned left towards the open gate into the main garrison. As he walked, he thought with some apprehension about the post-mortem he was soon to carry out. He was not bothered about the actual procedure itself, though in spite of his earlier response to the CO, he had virtually no experience of gunshot wounds, having only once watched his boss in Newcastle deal with a shotgun suicide. However, he had got up early to read the relevant chapter in his well-thumbed copy of *Glaister's Forensic Medicine* and reckoned that he could just about flannel his way through.

No, it was the prospect of having the widow there to identify James's body that worried him. Back home, he had several times been present when grieving relatives had to view the bodies of their loved ones and he still remembered the sobbing, the wailing and even the odd faint, even though most people seemed to be overtaken by a numbed silence as they looked through the glass panel into the viewing room of the mortuary. He wondered how Diane Robertson would take it. There were all the rumours about the Robertsons' marital discord and she seemed a pretty hard character, he mused – but one never really knows how someone will react.

These thoughts occupied him until he reached the inner gate to the garrison and once inside he turned right to reach another smaller compound. This occupied the furthermost corner of the stockade, divided off from it by another high double fence. The outer layer was of chain-link, topped with coils of barbed wire and just inside was a tall palisade of corrugated iron to screen the inmates from the rest of the garrison. A lofty gate of similar material had a small steel-mesh door set into it, beyond which a red-capped MP corporal stood on guard.

When he saw the officer approaching, he stamped his shiny boots across to the door and gave a cracking salute, which Tom returned in the half-embarrassed way that most newly enlisted doctors employed.

'Morning, sah! Identity card, please, sah!'

Though he came every morning, the pathologist held up his ID to the wire and with a rattling flourish of keys, the redcap let him in and locked the gate behind him. There was a single road running up the middle of the two-acre site, with the familiar long, low huts placed at right angles on each side. The first on the left contained the guardroom, Commandant's office, mess room and stores, while on the other side of the lane was the sickbay with other unidentifiable rooms beyond it. A dozen drooping figures stood on the verandah outside, with another MP corporal stalking up and down the line, his chest stuck out like a turkeycock.

When he saw the officer approaching, he slammed himself to attention and screamed at the patients to do the same. All hauled themselves upright, except for one, who seemed to be bent in half from some back trouble.

The corporal gave Tom a vibrating salute, which he again returned half-heartedly and went into the sickbay. It was a bare room, with a table and chair for the doctor, a spartan examination couch and a white bench with a cupboard above for the meagre medical supplies. Hovering near this was an elderly RAMC corporal, seconded from the 38th Field Ambulance at Taiping.

Sid Hooper was a burly, impassive man, with a row of medal ribbons on his tunic, half-hidden by the creased white coat he wore as his badge of office. He gave the weary impression of having seen it all before and that none of these bloody shirkers outside were going to put one over either on him or his doctor.

'The usual bunch of lead-swinging layabouts today, doc,' he announced. 'One of 'em might possibly have something wrong with him.'

Tom took off his hat and dropped it on to the table, before sitting down.

'Wheel them in, corporal. Let's make it quick, I've got a lot to do this morning.'

The corporal went to the door and after some more screaming from the MP outside, a man charged in, his nailed boots clattering on the floor at the tempo of a double-quick march. With a final crunch, he stopped in front of the table and stared fixedly at the wall beyond Tom's head. Hooper came across with a tattered document in his hand.

'Gunner Andrews, sir. Crime sheet as long as your arm. Sunburn.'

The man was dressed like most of the prisoners, wearing only green shorts above heavy boots and socks. The upper half of his body was bright red from the sun, as most of the men were sent out on working parties to cut grass or clear monsoon drains around the large garrison enclave.

'S'me back, sir,' was his only complaint and within seconds, the sickbay sergeant had slapped the paperwork before Tom, on which was already written the word 'calamine lotion', obtained a signature and harried the patient out through the door to wait for his treatment after the doctor had left. As he went, Tom saw that the blistered skin across his shoulders was peeling off in strips, but he was given no time to make any other examination.

The rest of the sick parade went in a similar fashion. For sunburn they had calamine, for foot rot they had anti-fungal powder or were 'excused boots' in favour of plimsolls for a few days. For alleged stomach ache they had magnesia, for headaches they had aspirin and for the 'runs' they were prescribed kaolin-and-morph mixture. All this was decided by Hooper and only if the medical officer suspected something more sinister were they examined more closely. Any really suspect conditions meant that they would have to be sent over to Casualty in BMH, a procedure which raised frowns from the prison staff, as it meant finding them an escort and disrupting the iron regime of the Military Corrective Establishment.

This morning, there was nothing to suggest any mortal conditions amongst the supplicants, most of whom used the sick parade to wangle an hour off grass cutting. Even the man with the bent back seemed to recover when screamed at loudly enough by the MP corporal.

As he walked back to the hospital, Tom wondered whether he had really needed five years in medical school for the sort of practice in which he now seemed to be involved. Even the prospect of a post-mortem seemed more attractive than signing chits for calamine lotion and 'excuse boots'.

Back in his office, he spent what was left of the morning in checking the positive blood films for malaria and looking at the bacterial cultures which had grown overnight in the incubator. Sergeant Oates was equally as proficient at recognizing them and diplomatically speeded the process by gentle remarks such as 'I think this one is *Staph aureus*, sir, don't you?' The malarial films had already been screened by Aziz, who only sent in the positive ones for the officer to check. In fact, the MOR had already confidently written the type of parasite on the form and Tom found later that he was never to catch Aziz out in all the time they were at BMH.

After another infusion of sweet tea, he sat signing report forms and waiting for the phone to ring, heralding the arrival of the autopsy delegation. At eleven thirty, the guardroom rang and he went down to the front of the hospital where he found Steven Blackwell and Inspector Tan waiting in Alf Morris's office with Diane Robertson.

She wore a black skirt, perhaps as a concession to mourning, topped by a white silk blouse, but otherwise looked her usual glamorous self.

'You're the new pathologist – it's Captain Howden, isn't it?' she said brightly. 'I've seen you in The Dog once or twice.'

Tom mumbled something about being sorry to have to meet in these sad circumstances, but Diane appeared unfazed by the fact that he was shortly going to dissect her husband.

'The Army police chaps will be along by twelve,' volunteered Blackwell, intending to cover up any awkwardness in the situation.

'So shall we get this over with first?'

As they left the office, Tom whispered quickly to the Admin Officer.

'Alf, is the colonel coming to this?'

Morris shook his head. 'Not as far as I know, though you never can tell with him. He's told me to make sure everything is laid on. As a former public health wallah, I don't think he's too keen on dead bodies.'

They followed the two policemen and the widow up the main corridor, Diane taking Steven's arm. Tom suspected that she was feeling that she ought to put on some sort of show of being a bereaved widow for the many curious faces that peered out of ward doorways as they went. She was never one to miss the chance to hold on to a man, even if he was a bald, middle-aged married policeman. At one point, Diane turned around and gave Tom a dazzling smile and asked if he was settling down well. In spite of the bizarre circumstances, he felt a twitch of desire as he appreciated again what a gorgeous woman she was.

At the point in the corridor level with where the mortuary lay, Lance Corporal Cropper was standing at attention. Tom Howden groaned at the sight, as the self-important technician had obviously appointed himself as guide. After he had jerked his hand up to his crumpled beret in salute, he marched in front of the posse across the stunted grass and the perimeter road. Tom felt that Cropper only needed a black top hat with a crêpe band to look like an undertaker's mute leading a funeral. When they reached the isolated hut, the corporal ceremoniously threw open the door and stood aside.

Alf Morris had seen to it that a couple of orderlies had brought the body out of the post-mortem room and arranged it on a ward trolley in the tiny anteroom just inside the door. Covered with a couple of clean sheets and with a vase of flowers temporarily borrowed from a ward placed on a nearby shelf, the scene was at least innocuous, if not actually dignified.

'We'll make this as quick as possible, Diane,' said the superintendent gently. 'It's a legal requirement, I'm afraid. All I want you to do is to confirm to me and Dr Howden here, that this is the body of James Robertson, OK?'

He led her through the door and though Tom tried to block Lewis Cropper, the corporal dodged past him and advanced to the head of the trolley, taking the ends of the sheet in both hands.

Tom and Alf Morris stood at the foot and the stringy Inspector Tan hovered behind, as Steven Blackwell nodded at Cropper, who reverently folded back the sheet to expose the face of the dead man. There was a tense silence as they all looked at Jimmy Robertson, who even in death seemed to have a bad-tempered look on his face.

Tom waited for sobs, screams or moans, but Diane surprised them all.

'I've never seen a dead person before,' she observed conversationally. 'But yes, that's certainly my husband.'

As she turned and walked out into the brilliant sunlight, Diane asked Alf Morris about funeral arrangements. 'I've no idea what to do. I've sent a cable to his brother in England, he'll tell my mother-in-law.'

As they walked away, Tom heard the Admin Officer telling her that once the coroner had completed his formalities, the Church of England padre from the garrison was the best person to help her. He should have been here this morning, said Alf, but was on a long weekend leave in the Cameron Highlands.

The two policemen went to see her to her car at the front of the hospital, saying that they would be back in a few minutes and Tom was left with his officious corporal, though in truth, he was now quite glad of his help. They wheeled the corpse into the inner room, which was half filled with a white porcelain slab on a pedestal fixed to the concrete floor. A column of soldier ants was marching from somewhere in the corner, up the pedestal and down the other side, causing Cropper to pump energetically at them with a Flit gun, filling the air with a mixture of paraffin and DDT insecticide.

A large kitchen sink against one wall had a single brass tap, with a long wooden draining board attached to one side. A small table stood under the slatted window and a broom, a long-handled squeegee and two buckets stood in a corner. A pair of rubber aprons with chains around the neck and waist hung from a nail on the wall.

'We had to move the ice to get him on to the trolley,' explained Cropper, pointing at a dozen chunks of cloudy grey ice, each the size of a breeze block, which now lay on the floor in a spreading pool of melted water.

They folded up the sheets, slid the now naked cadaver on to the slab and Cropper pushed the trolley out again, so that there was some space left in the small room for spectators. He had put his precious instrument box on the table and laid the weapons out in a row on the draining board.

A few minutes later, the two police officers returned, as smart as ever in their pristine khaki uniforms, though Tom noticed that the back of Steven's shirt was as black with sweat as his own.

'I think the main object of the exercise is to retrieve the bullet for forensic examination,' said Blackwell. 'Though I suppose knowing the range it was fired from might be a help, too.'

Taking off his uniform jacket, Tom hung the red rubber apron around his neck and hooked the chains around his waist, then put on some thick rubber gloves. The corporal did the same and by then, the clump of boots in the outer room heralded the arrival of the military men, Sergeant Markham from the SIB and Major Enderby from the provost marshal's department. They had brought a photographer with them, a sergeant from the Intelligence Corps, who proceeded to take a series of pictures of the body with a rather large and clumsy MPP Press camera. The pathologist wisely got him to take some of the bullet entry wound from as close as he could possibly get the lens.

'No burning, smoke or powder marks on the skin around

it,' he pointed out to the spectators, carefully checking all the points he had mugged up in 'Glaister' that morning. 'Nor were there any on the shirt, so it wasn't a close discharge.'

The two civilian police seemed immune to the proximity of a corpse, having seen plenty during the years of the 'Emergency', as it was euphemistically called. The SIB sergeant seemed to have a similar indifference, but the major, who had been a lawyer before entering the service, and the photographer, were looking rather pale about the lips.

'You've got the clothing safe, superintendent?' asked the sergeant.

'All packed up, though I can't see it'll be of much use. The lab in KL isn't all that hot on some aspects, they're really a chemical analysis outfit rather than forensic, though they're trying to expand. We may have to send the shirt down to Singapore if necessary, but it's the bullet that really interests us.'

While they were talking, Tom got on with his examination, examining every square inch of the body, though he found nothing out of the ordinary apart from the small hole in the chest. He helped Cropper to lift the shoulders while they slipped a thick block of wood under them, then opened the body with one of the murderous-looking knives. He had to admit that his technician had done a good job of sharpening them and the dissection went ahead with no hitches.

'What about the size of the gunshot wound, doc? Can you tell what weapon was used?' asked Blackwell.

Tom shook his head. 'I'm not even going to guess, superintendent. I've read that the skin can stretch and shrink, so that the diameter is not the same as the bullet. The hole is seven millimetres across, that's all I can say.'

'What the hell is that in English, captain?' asked the major, a khaki handkerchief close to his mouth. Enderby was a burly, red-faced man in middle-age, with a large walrus moustache stained with nicotine. He had trained as a solicitor but on being called for wartime National Service, had stayed on as a Regular in the provost marshal's department.

'Just over a quarter of an inch,' grunted Howden, forgetting to say 'sir'.

The bloody part of the autopsy began and the three army men abruptly decided to go outside for a smoke.

'No exit wound, so thankfully the bullet must still be inside him, Tom,' said the superintendent, now putting them on first-name terms.

'If it was a rifle, then it must have hit bone, as far as I can understand from the textbooks,' agreed Howden. 'Unless it was fired from a great distance, when it may have lost much of its punch.'

'If it was a military weapon, like a three-oh-three or an FN, it could still kill someone a mile away,' said Inspector Tan primly, speaking for the first time. He was a mild, reticent man, speaking only when he had something worthwhile to say. Steven had considerable respect for Tan's intelligence and always listened carefully to his ideas.

A few minutes later, the question of the calibre of the fatal missile was solved, as Tom finally held it in his hand. Mindful of Professor Glaister's admonition not to damage the rifling marks, he carefully groped around inside the chest with his fingers, to avoid using hard tools which could scratch the missile. He found the front of the spinal column shattered in the middle of the chest and lying alongside was a deformed metallic lump, which he carefully drew out and placed in the palm of his other hand. Going across to the sink, he washed the blood away and with Cropper peering over his shoulder, he offered it to the two police officers. 'Here we are! One bullet, distorted to blazes.'

They all looked at it as if it was the Holy Grail, a dull metal nodule about the size of a hazelnut. The base was still circular, but the upper part was crumpled, like a witch's hat that had been folded back, then stamped on.

'Looks like a standard .303 rifle to me,' observed Steven Blackwell.

His inspector nodded agreement, but Tom took up a small plastic ruler that he had brought from the laboratory and carefully put it across the base of the bullet. Though slightly out of shape, he could see that it was about a third of an inch across.

'Better give the army chaps a shout,' he suggested. 'That sergeant probably knows most about firearms.'

Tan went to the door to call them in, but the pathologist went to the outer room to show them the trophy, not wanting to subject them unnecessarily to the sights and smells of the mortuary.

Sergeant Markham, a veteran of Normandy and Korea, agreed that the bullet was the same calibre as that used in the standard British rifle.

'Must send it to the experts, though,' he advised. 'Needs to be checked against those you dug out of the wall at Gunong Busar last week.'

Lewis Cropper found a small screw-top specimen bottle and padded it with cotton wool to nest the bullet in, preventing it from rattling against the glass and blurring the rifling marks from the barrel of whatever weapon had fired it. The superintendent carefully labelled, dated and signed it and stowed it away in his pocket.

'I'll send it down to KL on the night train – if needs be, I'm sure your army boffins can get it back for any further work on it.'

'We can get it sent to Singapore   or even flown back to Woolwich if necessary,' said Major Enderby, his colour now recovered. 'That's where all our Ordnance experts hang out.'

'The cartridge case would be more valuable, if we could find it,' grunted the big SIB man. 'The origin of the ammunition could be traced through that.'

Steve Blackwell looked a little irritated. 'We don't even know where the bloody shooting took place. Could be anywhere within ten miles of here. That's one of our first priorities.'

Half an hour later, Tom had finished the rest of his dissection, finding nothing more of significance. He took some samples for Blackwell to send to Kuala Lumpur for blood grouping and alcohol analysis, telling Cropper to get them packed in ice in a Thermos flask for the long journey down-country. The spectators left, promising a conference later that day to discuss the sparse results of the post-mortem, leaving Tom and his corporal to restore the body as best they could. They sewed it up again, washed it, then covered it again with a sheet around which they packed large fragments of ice, broken from the blocks with the hammer from the surgical instrument set.

After washing down the mortuary, Tom doing his full share in unconscious defiance of the Officer–Other Ranks convention, the two laboratory men left James Robertson in peace under a whirling fan and a shroud of melting ice.

SEVEN

'**B**it of a bloody cheek, I thought! Questioning us as if we were damned suspects.'

Peter Bright sounded indignant as he signed the chit for a beer that Number One held out for him. It was just before lunch in the Officers' Mess and most of the resident medical staff were sitting in the anteroom with their pre-prandial Tigers or Anchors. Drinking spirits in the middle of the day was not banned, but was felt to be 'a bit off' as most members had clinical duties during the afternoon. The old pre-war days of working only in the morning had long gone and even though this was a Saturday, the habit lingered.

The chief surgeon's complaint was echoed by David Meredith, the dark, moody Welshman. His deep-set eyes were overhung by thick eyebrows, which matched the mop of curly black hair that came too low on his neck to suit Alf Morris's military mind.

'Why should Steve Blackwell come to me first, that's what I'd like to know? At least you were down at Casualty last night, Peter – but I never went near the damn place. First thing I knew about Jimmy Robertson was at breakfast.' His annoyance brought out a slight Welsh accent, but Tom knew from Alec Watson's gossip that Meredith had gone to school and university in the Midlands.

Before attending the post-mortem, the police superintendent had made a few calls and with Inspector Tan taking notes, had taken statements from several people about their movements last night, including the surgeon and anaesthetist.

As usual, Alf Morris set out to smooth the ruffled feathers.

'We'll all be asked the same things, eventually, so don't fret that you're being picked on,' he said soothingly. 'He'll be doing the same at the Sisters' Mess and amongst the members at The Dog.'

No one was tactless enough to mention that Peter Bright

was an obvious early target for the police, given that Robertson's death had now cleared the way for his pursuit of Diane, if she was still interested.

'Steve Blackwell wanted to know if I had a gun!' complained Meredith. 'He knows bloody well that I don't. What in God's name would an anaesthetist want with a gun out here?'

'The same with me! Damn silly questions these coppers ask,' added the senior surgeon.

Alf Morris persisted with his placatory role. 'I suppose it's what all policemen call "routine",' he said. 'If they don't ask everybody everything, they can get a rollicking later on.'

David Meredith shook his head sadly. 'Steve Blackwell's the nicest chap you could wish for when he's in The Dog – but he's a different person in uniform. It's like Jekyll and Hyde!'

'Must be difficult for police in a small place like this, having to be "official" with people you know so well socially,' observed Alec Watson. 'Conflict of interests and all that.'

'Yes, it's difficult for some of us, too – having to hobnob here with you murder suspects!' brayed Percy Loosemore, stirring things as usual.

Tom Howden sat quietly behind his beer, keeping as low a profile as possible. He also felt in a difficult position, as he was now technically an expert witness in the case of James Robertson and should not divulge anything except to the police and coroner. It soon became obvious that this was a forlorn hope in such an incestuous environment as BMH Tanah Timah.

'I hear it was a .303 you dug out of Jimmy's chest,' stated the brash Loosemore, confirming that the hospital bush tele-graph was in excellent working order. Tom immediately suspected Lewis Cropper as the source of the leak, but knew that the lance corporal would plaintively deny it if accused.

Once more, the Administrative Officer tried to come to the rescue.

'In the circumstances, I don't think Captain Howden should be asked about details by any of us – the whole affair is *sub judice*, understand?'

His attempt to save the pathologist any embarrassment was almost immediately doomed to failure. A sudden warning came from Alec, who was sitting facing the open door that had a view of the entrance path.

'Hell's bells, here comes the Old Man!'

The rare visit of the colonel to the Mess sent three of the members scurrying through the opposite verandah doors to hide in the toilets at the end of the block, but O'Neill arrived too quickly for the rest to vanish, though it had been known for the CO to find a completely deserted anteroom, with everyone crammed into the bogs.

He stalked in and everyone stumbled hastily to their feet in awkward silence. Dropping his hat amongst the others on the table inside the door, he ignored the assembly and spoke directly to the pathologist.

'Well, Howden, what did you find?'

Tom looked beseechingly at Alf Morris, but the major evidently decided that capitulation was the better part of valour and gave a tiny nod of his head. The new doctor tried to be as non-committal as he could.

'Confirmed the obvious, sir. A bullet lodged inside the chest, made a mess of the root of the right lung.'

The colonel stared coldly at him over the steel rims of his glasses.

'What sort of bullet?'

As the rest of the hospital already seemed to know, Tom decided that its Commanding Officer might as well join them.

'A three-oh-three, sir, according to the police and the SIB chap.'

'And the range of discharge?'

'Hard to say, sir. Certainly not close.'

Desmond O'Neill grunted, then glared around the circle of officers, who still stood awkwardly near their chairs, most wishing they had also made a dash for the toilets.

'Goes to confirm what I thought. This was a bandit taking a pot-shot at a planter. Enemy action, poor fellow. Ironic he was a civilian.'

The colonel's staccato style of speech produced a few reluctant murmurs of agreement from his staff, then taking up his usual role of pourer of oil on choppy waters, Alf Morris tried to make the CO more welcome in his own Mess.

'Are you staying for lunch, sir? Can I get you a drink?'

O'Neill shook his head and stared around disapprovingly.

'No, thank you. Don't go along with doctors drinking at lunchtime, slows you down for the afternoon.'

With another of his mercurial changes of mood, he gave a ghastly death's head grin at them all, then turned on his heel and walked rapidly out of the room, grabbing his cap on the way. A moment later they watched him walking quickly on to the perimeter road with his peculiar springing gait, lifting himself from heel to toe at every step.

Once out of sight, there was a collective sigh of relief in the anteroom, as people sank back into their chairs.

'What the devil was all that about?' demanded Percy. 'He could just as well have phoned you or called you down to his office, Tom.'

Howden shrugged, relieved that he had got off so lightly. 'Search me, why is everyone so interested in what sort of damned bullet it was?'

This was a question that would be central to the meeting to be held with the police late that afternoon.

It was just as well that terrorist activity had quietened down in previous weeks, as it allowed Steven Blackwell more time to devote to the death of James Robertson. True, there was still plenty of work, but he had three inspectors and half a dozen sergeants to carry on with the other cases, supervising the donkey work of thirty constables working out of Tanah Timah Police Circle. There were the usual run of robberies, thieving being a national tradition in Malaya, as well as a few serious assault cases, mainly among the estate workers. But on this Saturday, the superintendent felt obliged to devote all his time to the only case involving a European.

After leaving the mortuary at BMH, he forsook his lunch to drive with Inspector Tan up the road to Gunong Besar, aware that the first priority was to discover where the shooting had occurred.

'Robertson's car arrived at the club, but there was no

indication of which direction it had come from,' he said, using the attentive Chinese as a sounding board for his own thoughts. 'I'm just guessing that he was on this road somewhere.'

The Dog was the last building in Tanah Timah on the road to the Gunong Besar estate, being on the hill just beyond the little bridge that lay a few hundred yards from the junction opposite the police station.

Blackwell told the driver to go very slowly from that point and both of them scanned the track and verges closely as they went. 'Thank God it hasn't rained yet today,' he said, staring at the red laterite dust of the rutted surface.

They stopped a couple of times when one or other thought he saw something, hoping for a spent shell-case. But one was a piece of wrapper from a cigarette packet, the other a lost wheel-nut from some vehicle.

As they drew nearer the rubber estate, their luck improved. As they approached the cutting through the bluff of red rock which rose up fifteen feet above them, Tan, who was sitting in the back of the open Land Rover, suddenly tapped the driver on the shoulder.

'*B'renti sini*!' he snapped in Malay and as the constable jerked to a stop, he clambered over the tailboard to walk the few steps to the left-hand edge of the road, where Blackwell joined him. The inspector pointed to the lush growth of weeds that grew on the edge of the ditch between them and the rock beyond.

'Surely that is blood, superintendent?' he said quietly, his forefinger hovering over leaves that carried splashes of brown against the green.

Steven bent down to look at the nearby grasses and weeds and saw more fine blotches. There seemed to be none on the ground, but the adjacent road ballast was gritty and powdered, not offering a good surface for the retention of stains.

'Let's have a good look around here,' he ordered and with the driver, they combed a dozen yards up and down the road for any other signs.

'There were a lot of police and army vehicles up and down here last night, sir,' said the inspector. 'No chance of distinguishing Robertson's Buick tyres – anyway, he drives up and down here every day.'

'I'm not concerned with his car, there's no way we could tell if it was stopped here. But that blood – if it is blood – is all we've got.'

He looked up at the tops of the two bluffs, one on each side of the narrow road. They were partly covered in coarse grass, but due to the rocky nature of the outcrops, they were well clear of the trees.

'Tan, get some men up here to search along a couple of hundred yards on each side,' he ordered. 'Tell them to look out for cartridge cases. And we'd better take some of those stained weeds to check if it's blood – and if it is, whose blood!'

There were some cellophane exhibit bags in the Land Rover and between them, they carefully picked off every leaf and blade that showed some of the brown splattering, and placed them in the bags.

'I'll see if that young pathologist can do a quick test, though the stuff will still have to go down to KL with the rest of the samples,' said Steven.

As they were so near Gunong Besar, he decided to make a quick call on Diane Robertson to check on her welfare, as he suspected that her nonchalant manner at the mortuary was a cover for a later breakdown, but again he was proved wrong.

When they arrived, Inspector Tan went off to interrogate the servants who lived behind both bungalows and Blackwell climbed up to Diane's verandah, half expecting to find her either in a state of sobbing collapse or half drunk. She was neither, though she had the inevitable glass in her hand as she sat on the settee talking to Douglas Mackay, who sat opposite, primly upright on one of the armchairs grasping a tumbler of orange squash.

Refusing the offer of an early gin and tonic, the superintendent put his cap and stick on another chair and stood looking down at the pair.

'I just called to see how you are, Diane,' he began uneasily, for far from being a distraught new widow, the blonde looked her usual glamorous self, as she had done in the mortuary.

'I'm fine, Steve! Douglas and I were just discussing the future of the estate. He says there's no problem in his carrying on, at least until it's decided what's going to be done with the place.'

The gangling Scotsman nodded agreement. 'Production can carry on as usual, it's a pretty routine operation. I'm more worried about Mrs Robertson herself.'

'In what way, Douglas?' asked Blackwell.

'She insists on staying here alone. She could come over to our place – or Rosa could keep her company here, but she won't hear of it.'

He looked across almost reproachfully at Diane, but she tossed her head so that the mane of golden hair swirled about her neck.

'I'm quite alright where I am, thank you, Doug. I've got my servants here and you're within shouting distance. I expect I'll be going back to the UK very soon, though perhaps I'll take a few days in Penang first. Until then, I'm sitting tight, as long as those damned CTs don't come calling again!'

The police officer shook his head.

'I'm sure this awful thing isn't down to them. It's not their style to pick off one man like that.'

The manager frowned his disagreement. 'What about the assassination of Sir Henry Gurney? He was ambushed and killed on the road at Fraser's Hill a couple of years ago?'

'With all due respect to James, he wasn't the British High Commissioner,' responded Steven. 'In fact, last night's tragedy makes me even more confident that the shoot-up here last week wasn't a terrorist attack. I'm sure the two things are linked in some way.'

Mackay continued to look doubtful, but said nothing. He was always a man of few words, thought Blackwell. They talked for a few more minutes, Diane remaining adamant that she was staying put at Gunong Besar. She had a phone call booked to James's brother, an auctioneer in Norwich and expected the international operator to get back to her any time now.

'There's no way any of the family can get out here for the funeral,' she said in a matter-of-fact tone. 'His father's dead, my mother-in-law's got bad arthritis and his brother George will never get a flight in time, even if he wanted to come.'

There was an unspoken understanding between them that in the Malayan climate, burial was necessary within a very few days. Civilian air travel to the Far East was not easy and the propeller-driven planes of BOAC took several days to get to Singapore, even if a vacant seat could be found at such short notice. Further discussion established that the lawyer who handled the estate and presumably also James Robertson's personal affairs, was the same solicitor in Ipoh who acted as part-time coroner.

'That'll make it easier when it comes to releasing the body for the funeral and in sorting out the will,' observed Blackwell, emboldened by Diane's resilience into being direct about these practical matters. 'I'm told this padre chap is back tomorrow. Alf Morris has left him a message to contact you as soon as possible.'

'He's a good man, I know he'll do all he can to make the arrangements go smoothly,' added Mackay in his soft Scots accent. A regular churchgoer, the manager was familiar with the local religious figures.

Steven picked up his hat and stick and moved towards the verandah.

'I'll be up to check again tomorrow. Diane, you've got my number if you need anything.' He turned to the estate manager. 'Could I have a quick word outside, Douglas?'

At the bottom of the outside steps, they stood between two tropical lilies, their large red blooms standing shoulder-high between spiky leaves. Somewhere nearby, a monkey yelled shrilly in a tree and the ever-present twitter of cicadas formed a background to their conversation. Steven put on his uniform cap to keep the sun from his ruddy scalp.

'I know my inspector has already taken a statement from you, Doug, but I like to get things straight from the horse's mouth. You weren't at The Dog last night, I gather?'

Mackay shook his head, his sallow features devoid of expression.

'No, I'm not much of a one for dancing, I only go for Rosa's benefit now and then. She's younger and deserves a bit of life occasionally. It's a lonely place for a wife up here – and I'm afraid she and Diane don't get on all that well.'

Steven avoided any pursuit of that topic. He knew that Douglas was almost a teetotaller, apart from the odd beer. Keen on classical music, he was a devout man, going every Sunday morning to the garrison chapel, though he was really a Presbyterian, rather than a 'C of E' man.

'So you were at home all evening?'

'Yes, I did the usual last rounds of the sheds and tapper's lines about six thirty, before it got dark. James was away, gone to Taiping, so he said.'

Steven noted the slight sarcasm in the manager's voice.

'Then I went in and had a meal. We listened to the radio for a bit, then Rosa said she was tired and went to bed about ten, I suppose.'

'Both of you?'

'No, I did some paperwork and made up the servant's pay packets for this morning. Then I listened to records for a bit and went to bed about eleven, I suppose. Rosa was fast asleep and I'd only just nodded off when you and half the British army descended on us.'

Blackwell nodded, he'd had this already from Tan.

'What guns d'you have up here, Douglas?'

The manager stared at him. 'Guns? Well, we've accumulated a few since the troubles began. There were a couple here when I came and we've added some since. Last week was the fourth attack we've had over the years, so we needed them.'

'What exactly have you got?' persisted Steven.

Mackay steepled his hands to his chin as if in prayer.

'Both James and I each have a thirty-eight revolver and a Lee-Enfield rifle. Then there are three twelve-bore shotguns about the place, though they're mainly for rats and other vermin.'

'Where are they all kept?'

'The pistols and rifles are locked away with their ammunition in gun cupboards in each of the bungalows. I'm afraid we're more relaxed with the shotguns, they're usually stuck in a corner somewhere, though we keep the cartridges in the estate office across the road.'

'Have any of the house servants or estate workers got weapons?'

Douglas looked shocked. 'I certainly hope not! You know better than me that it's a hanging offence under the Emergency laws. Though I'll admit that occasionally one of the *serangs* will use a twelve-bore to have a go at the rats that infest the tapper's lines.'

Blackwell's experience at other places told him that illicit firearms were not all that uncommon, but he made no comment.

'Eventually, we may have to test fire all rifled weapons held by estates around TT, just to eliminate them. That's after we get the ballistics reports on the bullets I've sent down to KL.'

Mackay looked dubious. 'Sure, but it'll be a waste of time checking ours. James and I had them with us when we turned out to deal with the swine who shot us up the other day. And poor old James didn't shoot himself.'

The policeman shrugged. 'Just routine, Douglas. With all the arms held by the garrison, I agree it seems a bit futile just testing the few outside. Yet it looks as if James was hit just down the road, so what with last week's attack here, we have to eliminate the local weapons.'

The manager's sparse eyebrows rose. 'You know where it happened then?'

'I didn't mention it in front of Diane, not until we're sure, but we found what looks like blood just where the road goes through that cutting.'

The manager nodded slowly, his lean face looking even more solemn than usual. 'Just the place for an ambush, Steven. I'm still not convinced by your argument that this wasn't the work of the CTs.'

Inspector Tan came across from the curing sheds at that moment and after muted farewells, they climbed into the Land Rover and were driven off, leaving a pensive Douglas Mackay staring after them.

*   *   *

Around five o'clock, a meeting was held in the Police Circle building in Tanah Timah, mainly to discuss the significance of the post-mortem findings. Alfred Morris was sent by the CO to represent the hospital's interests, as the victim had died there and the pathologist was one of its officers. The Admin Officer drove Tom Howden down to the town in his Hillman, both wearing civilian clothes, as was usual on a Saturday. Their identity cards got them past the constable on the gate and, inside the high-walled compound, Tom saw that it was largely a vehicle park and workshops, with a police barracks at the rear.

The headquarters building itself was typical colonial government – two-storey white cement under a red-tiled roof, with wide balconies running around the upper floor. They went up the steps to the front entrance and found themselves in a large hall with busy policemen behind a long counter. A Malay desk sergeant escorted them up an imposing central staircase and out on to the balcony, which had doors at intervals. Tapping at one, he motioned them in and they entered a bare, high room with the inevitable fan turning below the ceiling. There was a large desk, a table, some hard chairs and walls covered with maps. Steven Blackwell rose from the table, where he had been talking with Major Enderby, Sergeant Markham and Inspector Tan.

'Come and sit down with us, chaps. We were only gossiping until you arrived.'

They sat down and an Indian servant came in with a tray of opened bottles of cold orange squash and grapefruit soda, each with a straw stuck in the neck. When they had settled down again, the superintendent began the meeting.

'Firstly, I must thank you, Captain Howden, for so readily agreeing to do the post-mortem. If you hadn't been here, there'd have been at least a few days' delay – and in this climate, that doesn't help to preserve any evidence.'

Tom nodded his appreciation, though privately he knew he had had no choice, with the CO breathing down his neck.

'I've written out a rough draft of the report,' he said, holding up a thin cardboard folder. 'Only handwritten at the moment, I'll get it typed up when the office opens on Monday.'

The major from the provost marshal's department stopped sucking on his straw for a moment. 'Fine! We were there, so we know the gist of it. But can you give us your interpretation of the findings?'

The pathologist shifted his bottom uneasily on the hard seat.

'Look, I'm a pretty junior bloke, you know. I've had almost no experience of this kind of thing, all I know is from the books.'

'Just do your best, Tom,' said Steven kindly. 'I'm sure you know a hell of lot more about it than us.'

Opening the file, Howden looked down at the two sheets of lined quarto paper, with the government crest at the top. He had no need to read it, as he already knew every word.

'James Robertson was perfectly healthy, so death was entirely due to a gunshot wound,' he began. 'There was a single entrance wound to the left of centre in the front of his chest. The bullet, which you saw was a .303, was still in the back of his chest cavity, so there was no exit wound.'

Sergeant Markham looked up at this. 'Thinking about it, sir, isn't that a bit unusual for a service rifle? I've seen a few in my time and most them went in one side and out the other.'

Tom nodded his agreement. 'From what the books say, it's very common for a high-velocity projectile from a military weapon to make a through-and-through wound. But here the bullet happened to hit the spine at the back of the chest. It made a hell of a mess of it, completely disintegrated one of the vertebrae, but the thick, hard bone must have stopped the bullet.'

A sudden thought occurred to him and by the look on Blackwell's face, it must also have dawned simultaneously on him. The pathologist beat him to it in stating the obvious.

'Hang on a minute, there's something wrong here! Though he may not have died instantaneously, he must have been totally disabled and almost certainly unconscious from the moment the bullet hit him!'

The three other Army men looked mystified, but Inspector Tan was quickest off the mark.

'So how could he drive his car to the Sussex Club from wherever he was shot?'

'Which now seems to be a few miles up the road towards Gunong Besar,' added Steven Blackwell.

'Are you sure about this?' demanded Enderby, leaning forward. Tom was confident about this aspect, however little he knew about firearm wounds.

'His spinal column was smashed through. There's a condition called "spinal shock" which even apart from his other internal injuries, would almost certainly make him lose consciousness instantly. And apart from that, he wouldn't be able to sit up to drive, with a broken back – though that would soon be impossible anyway, with massive bleeding inside his chest from the big arteries and veins ripped in the root of his lung.'

Tom looked a little crestfallen after giving this lecture. 'I should have thought of this earlier, but I had just accepted the business about Daniel finding him in the driving seat of his car.'

There was a tense silence for a moment.

'This puts a whole new complexion on the matter,' snapped Blackwell. 'There are only two explanations. One is that he was shot in the car park of The Dog – which is patently impossible, as no one there heard a shot. And you can't shoot a man in the front of the chest when he's sitting in the driving seat, unless there's bullet hole in the windscreen, especially in a car with armoured side windows!'

'And the other explanation?' asked Alf Morris, though he guessed the answer.

'Is that someone drove the car there from the murder scene, then buggered off before Daniel appeared!' completed the major from the garrison. After another brief silence while they digested this, Blackwell spoke again.

'Whatever else this tells us, it means one thing is definite – this was no terrorist shooting! Killing one man with one shot is damned unusual for them anyway, but it's ludicrous to imagine a CT driving his victim away!'

There were murmurs of agreement, then the Chinese police inspector voiced the next question.

'Why would the killer do such a thing? It must have greatly increased the risk of him being seen.'

Steven Blackwell shook his head. 'Not necessarily. If we're right in thinking that the blood found near that cutting was where the shooting occurred, he might have wanted to shift both the car and the body well away, to delay discovery.'

'Because of the increased patrols up and down that road, you mean?' asked Alf Morris.

'Exactly! If he could have quietly left the car in a corner of the car park, then it could have been some time before the body was found – perhaps not until the next morning.'

'But he goes and bashes into the back of a truck and brings poor old Daniel out to investigate,' said Enderby.

'Bloody lucky he missed seeing the killer, or he might have collected a bullet as well!' added the SIB man.

'Where's the car now, Tan?' asked the senior policeman.

'In the garage down below, sir,' replied the Chinese inspector.

'Better check the wheel for fingerprints, though both Daniel and presumably a police officer have driven it since the shooting.' Blackwell drummed his fingers on the table. 'I wish we had proper forensic laboratory facilities up here. They can do all sorts of things back home now, looking at the soil from shoes and God knows what.'

'I doubt if that would help much here – everyone has red laterite on their boots. I don't think any laboratory is going to crack this one for you, Steven,' said Enderby.

'Talking of that, Captain Howden, can you do tests for blood in your lab over at BMH?' asked Blackwell.

Tom looked dubious. 'We can easily do a presumptive test for blood, though many other things give a false positive. I can certainly tell you if it's not blood!'

'Any hope of confirming it's human and possibly what group?' persisted the superintendent.

The pathologist shook his head. 'I honestly don't know. If it's very fresh, maybe we could get a group out of it, but it's way out of my line, dealing with stains rather than fresh blood.'

'Well, give it a go, there's a good chap. Tan can give you

some of those apparently bloodstained leaves we picked up on the Gunong Besar road. We'll get a report from KL eventually, but I thought it might help to get a quick answer.'

'Going back to this post-mortem, Captain Howden,' grunted Major Enderby. 'Any idea of the range of the shot?'

'It certainly wasn't close, as I said this morning,' replied Tom. 'No scorching, smoke staining or powder tattooing on the clothing or skin. The books say that the distance over which that occurs is very variable according to the type of weapon and ammunition, but in any case, wouldn't happen if the muzzle was more than a few feet away.'

'So not a very close discharge – but it could be ten feet or half a mile!' said the major. 'Any idea about the direction?'

Tom rubbed his chin and looked at his papers while he made time to consider his answer.

'Anatomically, it was a bit downwards through the chest and slightly from left front to right middle, as it smashed the spine. But of course, it all depends how the deceased was standing or sitting when he was hit.'

'How d'you mean?' asked Steven.

'Well, the books warn against assuming that a downward path means that the shooter was firing from above. If the victim was leaning forward a bit, then even a horizontal shot would incline downwards through the body?'

There was a silence as they digested this. Then the inscrutable Inspector Tan spoke, again picking up something that the others had so far missed.

'Superintendent, you said just now that a driver couldn't be shot straight through the front of the chest while sitting at the wheel, especially in an armoured car like that Buick. So that must surely mean he was shot when he was *out* of the vehicle?'

They all thought about this, but it was Blackwell who responded first.

'Of course! And it had to be like that, otherwise how could that blood have got on to the grass at the side of the road!'

'If it is blood,' muttered Enderby, with typical lawyer's caution.

'Let's assume it is for the moment,' said Steven, rather

impatiently. 'So why the hell would a man get out of his car on a lonely road late at night, not many days after a presumed terrorist attack less than a mile away?'

'Because he recognized someone he knew,' snapped the SIB sergeant.

'Someone whose own car had broken down – or who pretended it had,' offered Enderby.

'But then the killer would have had to leave his vehicle at the scene, if he drove the body down to the club in Robertson's car,' objected the implacably logical Chinese inspector.

Steven Blackwell raised a hand. 'Let's not get too far in front of ourselves, chaps. At this stage, I don't think that matters all that much. We've learned something very important from Dr Howden, that James Robertson must have been driven to The Dog by someone, presumably the assailant.'

The taciturn sergeant joined in the discussion.

'I wonder how he got away so quickly? Surely he didn't drive away, or that manager chap would have seen or heard a car, as he seems to have gone out straight away when he heard the crash.'

'He wouldn't have a car there, anyway, if he drove James's down from the murder site,' reasoned Enderby.

'Unless he was someone who was in the club earlier and had left his car there, then footed it up to that cutting. It's only a couple of miles away.'

Alfred Morris's observation suddenly brought home the fact that the murderer, now known not to be a terrorist, could quite well be one of their own acquaintances. It was an unpleasant realization, unwelcome to them all. Steven Blackwell sighed, thinking of the difficult work that lay ahead, interviewing people who he knew all too well.

'This means that we will have to concentrate on all weapons that could possibly be involved, both in civilian and military use. A hell of a job, I'm afraid.'

He looked at the two majors. 'This is going to be bloody difficult! It's going to be a nightmare testing even the relatively few guns in civilian hands, amongst the planters, let alone the military weapons. The chaps on the estates are not going to take kindly to being deprived of their shooters, even for a short time.'

'Will they all have to be sent down to the forensic lab in KL?' demanded Enderby. 'I can't see the Brigadier suspending his war for you, even for a murder!'

'That's out of the question, of course,' said Steven. 'We'll have to be very specific about what guns we test, to limit the numbers.'

Sergeant Markham chipped in again. 'Getting a test bullet to check on the rifling marks can be done on the spot. Firing into a tank of water or a big box full of wadding is sufficient. That stops a bullet without damaging it.'

'Let's wait until we get a report back on those shell cases from the attack on Gunong Besar, before we start on the rifles,' advised Blackwell. 'I'm convinced now that that episode is linked somehow to this killing.'

He turned to his inspector. 'Tan, you said your constables found no sign of a spent cartridge along the road near that cutting, but we need to find the one that carried the bullet that killed poor James. Send another team up there tomorrow and widen the search, OK?'

After a few more minutes of discussion, which got them nowhere in particular, the meeting broke up and Morris drove Tom back to the hospital. Just before the garrison entrance, a red-capped military policeman held them up as a procession of vehicles streamed out of the gate. Three Ferret armoured cars, four Saracen troop carriers, half a dozen three-tonner Bedford TCVs, two Land Rover ambulances and a radio van lumbered off down the road towards the town.

'What's going on?' asked the pathologist, suddenly aware that he actually was on Active Service and that one man with a bullet in his chest was pretty small beer compared to the potential mayhem in which this convoy might soon become involved.

'Looks as if the Brigadier has decided on disinfecting some part of the jungle,' replied Alf, laconically. 'They're probably going down the main road to the turn-off for Grik and then going up north for a punch-up.'

Dusk was approaching as they entered BMH and as they

parked behind the Mess, a glorious sunset filled the western sky. Streaks of salmon pink and scarlet vied with the blue vault above, masses of cumulus on the horizon being tinged with brilliant gold. Though Tom had seen this almost every evening, he was still spellbound by the sight, so different from the grey haze that hung over Tyneside when he had left a couple of weeks earlier. His feelings of unreality hit him with full force, but he managed to shake them off and follow Alf into the anteroom for a reviving Tiger before dinner.

With his wife away, Steven Blackwell found that one day was much the same as another and that weekends merged into a continuous pattern of work. So though the next day was a Sunday, he found no problem in seamlessly pursuing the enquiry by interviewing the potential witnesses. In fact, it was easier, as most of them were off duty on the Sabbath.

He had an early breakfast in his quarters, which was a bungalow at the back of the police station. It was within the safety of the encircling wall and high fence, but far enough away from the constable's barracks to be relatively private. With Margaret away, he was looked after by an Indian houseboy and their Chinese cook who came in each day from the town.

He spent a couple of hours in his office dealing with other matters and conferring with the duty inspector about the day's patrol schedules, then called his driver and was taken in the Land Rover up to Gunong Besar. Here he met his first obstacle, as the Robertson's servant gravely informed him that his mistress had gone to church. At first, Steven wondered if James's death had driven her to a return of faith, as to his knowledge, Diane had never before set foot in the garrison chapel. Siva soon enlightened him, explaining that she had gone to see the padre to make arrangements for the funeral.

'The priest telephoned, sir. He said his Sunday morning duties made it difficult for him to come up here until after lunch, so Missus said she would drive down to see him.'

Though Tan had already grilled all the servants, the superintendent took the opportunity to question Siva, who was an unusually tall man for a Tamil. Politely, but firmly, the servant said that he had heard and seen absolutely nothing out of the ordinary on the night of the murder.

No, there had been no strangers hanging about the estate lately, the only visitor in the past few days being Mr Arnold from Batu Merah, the next plantation a couple of miles further up the road.

Blackwell had no luck at the other bungalow, as the Mackays were also at church, though he half expected this. Douglas was known to be a keen Christian and although his wife was a Roman Catholic, she went with him to the Anglican services on Sunday morning. Steven knew that she also went down each Thursday evening, when a Catholic padre from Sungei Siput came up to say Mass for the relatively few of that faith in the garrison.

Frustrated, he decided to avoid totally wasting the journey, by going up to Batu Merah to talk to Les Arnold, as he knew that there was no chance of the laid-back Australian being in church. Indeed when he arrived at the next estate, he found the owner lounging comfortably in a striped deckchair outside his bungalow, which was very similar to the ones down the road. He had a bottle of beer in one hand, a copy of yesterday's *Straits Times* in the other and looked very much at ease.

Arnold lived alone, the gossip saying that he had been divorced before coming up from Darwin soon after Malaya was liberated from the Japanese. Blackwell knew that he had been in the Australian army during the war and had seen service in New Guinea. He had made a real success of running Batu Merah, which was said to be one of the most profitable estates in the valley – probably aided by Arnold's reputation for ruthless business dealings and his strict control over his workers.

Les hoisted his lanky frame from the chair and as the policeman climbed from his vehicle, yelled at his houseboy to bring out another chair and a beer from the house. Though it was not yet eleven o'clock, Steven Blackwell accepted a sit down and a pewter tankard of Anchor, as the morning seemed even more oppressively hot than usual. Unlike the

Robertsons' place, this bungalow sat in a dip, the rubber
closely around it on all sides. Perhaps coming from the
tropical Northern Territories, Les Arnold was more used to
the heat, but Steven's bald head was as red as a ripe tomato
and his uniform shirt was blackened with sweat. Though he
had been out from 'home' for years, he knew he would never
get used to the oppressive climate and already ideas of early
retirement were beginning to germinate in his mind, especially since his wife had gone back for a six-month stay. He
took a long draught of the cold beer and sank back thankfully
in the chair, then forced himself to attend to the business in
hand.

'Look, Les, this is difficult for all of us, especially me. I've
got a job to do and I'll get no thanks for having to pry into
people's affairs – especially as most of them are friends and
acquaintances.'

The long face of the planter split in a grin.

'Don't worry yourself, mate. We all understand – and those
who don't are just thick! Fire away, I've got a clear
conscience.'

'Right, then. I've got to ask everyone about their movements
on Friday night. I guess you were in The Dog?'

'Yep, propping up the bar most of the evening. Got there
about eight, had a bit of tucker at the buffet at half ten, drove
back here around eleven thirty or thereabouts.'

'Thereabouts? You can't be a bit more exact?' asked
Blackwell.

'Jesus, no! I'd had a good few beers, as always. Even had
a bit of a dance, before and after the grub. Do you want to
know who with?'

His tone was bantering, a half-amused smile on his face.

Steven shook his head. 'You saw no one on the road from
Tanah Timah, I presume? It would help if you knew the time
you came up, so that I could try to place where James Robertson
was then.'

Arnold took another mouthful of beer and tried to look more
serious.

'Just can't be that exact, mate. Time doesn't mean a hell
of lot in a place like this, getting the date right is hard enough.

But I think I got to bed about midnight, give or take a few minutes.'

'And you saw nothing on the road?'

'Damn all, Steve.' He looked quizzically at the superintendent. 'Why this interest in this road? Was that where it happened?'

It was inevitable that everyone would soon hear about the blood on the grass, so he made no attempt to avoid the question.

'I'm not absolutely sure, Les, but I think the shooting happened near that cutting just below Gunong Besar.'

The Australian shrugged. 'That's a long way from here. I wouldn't hear any shots this far off. I didn't even hear when they blasted the place a couple of weeks ago and that's almost a mile closer.'

Blackwell took a long swallow of his beer, imagining that he could feel it come out as perspiration on his forehead as soon as he drank it.

'This is the awkward bit I have to ask people, Les. We're sure this wasn't a CT attack, it was more personal, so we need a motive. How did you really get on with James and Diane?'

Again a crooked grin appeared on the planter's face. 'What d'you expect me to say, for Chrissake? Jimmy Robertson was a pain in the arse, but he was harmless.'

'And Diane?'

'Come on, Steve, you've got eyes and a pair of balls! She's bloody gorgeous and I could do her a good turn any day of the week – though I'd have to join the queue!'

'And did you?'

Arnold's expression hardened a little, the smile fading. 'Look, Steve, you're sitting in my place, drinking my beer. Do you seriously think I'm going to admit to you that I was knocking off Jimmy's wife?'

Blackwell carefully put his empty tankard on the ground alongside his chair.

'Is that a "yes" or a "no", then?' he asked.

'It's a "no comment", and that's all you're getting, Stevie boy,' he grunted. 'It's got bugger all to with this affair, anyway.

I'll admit I fancied her something rotten, as did every red-
blooded chap within ten miles, but that's sweet Fanny Adams
to do with Jimmy getting killed.'

The planter uncoiled his six feet from the chair and Steven
sensed that he would get nothing more from him at present.
Not wanting to antagonize people with whom he had to asso-
ciate – and who he would no doubt have to return to question
yet again – he decided to retire gracefully while he was still
ahead.

After a few rather stilted platitudes, the social temperature
having dropped somewhat, the police officer climbed back
into his Land Rover, wishing the air temperature would do
the same.

When they got back down the road as far as Gunong Besar,
Steven Blackwell saw that a black Ford V8 Pilot was just
turning into the manager's driveway. A quick glance up to the
Robertson house showed him that there was no sign of Diane's
Austin under the bungalow, so he told to his driver to follow
the Ford. As they drove up to the front of the bungalow,
Douglas and Rosa were just getting out of the V8, stopping
to stare at the police vehicle as it pulled up. The Scotsman
wore a rather creased linen suit and a wide-brimmed straw
hat, Rosa being as neat as usual in a blue-and-white flowered
dress with a wide skirt. She had a small blue hat on the front
of her raven hair and even carried a pair of white gloves,
obviously her formal churchgoing outfit.

Leaving his driver with the vehicle, Steven got out to greet
the manager and his wife and was invited up into the bungalow,
a slightly smaller version of the one next door. In the wide
lounge, Douglas invited the police officer to sit down, after a
rather apprehensive Rosa took off her hat and sat opposite,
perched stiffly on the edge of a settee.

'I've only a beer to offer you, I'm afraid,' said Douglas
softly. 'We're not great drinkers here, you see.'

Blackwell waved away the offer, but accepted Rosa's suggestion of a fresh lime. She rang a small brass bell that stood on
a coffee table between them and gave an order to a silent
Chinese *amah* who glided in from the back of the house.

'What can we do for you, Steven?' asked Douglas. 'More questions, I expect.'

He said this without rancour and sat alongside his wife, looking expectantly at the superintendent.

'Sorry about all this, but I've got to start doing the rounds of everyone who had more than a passing acquaintance with poor old James. I've just been up to talk to Les Arnold.'

Douglas Mackay gave a slight sniff at the mention of his neighbour. Steven recognized that though Douglas was a most Christian soul, full of compassion and forgiveness, he was not overly fond of the Australian, a cynical, hard-drinking and sometimes aggressive fellow.

'How did James get along with Arnold?' asked the policeman. 'We all saw them together often enough in The Dog, but that doesn't really tell me much.'

Douglas looked down at his wife's smooth features, then warily raised his eyes to his visitor.

'I'm not much given to gossip, Steven. People's affairs are their own. But as this is a police matter, I have to say that they were certainly not bosom pals. Arnold used to needle James quite a bit, sort of sarcastic leg-pulling. I felt he thought James a bit of a "pommie snob", to be honest.'

'Anything more than that?' persisted Steven.

Mackay hesitated and again looked across at Rosa, who sat impassively alongside him. 'I think he used to get annoyed at Les flirting with Diane – but Les did that with every woman he met, it doesn't mean that it was at all serious. Though perhaps James may have thought it was – he wasn't the most perceptive of people. But one shouldn't speak ill of the dead.'

The *amah* brought a tray of drinks, tall glasses with a crush of heavily sugared limes. They each took one and rattled the ice with the straws before gratefully sucking down some of the delicious pale green juice. Then Blackwell went over once again their movements on the night before last, this time in meticulous detail, though nothing new emerged.

'I'll have to borrow your rifle in the next few days, Doug – and the one that belonged to James. A damned nuisance, I know, but every .303 in sight will have to be test-fired, just as a routine. We'll only need them for a day, the Ordnance guys in the garrison can do the business.'

Mackay's fair eyebrows rose at this. 'How the dickens can you do all of them, Steven? There must be hundreds down in the Brigade!'

The superintendent shrugged helplessly. 'I know, it's almost impossible. We'll start with those in civilian hands, like yours, then gradually work selectively through those which must have been in the garrison both on Friday night and when your bungalows were shot up the other day.'

'Will the army let you do that?' asked Douglas.

'They're very cooperative. There's an SIB chap working with the provost marshal's office. I think they may be afraid that the culprit may turn out to be in the military.' Steven said this in a neutral tone, but they all knew that the possibility was that an officer was involved.

The superintendent sighed to himself. He felt he was getting nowhere fast in this investigation

'And there's been no trouble recently between James and his workers, has there?' he asked.

Douglas shook his head. 'Nothing at all lately. James was always a little brusque with the men – some would say over-bearing and rude, but I was usually able to smooth down any ruffled feathers. We had better labour relations than Les Arnold, that's for sure!'

After a few more rather futile questions, Blackwell finished his drink and rose to leave. As they walked out on to the verandah, he heard a car changing gear and crunching up the drive next door.

'That must be Mrs Robertson,' said Douglas. 'I was told she'd been into the garrison to see a padre about the funeral.'

Rosa nodded. 'That would be John Smale, one of the Anglican chaplains. He's a very nice man.' A mention of the priesthood seemed to draw her out of her usual reticent manner.

The pair watched him clatter down the steps and walk away through the bushes up towards the Robertson bungalow, waving to his driver to take the Land Rover around into the other driveway.

As they turned to go back into the lounge, Douglas put his arm around his wife, who began weeping quietly, burying her face in his jacket.

When Steven learned from Diane that James's burial was to be the next day, he abandoned his intention of questioning her more rigorously, until the funeral was behind them. Declining her offer to join her in an early gin, he stood with the blonde on her verandah, saying that he couldn't stay, but only wanted to check that she was alright.

'Have you heard from James's family yet?' he asked solicitously.

'His brother phoned back late last night – lousy line, I could only just hear what he was saying.' From her tone, Steven guessed that she had little affection for her in-laws.

'How did his mother take it?' he asked. 'Must have been an awful shock for the family. And being so far away, they must feel helpless.'

Diane shrugged, as she flicked her cigarette ash over the balcony rail.

'They're a pretty tough bunch, the Robertsons. Hunting, shooting and cussing, that's their style. But George did sound cut up, what little I could make out over the wires.'

She was dressed in the same outfit as she was at the mortuary, a black skirt and crisp white blouse. It was obviously her version of a mourning outfit and Blackwell wondered what she would wear at the actual funeral.

'This padre chappie was very helpful,' she said calmly. 'He rang around and fixed the ceremony for tomorrow afternoon, at the English church in Taiping.'

Steven nodded. 'The coroner is issuing the release certificate in the morning, so I'll give you a driver to take you to Ipoh to collect it and go to the Registrar.'

Diane looked surprised at this. 'Oh God, do I have to go myself?'

'Afraid so, you are the only eligible informant. It's only a formality, you'll be back before lunchtime.'

As he moved towards the steps, he turned back to the new widow.

'We'll all rally around at the funeral, Diane. A few of the people from BMH want to be there, as well as some other members from The Dog. You'll need some support, with no one from his family able to be there.'

Diane murmured some thanks, but Steve felt she was not overcome with gratitude and suspected there were a couple of female faces that she would prefer not to see in Taiping.

As he drove away, his last glimpse was of her in her typical posture, leaning on the veranda rail with a glass in one hand and a Kensitas in the other.

Sunday lunch in the RAMC Mess was something of a ritual, a hangover from the days when many officers were ex-Indian Army and demanded their curry on a regular basis.

Though Meng was nominally the cook, she was assisted by Vellatum, an Indian kitchen 'boy', though he was actually a wizened fellow in his forties, who had been badly beaten up by the Japanese during the Occupation. On Sundays, Meng took the day off to go on the bus to visit her sister in Kuala Kangsar and Vellatum was given a free hand to prepare the weekly curry.

The general idea was for the residents to eat as much of the eye-watering mixture as they could manage, chase it with a few Tigers, then crawl satiated to their room to pull on a sarong and collapse sweating on to their beds for a few hours. Such a novel Sunday lunch was a new experience for Tom, as Tyneside had yet to see any oriental eating houses. Yet he rapidly took to the fiery concoction that Vellatum served up and happily spooned down the colourful food, alternating with mouthfuls of beer to put out the flames in his gullet.

'I like all these little bits on the side,' he said, after blowing through his lips that were burning from a shred of red chilli. He pointed to the tray in the centre of the table that held small dishes filled with shredded coconut, banana, mango chutney, cashew nuts and other unidentifiable substances.

'What are these things?'

'That's Bombay duck,' answered Eddie Rosen. 'Little dried fish, actually.'

Tom shook his head in wonderment at the strange ways of

the East, as he accepted some more rice, the Indian coming around the table with a tureen filled with the fluffy white grains. When the curry was finished and they were waiting for their dessert, the conversation inevitably turned to the dramatic events of the weekend.

'The CO's in an unusually benign mood,' announced Alf Morris. 'He's said that anyone whose duties allow, should attend James Robertson's funeral tomorrow. We should try to get there to give some support to Diane, as she'll have no family there at all.'

There was a murmur of agreement around the table.

'Is our dear colonel going himself?' asked Percy Loosemore, managing as usual to inject sarcasm into his voice.

'No, he says he's too busy, with the ADMS coming up from Singapore next week – though I can't see what that's got to do with it,' added Alf, with a rare hint of disloyalty to his senior officer. Tom had already added 'Assistant Director of Medical Services' to his compendium of acronyms.

'We'd better work out a travel plan,' suggested David Meredith. 'No point in everyone taking a car to Taiping.'

'Especially those who don't have one,' said Eddie. 'Tom and I will need a lift from somebody.'

'I can't go, I'm afraid,' said Peter Bright, stonily. 'I'm on call and Roger Lane says he can't stand in for me tomorrow.' Most of his colleagues around the table assumed that this was a tactful gesture to avoid seeing off the man they suspected he had been cuckolding.

'Is this going to be a funeral procession all the way?' grunted the sardonic Percy. 'Who's taking the corpse – and how? On a gun carriage or in the back of a three-tonner?'

Alec Watson made a noise suspiciously like a giggle, but the Admin Officer glared at Percy.

'He was a civilian, remember?' said Alf. 'A hearse is coming up from Ipoh in the morning. The only Western-style under-taker in Perak. We're all to meet up with him in Taiping at three thirty.'

'And that's at the Anglican church, not the military ceme-tery!' added Clarence Bottomley sternly. Montmorency had little sense of humour and Percy's waspish tongue got up his long aristocratic nose.

'Everyone in civvies, not uniform,' commanded Alfred. 'The colonel was insistent on that.'

Vellatum came in with a tray of glass dishes containing *gula malacca*, the traditional dessert served after a curry. Tom found he liked this as well, a sweet, sticky mound of sago swimming in palm sugar and coconut milk. After they had all ingested this antidote to the cook-boy's culinary dynamite, the talk went back to tomorrow's excursion.

'Is it a men-only affair or are the ladies attending?' asked Clarence.

'As the widow is the only official mourner, the Matron suggested that it might show some feminine solidarity if a few of the QA officers went along as well,' said Alfred Morris. 'Maybe someone could give them a ring later and see if any want transport, as only a couple have cars.'

Tom's thoughts immediately fell to hoping that Lynette might be going, especially if she could come in the same car and resolved to hint to Alf that he offer them space in his Hillman.

Coffee was next on the agenda before everyone crept off to their pits to sleep off the meal, but in the anteroom next door, the disgruntled anaesthetist brought up the murder once again.

'Has the local Gestapo been around you all yet?' Meredith asked sourly. 'Steve Blackwell was almost rattling his handcuffs when he came to see me yesterday.'

All except Peter Bright denied being interrogated, giving Percy the chance to tactlessly claim that obviously the surgeon and his gasman were the prime suspects.

'The superintendent told me that he would be around later today and again in the morning,' announced Alfred, whose 'Admin' job made him the official contact with the outside world, which included the police. There was a groan from several of them and Eddie rattled his cup back into its saucer and stood up.

'In that case, I'm off to my scratcher now, to get a bit of kip before the constabulary come to beat the truth out of me.'

As he stumbled across the coarse grass towards his room, he was followed by a straggle of bloated and sleepy medical officers.

It was early evening before Steven Blackwell arrived at the hospital and most of the residents were dragging themselves from under their mosquito nets to wash and dress ready for dinner. A few were sitting writing letters home or having a beer on chairs dragged out on to the concrete verandah, where they could enjoy the glorious sunset.

Alf Morris, in his usual role as organizer and go-between, asked several officers to go over one at a time to the empty anteroom to talk to the policeman.

'He realizes it's bit near dinner, so it won't take long,' he said reassuringly. Steven had brought Inspector Tan with him, who silently recorded the interviews in his notebook, to turn into statements which the witnesses could sign after they were typed up back at police headquarters.

Eddie Rosen ambled over first, still in his gaudy red-and-white check sarong that he wore in bed. He had little to tell Steven, other than he was fast asleep in bed from ten thirty on Friday evening and knew nothing of the tragedy until breakfast.

'He could be an obnoxious so-and-so, could Jimmy Robertson,' observed Eddie ruminatively. 'A top-class snob was James and a bit thick with it. But I'm appalled that someone has topped the poor devil. There must be a woman at the bottom of it somewhere, surely. That was his only interest in life, apart from booze. He didn't even play golf!'

The superintendent thanked him and mentally wrote him off as a suspect. The little doctor was hardly a heart-throb and Steven knew he had left a wife and two babies back in London, making him an unlikely candidate for a crime of passion.

He felt much the same about the next interviewee, Alec Watson. The Scot looked more like a schoolboy and Blackwell had difficulty in believing that he must now be at least twenty-five to have qualified and done his house-surgeon time in Edinburgh. Like Eddie, he claimed to have been tucked up in bed at the material time and Steven had no reason to doubt him. Though he was an inveterate gatherer of gossip, Alec was a canny-enough Scot not to offer Blackwell either his opinions or his scraps of tittle-tattle about James and various ladies, so the interview was short and sweet.

The next man was Lieutenant Clarence Bottomley, who was rather pompous and formal with the policemen. Far from being in a sarong like Eddie, he was gorgeously arrayed in full mess kit, as he announced that he had been invited over to a Mess Night at the West Berkshires. A starched white monkey jacket sat stiffly above his dark blue 'Number One' trousers with their cherry-red strip down the outside of the legs. A matching cummerbund around his waist contrasted with a gleaming white shirt, which displayed small gold studs and a carefully tied black bow.

'This goes against the grain a little, superintendent,' he complained, as he sat erect on the edge of the chair opposite the policeman. 'We're officers on active service, y'know. Shouldn't be chivvied around by civilians like this.'

Steven, who was almost old enough to be his father, sighed but held his tongue. 'Just routine, doctor. As for being a civilian, I think you may find that your own military police may be taking an interest in this matter before long.'

This brought Montmorency up short and he had no answer to offer. Steven went through the same questions, asking where Bottomley had been when James Robertson was shot. This time he got a different answer to being in bed, as the others had claimed.

'I was out with a couple of chaps in Ipoh, as it happens. Fellows I knew at school, actually.'

It seemed that a subaltern from the Rifle Brigade and another from 22 SAS had joined up with Clarence to visit a new nightclub in Ipoh. The superintendent ruminated on this as Inspector Tan painstaking wrote down all the details that Steven drew from the reluctant lieutenant. Quite a number of these rather seedy joints had appeared in the towns of North Malaya, depending heavily on the military for their clientele. The usual venue was a large house, with a dimly-lit bar, a minute dance floor and a record player. The patrons were a mixed bag, as although most of the men were officers, there was also a number of Chinese and Indian businessmen. Malays were uncommon, mainly because they eschewed alcohol. The usual shortage of European women was made up for by ladies from the same two races and although the clubs were far from being houses of ill repute, certainly many a liaison was contracted before the evening was out.

Steven had no interest in pursuing Bottomley's activities in Ipoh, but wanted to know what time he arrived back at Tanah Timah.

'Must have been about two, I suppose,' said Montmorency airily. 'I dropped my chaps off at their messes in Sungei Siput and then drove home.'

He made no mention of any activity around the Casualty Department at BMH, but Steven supposed that most of the panic must have died down by two in the morning.

'You drove back alone?'

The tall, thin officer looked indignant at this mild enquiry.

'Of course! Look, what is this? Am I under some sort of suspicion or something? Can't you take the word of an officer?'

Steven felt that Montmorency had almost said 'officer and gentleman' and hastened to smooth his ruffled feathers.

'Just routine, Clarence! We have to know where everyone was at the material time, you see. And to get corroboration where possible.'

'Well I was in my jolly old Riley at the material time, miles from here,' he snapped crossly. Then he stood up, deciding that the police had had enough of his time.

'And I have to be at the Garrison Mess in five minutes. Dashed rude to turn up late, the Brigadier will be there tonight.'

With that, he nodded curtly to them and stalked out.

'Cocky young devil,' muttered Steven, but Tan kept a discreet silence.

The senior policeman looked at a list on a sheet of paper and ticked off a few names. 'No point in bothering Dr Howden or Major Morris – we know well enough where they were on

Friday night.' He dabbed his face with a handkerchief, wondering if another nine years in this country would finally acclimatize him to the heat. 'Right, let's call it a day, Inspector.'

'What about the lady nurses and the colonel, sir?' the Indian reminded him softly.

'Tomorrow morning, Tan. They're not going anywhere.'

EIGHT

The funeral cortège went at a steady forty miles an hour northwards through the flat land between Ipoh and Taiping, green hills and mountains rearing up on the right. The pre-war hearse led the way, as this was a 'White Area' with no curfew nor restrictions on travel. In many parts, such as the long winding road up to the Cameron Highlands hill station, only convoys shepherded by armoured cars were allowed.

Behind the vintage Daimler came a motley collection of about a dozen vehicles, ranging from Alf's old Hillman to Clarence Bottomley's sleek Riley. There were several other cars belonging to other planters and to garrison and hospital staff, including an Armstrong-Siddeley Typhoon belonging to the matron and Alec Watson's creaking Morgan. Steven Blackwell's police Land Rover brought up the rear. He had no car of his own and was quite comfortable with using an official vehicle and driver for every purpose, as he considered that he was never really off duty.

'Cracking on a bit for a funeral, aren't we?' said Percy Loosemore, in the front passenger seat alongside Alfred Morris. 'Seems as if they're trying to get shot of poor old Jimmy as quickly as they can.'

'Got to keep up with the hearse,' said Alf. 'It's a fair old trot from Ipoh up here.'

Tom Howden's plotting had been successful and he sat in the back alongside Lynette. Few of the women had clothes really suitable for a funeral, but most had managed to find something relatively sombre in a place usually renowned for its summer dresses. Lynette wore a black skirt and grey silk blouse and Tom thought she looked lovely. He was rapidly falling for her and something told him that the feeling was mutual, so he was feeling very contented, in spite of the solemn occasion.

Taiping was a pleasant town at the foot of Maxwell Hill, a

three-thousand-foot jungle-covered ridge with a hill station at
the top, where there was a Rest House with a real log fire. A
long dead-straight Main Street lined with shophouses led to
the Lake Gardens, a landscaped park made from a reclaimed
tin mine, where lay the New Club, a larger version of The
Dog in Tanah Timah.

'Could call in there for a snifter on the way back, as we're
not having a proper wake,' suggested the irreverent Percy. No
one bothered to answer him as the procession carried on
through the town and down a long avenue of stately trees.

'This goes to Kamunting, where the other BMH is,'
explained Alfred. 'Like our place, there's a big garrison almost
next door, the 28th Independent Commonwealth Infantry
Brigade.'

The cortège slowed down long before these were reached
and turned off Assam Kumbang Road into the Christian
Cemetery, a quiet park-like field, edged by trees.

'Is this a War Graves place?' asked Lynette in a hushed
voice as they stopped behind the other vehicles on a parking
area inside the gates.

Alf Morris shook his head as he opened the door for her.
'It's been here since the last century, since Europeans came
out to run the tin and rubber industries. But now unfortunately
a large part is kept for the military and their dependants, since
the Jap invasion and now the Emergency.'

All the travellers disgorged from the cars and quietly made
their way forward towards the front of the cavalcade, where
the only hired car was the one belonging to the undertaker,
another aged but stately Daimler. From this stepped the garrison
padre, who ushered out Diane Robertson, today attired in a
grey shantung silk dress and jacket that was the nearest she
could muster as a mourning outfit. Also in the Daimler was
her manager Douglas Mackay and his wife Rosa, both women
trying to look as if the other was invisible. Together with half
a dozen sisters from the hospital clustered behind their matron,
a couple of planters' wives made up a respectable contingent
of ladies to support the new widow.

From his position as the rearguard of the convoy, Steven
Blackwell looked at the small crowd ahead with concerned

interest. In cases of murder, it was traditional for the investigators to attend the funeral of the victim, though he had never
yet heard of any advantage coming from it.

The coffin was lifted from the Daimler by four of James's
fellow planters, including Les Arnold, and placed on a rather
rickety trolley belonging to the cemetery. A large bunch of
tropical flowers, which Steven assumed had been ordered by
Diane, lay on top. A few of the onlookers stepped forward to
add their own sprays of colourful blooms, including Doris
Hawkins who contributed one from the Sisters' Mess.

With the mourners following, the chaplain set off behind
the coffin as it was trundled down a path between rows of old
graves, some moss covered and dating back scores of years.
John Smale wore a surplice over a light cassock with a purple
stole around his neck, as he walked ahead of Diane and the
Mackays.

The procession drifted along in silence, until the roar of an
engine caused most heads to turn, as a black Vauxhall swept
in from the road to the parking area.

'Bloody hell, it's the Old Man!' muttered Percy Loosemore
irreverently, as Desmond O'Neill hopped from the driving seat
and hurried after the funeral procession. Not only did the
colonel catch them up, but he pushed past the stragglers and
with his jerky up-and-down gait, went straight to the front and
squeezed himself between Diane Robertson and her manager.
There were some scowls and muted murmurs from the throng,
but as he was the most senior officer present, nothing was said
aloud. The new widow looked quizzically at him, then turned
her attention back to the proceedings, as they had by now
arrived at the graveside. Steven Blackwell watched this tableau
from the rear, putting O'Neill's behaviour down to his well-
known eccentricity, as the gaunt colonel put his hand on
Diane's elbow and solicitously steered her to the edge of the
open pit.

'What's the old bugger up to now?' hissed David Meredith
to Alec Watson. Any reply was stifled by the start of the burial
service, as the coffin was unloaded on to two planks placed
across the fresh excavation. There was no church service, as
Diane had impressed on the padre that neither she nor James

had had any religious beliefs, but for convention's sake, the Reverend Smale went though an abbreviated version of the service at the graveside. The police superintendent watched all the bowed heads as they listened dutifully to the calm voice of the priest, but saw nothing that rang alarm bells in his head hinting at someone's guilt. Even the colonel's peculiar actions could be put down to a middle-aged fantasy over a beautiful woman.

Within a few minutes the soliloquy was ended, the planks removed and James Robertson's mortal remains were lowered into the ground.

Tom Howden stood dutifully alongside Lynette and the words of Rupert Brooke's poem came into his head. He felt that 'a corner of a foreign field that is forever England', was most appropriate to this scene. Tom had another wave of unreality passing over him, momentarily disbelieving that he was standing in sticky heat below jungle-covered hills, watching a murdered man disappear below ground, instead of being in the cold drizzle of a December Tyneside.

There was no morbid ceremony of handfuls of earth being thrown on to the coffin and almost casually, the group turned away and left two Indian labourers to fill in the grave. Diane and the chaplain again led the way back to the cars, where a rather ragged series of commiserations were offered by those attending the service, before everyone went off to find their transport.

'Look, the undertakers are doing a runner!' exclaimed Alec Watson – and sure enough, the two Daimlers took off empty, obviously going straight back to Ipoh. As the junior medical officers watched, they saw that a redistribution of passengers was taking place. Douglas Mackay and his wife went to Les Arnold's large estate car, while Diane was escorted to Desmond O'Neill's Velox.

'Looks like the old sod has taken a fancy to the blonde bombshell,' muttered Percy Loosemore. 'Good job our revered surgeon didn't come, he'd have blown his top.'

They pressed nearer the cars and as the colonel gallantly opened the passenger door for Diane, they heard her call out rather too gaily for the occasion. 'God, I need a drink after that! Desmond, call in at the New Club on the way back, there's a dear.'

The next two days were busy ones for the police in Tanah Timah and the death of James Robertson had to take a back seat as far as Steven Blackwell was concerned, though in truth, there was little to be done except take unhelpful statements from people who knew James.

The reason for the diversion was an armed robbery at one of two banks in the town, which involved a shooting. At one end of the main street was the Chartered Bank and almost opposite, the Hongkong and Shanghai Bank. They were small establishments, just a couple of rooms with a Chinese sub-manager and a few Chinese and Indian tellers and clerks. Outside the door of the Chartered Bank was the usual guard, a turbaned Sikh *jaga* sitting on a wooden chair, cradling a twelve-bore shotgun and chewing red chillies as if they were crisps.

At mid-morning on Tuesday, a battered Ford pick-up stopped outside and two men rushed into the bank, another two overpowering the startled Sikh before he could even raise his gun. They hit him on the head and lashed him to his chair, before joining their accomplices inside, where amid much screaming from both robbers and customers, the threat of a pair of sawn-off shotguns made the terrified staff scrabble together as much money as they could muster. Though the police headquarters was only a few hundred yards away, it was beyond the other end of the street and out of earshot of the fracas in the bank.

Within minutes, the thieves had grabbed all they were likely to get and rushed out of the bank. By now the very angry *jaga* had freed one of his arms from the rope and as the men were scrambling aboard their stolen truck, he managed to reach his twelve-bore and let off a blast which peppered several of the robbers. As they revved away, one them fired a shot in return, which hit the Sikh in the legs. At that distance, the discharge was not crippling, but the guard's roars of pain and outrage were added to the cacophony coming from the bank.

The sound of shots brought the police racing down the street and soon there was a full scale pursuit in operation. The Ford had vanished in the direction of Ipoh, but was soon found abandoned near a patch of secondary jungle halfway to Kampong Kerdah. Steven Blackwell and many of his officers were busy for the rest of the day organizing a search through the heavily forested land nearby, but without success.

The superintendent was concerned that this might be a terrorist-linked incident, especially as the witnesses confirmed that the attackers were all Chinese. Though this was by no means conclusive, it was known that the Malayan Communist Party sometimes resorted to robbery to get funds to sustain its desperate campaign.

At the back of his mind, Steven also worried about the possibility of a connection with the attack on Gunong Besar and the Robertson murder, even though all common sense indicated that Chin Peng's men could have nothing to do with James's corpse arriving at The Dog.

By Thursday, this enquiry had fizzled out for lack of any more evidence and Blackwell's attention was once more drawn back to the Robertson case. As a result of making some early phone calls, the afternoon again saw him at the garrison head-quarters, meeting this time in Major Enderby's office in one of the 'spiders', the long wooden huts that jutted from the central roadway. The SIB sergeant from Ipoh and the tubby intelligence officer, Captain Preston, were there again to discuss the situation.

As he was on his home ground, Enderby, the head of the Brigade's military police, appointed himself chairman and shuffled some papers on his desk as the other three men pulled up chairs. He stared at them fiercely, this being his usual expression, which he felt obliged to maintain as the local upholder of Queen's Regulations.

'As you rightly said on the phone, superintendent, in this rather isolated town, we cannot disregard the possibility that the perpetrator is a member of Her Majesty's Forces.'

Steven smiled disarmingly at Enderby, as the latter continued.

'As we've decided that it seems unlikely that any of the local native inhabitants did this, then statistically there are far more Service people around here than the relatively few planters.'

Preston, the Intelligence man, bobbed his moon face, yet immediately qualified his agreement.

'Can't dismiss them entirely, though. After all, Jimmy Robertson was an estate man himself.'

The craggy-faced staff sergeant scowled down at his gleaming boots as he spoke. 'In my experience, sir, any bugger can commit any crime!'

Markham always managed to give the impression that he thought all commissioned officers were ineffectual prats, though nothing he ever said could be construed as open criticism.

Steven Blackwell opened a thin manilla folder and laid it on Enderby's desk. 'I've had the first report up from the Government Chemist's laboratory in KL,' he said briskly. 'James Robertson had a moderate amount of alcohol in the blood sample taken at the post-mortem. It was just over a hundred and forty milligrams per hundred millilitres.'

'What's that in English?' demanded Enderby, his cigarette-stained moustache bristling.

'Certainly shouldn't be driving a car, but given Jimmy's capacity for drink, I'd say it was about average for a night in The Dog.'

'No surprise there, then,' grunted the major. 'Anything more helpful?'

Blackwell turned over a page in his slim folder.

'Those half-dozen bullets my inspector dug out of the walls of Gunong Besar – they were all .303s and all came from the same weapon. From the rifling pattern, it was a Lee-Enfield, not a Bren.'

None of the others looked impressed.

'Doesn't tell us anything we didn't expect, does it?' grunted Markham, adding 'sir' as a reluctant afterthought.

'Were they from the same weapon as the one that killed Jimmy?' asked Preston.

The policeman shook his head. 'Don't know yet. These went down to the lab first, after that attack on the bungalow. I hope to hear more tomorrow.' He picked up another piece of paper.

'Dr Howden in BMH has had a look at the leaves and grass

that Tan collected from the roadway on the way up to the estate. He confirms that the staining was blood and that it was human, but he's got no facilities for telling if it was Robertson's blood group. I've sent it down to the Petaling Jaya lab, but I see no reason to doubt that it marks the spot where he was shot.'

Major Enderby turned his watery eyes on to the SIB man. 'Did you hear anything yet about those cartridge cases?'

Markham pulled a folded paper from the top pocket of his starched jungle-green jacket. He opened it and scanned down the page.

'I've just had this signal from Command Ordnance HQ in Singapore, where I sent half a dozen of the shell-cases from Gunong Besar. It seems that .303 ammunition is a hell of a mixture, some of the stuff still in use going back to 1942! The date stamped on it is when the casing was made, but not necessarily when it was filled with propellant.'

The three other men looked at him blankly.

'So what?' growled Enderby.

'Well, if we wanted to know if this was stuff dropped to the CTs when they were fighting the Japs – or if it was pinched from the army recently, there's no way the date stamping can help, unless it was, say 1954. And none of these were, they were all '44 or '48.'

There was a silence. 'So we're none the wiser about when they were made?' asked Preston.

The staff sergeant's dour face almost cracked into a smile.

'The clever sods in Singapore tested the residues in the shells, sir,' he said smugly. 'Seems until about five years ago, all .303s made by the Greenwood and Batley factory were filled with cordite, but after that, they used nitrocellulose, even into empty cases dated years before. Some of these shells were made by Kynoch, but again they could have been filled later.'

'What are you trying to tell us, sergeant?' asked Preston rather irritably.

'Some of the cartridges had been filled with nitrocellulose, so they can't be earlier than the late forties, early fifties.'

Again there was a silence. 'Does that help us at all?' asked Steven Blackwell.

The SIB man shrugged indifferently. 'Only that it makes it a lot less likely that these rounds were fired by bandits, sir. Unless there's been a fairly recent capture of munitions by them, most of their stuff is left over from the Jap occupation, when we supplied the Malayan People's Anti-Japanese Army with masses of weapons and ammunition.'

Preston, the Intelligence man, shook his head. 'Nothing lost to the CTs here in the north for several years.'

Major Enderby slapped his hands on his table. 'Thank you, sergeant. Interesting and confirmative, but we guessed that already from the circumstances.'

'What will be even more interesting is to know if the bullet that saw off poor Jimmy came from the same weapon,' grunted Preston.

As Markham handed his paper to the superintendent to put in his file, Enderby changed the subject.

'Let's get back to personalities, gentlemen. We agreed just now that the military certainly can't be excluded from our investigations.'

Blackwell cleared his throat diffidently and Enderby glared at him.

'You have a problem with that, Steven?' he snapped.

'Only that technically – and legally – it's my investigation. I'm not being awkward, but James was a civilian and he was almost certainly shot on the public highway. Naturally, I'm very grateful for your input and the police couldn't get anywhere without your cooperation. But I thought for the record, I must make it clear that any arrest and indictment is down to us.'

Major Enderby gave a loud sniff, but he seemed to accept the point.

'Sure, but we're getting ahead of ourselves, talking of an arrest. None of us have a clue at the moment.'

The captain from Intelligence looked uneasy.

'What happens if it does turn out to be someone from the Forces?' asked Preston.

Blackwell shrugged. 'That'll be up to the lawyers. The magistrates or even the Malayan judiciary would have to refer the matter to your Army Legal Branch and then sort it out between themselves. Thank God, that won't be my problem, all I want to do is arrest the man who did this.'

'Or woman,' growled Sergeant Markham.

The other heads swivelled towards him.

'Woman? Are you serious?' brayed Preston.

'As I said earlier, sir, anybody can do anything. Doesn't take much strength to pull a trigger, even on a Lee-Enfield.'

Enderby tapped the table impatiently.

'Let's get back to brass tacks,' he demanded. 'As it's possible that military personnel might be involved, I've had a word with the Adjutant and he's spoken to the Brigadier. It's agreed that we can divulge any Service records and even Confidential Reports to the police, on a strictly "need-to-know" basis.'

He slapped his hairy hand on to a pile of folders lying on the desk.

'I've had the records pulled of everyone who had anything to do with the Robertsons – and quite a few others besides.'

Steven's eyebrows climbed up his sun-reddened forehead. The provost marshal's office had certainly been busy.

'Does that include people from BMH?' he asked.

'Include? They're the main customers, Steven!'

That night, Tom Howden was again Orderly Medical Officer and sat abstemiously in the Mess after dinner, drinking grape-fruit soda while his fellow officers replenished their body fluids with Anchor or Tiger.

A violent thunderstorm was going on outside and rain lashed down like the proverbial stair rods. As Tom looked out through the open doors of the anteroom, he could see a row of regularly spaced cascades pouring vertically from the edges of the corrugated roof into the deep monsoon drains at the edge of the verandah. One of the frequent flashes of lightning showed a figure dashing from an Austin K2 ambulance for the shelter of the covered way. A moment later, Eddie Rosen came in, the shoulders of his green uniform shirt black with rain.

He called to Number One to rustle up some food, as he had missed the regular evening meal, then dropped into a chair.

'Been assisting the Great Surgeon with a compound fracture, an Aussie who lost an argument with a three-tonner,' he announced. 'Peter's still down in theatre with the gasman. We started late, as Blackwell of the Yard turned up to give the third degree again to the other two fellows.'

Percy Loosemore leered across from the depths of his chair, where he had been studying an old copy of *Men Only*.

'They must be the prime suspects, then. Wonder which one of them did it?'

Alfred Morris put down his airmail copy of the *Daily Telegraph* and frowned at the speaker. 'That warped sense of humour will get you into trouble one day, Percy,' he said severely.

'I wasn't trying to be funny, Alf! Did you lot know that Dave Meredith was a crack shot? When he was a student, he was in the University of Liverpool's Small-bore Rifle team and competed in Bisley.'

No one asked him how he came by this nugget of information, but neither did anyone challenge his news. However, Robbie Burns couldn't resist some sarcasm. 'And I suppose you'll tell us that Peter Bright was an Olympic gold medallist with the Bren gun!'

The pox doctor sniggered, determined to get the last word.

'No, but Posh Pete was a dab hand with a shotgun. I heard him bragging once about how often he went murdering pheasants in Sussex with his father and his fancy Tory pals.'

The Admin Officer rattled his newspaper irritably.

'That's enough, fellers! This affair isn't something to joke about, so let's drop it.'

The somewhat awkward silence was broken by Eddie Rosen.

'Tom, if you're OMO, keep your eyes peeled for the CO. He's been acting strangely lately.'

'Nothing new about that! When was he ever normal?' The quartermaster's nasal Scouse tones sounded bitter, as he suffered more than most from the colonel's eccentricities.

'No, I mean really odd,' said Rosen. 'I was OMO last night and on the way to the arms kote, I saw him prowling around the hospital with a flashlight. Later, I caught a glimpse of him

shining the torch into the windows of one of the barrack blocks
. . . and I think it was where the QA Other Ranks sleep.'

A few eyebrows were raised at this – the antics of their
Commanding Officer were always fertile ground for gossip.

'Dirty old bugger!' said Percy Loosemore. 'That's what
comes of his wife buzzing off back to Blighty – he's gone
randy.'

With a sigh, Alfred Morris put down his newspaper and
came to the rescue of his colonel's reputation. 'If you must
know, he's been concerned about security lately, especially
since the murder and the attack on Gunong Besar. Now there's
been this bank hold-up in town, and he's got into his head
that we should all be more security conscious.'

'Funny place to start, the QA's dormitory,' grunted the
quartermaster.

'He's been trying doors and windows, to see if they've been
locked at night, that's all,' said Alf defensively.

'What, is he afraid that Chin Peng is going to nick the
ashtrays from the Sergeants' Mess?' asked Alec Watson. 'I
saw him snooping around there after midnight when I was
duty officer last week. Then he went up to the armoury and
started yelling at the poor little Malay corporal through the
door.'

'What was that about?' asked Alfred, curious in spite of his
ingrained loyalties.

'Dunno, I kept well clear!' replied Alec. 'But his obsession
with the armoury has got worse since these shootings.'

The debate about the foibles of their chief was interrupted
by the arrival of the surgeon and his anaesthetist who both
dropped wearily into chairs and called for beers. As he took
their orders, Number One asked solicitously if they wanted
him to find them a late meal.

'No thanks, night sister rustled up sandwiches for us in
theatre,' answered Peter Bright. 'We had a late start because
Sherlock Holmes came again with a list of questions.'

'Which one of you confessed?' demanded the irrepressible
Percy.

Dave Meredith ignored him, but had a gripe of his own.

'Damned cheek. Steve Blackwell wanted to know all about

my ability as a marksman. How the hell would he know that, I haven't so much as touched a rifle since I joined the army!' He omitted to say that the police superintendent had also asked some pointed questions about his relationship with Lena Franklin, Robertson's latest paramour.

'He must have had sight of our Service records,' complained Peter. 'Some of the things he was asking me, not even you nosy devils know anything about.'

He failed to elaborate on this, but most of his colleagues had a fair idea that Diane Robertson's name would have featured in Blackwell's questions.

The Mess seemed to slide into gloomy silence after this, until their Admin Officer made a suggestion intended to raise the mood a little.

'I've been looking at the duty rosters for next weekend, chaps,' said Alf earnestly. 'Quite a few of you are free, so why don't we organize a trip to Pangkor? I know the colonel's going down to Kinrara to meet the ADMS, so we could get away early on Saturday morning and come back on Sunday.'

There was a stir of interest, except from those who were tied to the hospital that weekend.

'Be a nice change, we could see if a few of the QAs wanted to join us,' said Alec, always with an eye to female company. During the buzz of discussion that followed, a mystified Tom Howden asked Alec what this was all about.

'Pangkor? It's a tropical island just off the coast. Smashing place, only about fifty miles away. We leave the cars at Lumut, then get a small ferry across. The accommodation's a bit primitive, just a row of wooden chalets above the beach, but it's better than this place. You must come, Tom, it's great! Swimming, boozing, flirting!'

Alf winked across at the pathologist. 'See if you can get that nice Lynette to come, Tom. Swaying palm trees under a tropical moon, do your love life no end of good!'

It seemed that several other officers had the same idea, as when they got around to discussing which cars to take, David Meredith announced that his passenger seat would doubtless be occupied by Lena Franklin. Then Peter Bright effectively stopped the chatter by rather gruffly indicating that he intended asking Diane Robertson if she would like to join the party.

'She needs something to take her mind off things, poor woman!' he said defiantly, making it clear that he was personally intending to provide that something. He got a few knowing looks from his fellow officers and a leer from Percy, but no one pursued the matter and the conversation drifted on to details of the trip, Alf volunteering to contact the beach hotel and make the bookings.

Outside, the storm finished as abruptly as it had begun and gradually the crowd in the Mess began to drift away. Some of those not on duty went out to the cinema or visit other messes in the garrison, while a few sloped off to their rooms to write letters, read or listen to their record players.

An hour later Tom was left alone in the anteroom, apart from Eddie Rosen, who was snoring peacefully in one of the chairs.

The pathologist browsed through his thick dog-eared copy of *Muir's Pathology*, but his attention span was limited, even though he told himself that he must keep bashing the books, as he intended taking the Diploma when he got back home. Too many diverting thoughts marched through his mind, from puzzling about Jimmy Robertson's gunshot wound to the sounds and aromas of a tropical night that wafted through the doors. A recurring diversion was the face and figure of Lynette Chambers. He knew that she was not on duty tonight, but the promised weekend with her on this fabled island was a tantalizing prospect, with which Professor Muir's book had no chance of competing. He gave up the attempt at study and earlier than needs be, grabbed his hat and belt and went off down to the hospital to do his rounds.

Checking first with the orderly sergeant down at the front, he began working his way back up the corridor, stopping at each ward in turn. At Ward Five, his path crossed that of the night sister and they stopped for a cup of coffee in the office. Tonight QA Captain Joan Parnell was in charge and sitting in close proximity in the small room, he was aware of what an attractive woman she was. Glossy auburn hair peeped from beneath her white linen head-cloth and her smooth features always seemed to hold a slightly mischievous expression.

'You've made quite a hit with young Lynette, Captain Howden,' she said archly. 'Fast workers, you Geordies!'

Tom grinned sheepishly. She was an easy woman to talk to as they had no flirtatious hang-up to contend with. He had his eye firmly on Lynette and Joan was intent on prising Peter Bright away from the new widow woman.

'There's a plan afoot to make up a party for this Pangkor place next weekend,' he observed. 'Will you be able to come?'

'Is Peter going, d'you know?' she asked. 'Maybe we could drive down together.'

Tom felt that he was treading on sensitive ground here, but he could hardly avoid a direct question. 'He said that he was, but I think he's giving a lift to Mrs Robertson.'

Joan's luscious lips tightened at this.

'Then I'm definitely damned well going!' she exclaimed. 'I'm not letting her have him all to herself for a whole weekend.'

Tom wisely avoided any comment and tried to change the subject.

'Eddie Rosen and Alec both said the CO had been acting strangely the past few nights. Have you seen anything of him?'

Joan Parnell pulled her mind away from the prospect of their surgeon cavorting with a blonde on a tropical island and nodded.

'It's the talk of the Sisters' Mess this week. Matron said she's going to have a word with him, as he's been poking about the buildings until God knows what hour – including the QA's Other Ranks billet. The man's mad!'

'Have you seen him tonight?'

'I caught a glimpse of him in the distance about an hour ago, going up the corridor towards the armoury. I'm sure it was him, you can tell by that funny up-and-down walk of his.'

The pathologist drained the last of his Nescafé from a mug advertising a new lotion for treating scabies. 'Let's hope I can keep clear of him tonight. He seems to have taken an instant dislike to me.'

Joan gave him a glowing smile and reached out to touch his hand.

'Don't take it personally, Tom. He's like that with everyone, unless they've got boobs and long legs! The latest one to hate him even more than usual is Robbie Burns.'

'I've heard they don't get along, to put it mildly,' said Tom. 'But is this something new?'

'The colonel gives all the QM people a hard time, but now he's threatened to arrest Robbie and have him court-martialled,' explained Joan.

'This place is nothing like Newcastle's RVI, where I worked,' said Tom ruefully. 'What's he supposed to have done?'

Joan shrugged her slim shoulders indifferently.

'Some fuss over a fiddled Board of Survey, they say. Nothing out of the ordinary.'

Tom Howden had already been instructed in the art of handling Boards of Survey by Lance Corporal Cropper. Every department had to have its inventory of equipment checked every so often by an officer and a member of the QM staff. Any deficiencies had to be paid for out of the pocket of the officer-in-charge. Where the lab was concerned, the crafty Cropper informed Tom that all his predecessors had wangled their way out of debt by calling a 'Board of Survey' to condemn items allegedly worn or unserviceable. These were supposed to be destroyed immediately, but in fact, after replacements were obtained, the old ones were quietly brought back to replace anything missing from the inventory.

'In this man's army, you can get away with writing off a truck or a tank with no more than a ticking-off,' the corporal had confided. 'But break a bloody thermometer worth five bob and there's hell to pay!'

It seemed that the luckless quartermaster had fallen foul of the eccentric Commanding Officer over something to do with this time-honoured tradition.

'Apparently, Captain Burns is livid!' went on Joan. 'It seems the colonel has been persecuting him for months and now Burns has been heard to say that he's willing to swing for Desmond O'Neill! Let's hope they don't meet on one of our nights on duty!'

With this cheerful thought, the two went about their

business and after finishing his pilgrimage to the other wards, Tom made his final trip to the arms kote. As he went, he kept a wary eye out for the CO, but thankfully the only thing he saw at the top end of the hospital was a cat slinking along a monsoon drain. The excursion to the arms blockhouse also went peacefully, though again there was another new Malay OR locked inside, one Tom had not seen on his previous visits.

By midnight, he was back in his own bed, as the air-conditioned ward was occupied by a gunner with malaria. As he stared up in the gloom at the dim wraith of his mosquito net, he thought of the coming weekend. Visions swam into his mind of nubile maidens in grass skirts dancing on a palm-fringed moonlit beach – and they were all wearing the starched headdress of the Queen Alexandra's Royal Army Nursing Corps.

NINE

The next meeting of the investigators into the killing of James Robertson was held in the Police Circle building, partly because Steven Blackwell wanted to emphasize that this was primarily a matter for the civil police, rather than the military. The same people attended halfway through Thursday morning, gathering over Fraser & Neave grapefruit sodas in the superintendent's room upstairs. Inspector Tan was present, sitting in his usual self-effacing way with an open notebook on his knee. This time it was Blackwell who sat behind his desk as chairman and he opened the proceedings by pulling a sheet of paper from the now slightly thicker file on Robertson's murder.

'The first thing is another report from the lab at Petaling Jaya,' he announced. 'The blood on those leaves from the road up to Gunong Besar was the same blood group as the dead man's. It was a moderately common group, but I see no reason to think that it was anyone else's but his.'

He shuffled out another sheet and laid it on his desk.

'Perhaps more significantly, there is report on the bullet that the doctor here removed from James's chest.'

There was a palpable silence as the faces opposite waited for the result.

'It was *not* fired from the same weapon as that which peppered the estate buildings the previous week.' He emphasized the negative, to impress the fact on the others, who broke into a confused murmuring.

'So where does that leave us?' demanded Enderby, the major from the provost marshal's section.

Steven shrugged. 'Either the same guy using a different rifle – or two different villains!'

'Pity we don't have the shell-case from James's shooting,' offered tubby Major Preston, the Intelligence Officer.

'Wouldn't help much,' retorted the SIB sergeant. 'The ones

from the previous shoot-out were a complete mixture of ammunition from after 1948. Unless this one was a cordite-filled shell which greatly pre-dated the others, we couldn't say it was from a different source.'

'And it still wouldn't tell us who fired the damned thing,' added the superintendent, wearily.

Tom kept quiet through the ensuing silence, as the others digested this latest unhelpful information. He felt that after carrying out the post-mortem, he had nothing more to offer these professionals.

'So what's the next move?' asked Alfred Morris, mindful of the questions that Desmond O'Neill would be barking at him when he got back to the hospital.

'I've now got statements from virtually all the people who might either be involved or might know something useful,' said Steven Blackwell. 'These, together with the information kindly provided by the garrison on the military personnel, will have to be gone though with a fine toothcomb. We need to know who was where and when they were there, on that night.'

Morris stroked his bristly moustache in a gesture of concern.

'That's a hell a wide net to fling, Steven. Theoretically, it could be any of us – even me! I was in bed, but I can't prove it. Captain Howden is the only one of us who has a cast-iron alibi!'

Tom pushed his chair back, grating it on the concrete floor.

'Maybe I should leave now, if you are going to discuss colleagues of mine,' he offered.

Blackwell waved him down. 'I wouldn't be concerned about that, Tom. We're hardly likely to accuse anyone this morning! And we may need your advice if anything crops up about the actual shooting.'

Having made his point, the pathologist settled back, admitting to himself that he was intrigued by this business of detection. Maybe he would take up this forensic game when he went back home. The senior police officer shuffled his papers once again and picked out one to lay on top.

'I'll go through each of the people in turn, just to lay out the basic plot. The first is Major Peter Bright, your senior surgeon. He says he went to the usual Friday night dance at

The Dog, left about ten forty-five and drove downtown to the Rest House, where he sat alone and had a few beers, before driving back to the hospital soon after midnight. He arrived in time to see all the action outside the Casualty Department and we know that he came in at that point.'

Blackwell raised his head and looked enquiringly around at the others. Again Tom kept his mouth shut, but the staff sergeant felt no such inhibitions about an officer unknown to him.

'Why leave the club and go drinking alone in a local bar late at night?'

It was hardly accurate to call the Rest House a 'local bar', of which there were several in Tanah Timah. The Rest Houses were a chain of rather austere hostels originally meant for government officials to stay in when they were travelling on official business, but anyone could book in if there was a vacancy, and they were usually open for food and drink. However, the SIB man's question was still valid.

'I asked him that myself,' replied Steven. 'He was a little reluctant to be precise, but said that he got fed up with The Dog and felt like a change.'

He smoothed his bald head thoughtfully. 'I think we all know a little about his personal attachments and it seems probable that these were at the root of it,' he added delicately.

'And he says he was alone, not with a woman?' demanded Preston.

Blackwell nodded. 'I suspect the woman he would have liked to have been with was otherwise engaged. Anyway, he's got no alibi for the crucial hour.'

'The Rest House servants – do they confirm he was there?' asked the SIB sergeant.

'There was only one Indian boy on duty at that time of night. He said that a tall man with yellow hair was there, but was hopelessly vague about times.'

'What do we know about Major Bright that's relevant?' grunted Enderby, pointing a finger towards the files.

Steven Blackwell looked across at Alfred Morris. 'You must know everything that's in here, being the Admin Officer at BMH.'

Alf nodded. 'An exemplary military record. He's a Regular

Officer, a Senior Specialist in Surgery, in line to be pushed up to half-colonel when he finishes this tour in Malaya. Upper-class chap, his father's also a doctor, I understand. Hunting, shooting and fishing types.'

'What about personal character?' enquired Enderby.

'Divorced a couple of years ago when he was in Germany. No children. Don't know what else to say about him,' ended Alf loyally.

Steven nervously tapped a pencil on the desk. 'Let's not beat about the bush, chaps. It's common knowledge that Peter Bright was more than a little friendly with Diane Robertson.'

Alfred Morris bridled a little at this. 'A small place like Tanah Timah is naturally a hotbed for gossip. But we don't actually know that there was anything between them.'

Major Enderby snorted. 'Come off it, Alf! I'm not even in BMH, but even I know that Peter had the hots for the lovely blonde.'

'You're not suggesting that he shot her husband just to make her available?' said Morris indignantly.

'Stranger things have happened,' grunted the more cynical SIB man. 'A few drinks inside a fellow and a sense of griev-ance, anything can happen.'

'And a little bird told me that Diane might have been playing away lately,' added Preston, mischievously.

'I don't believe it for a moment,' huffed Alf Morris. 'Peter Bright is a real gentleman, murder would never enter his head!'

The police superintendent shrugged and turned to another sheet from the file on his desk.

'Captain David Meredith, your anaesthetist. What about him?'

Alf shook his head. 'A complete non-starter, I'd say. Having designs on Diane Robertson was the last thing he was inter-ested in – he was dead keen on one of the QAs, Lena Franklin.'

Steven regarded Alf steadily. 'But we know that that affair had cooled off a bit, according to my sources. And it was very likely Jimmy Robertson who did the cooling.'

'You've been listened to Percy Loosemore, our garrison gossip,' retorted Morris accusingly. 'His tongue will get him into trouble one of these days.'

'This Captain Meredith, isn't he the one who's a crack shot?' growled Markham. 'Bisley and all that?'

'Oh, come on, sergeant! There's the better part of a thousand soldiers in the Brigade, all taught to shoot well enough to hit a bungalow or a chap across a narrow road! You don't need to be an Olympic hopeful for that.'

'Anything in his Confidential Report that's relevant?' asked the Intelligence Officer.

'Not very bloody confidential any more,' muttered Morris, but no one seemed to hear him.

The superintendent rustled some more paper. 'Short Service Officer, originally Welsh, but his family now live in Wiltshire. Twenty-eight, unmarried – nothing else to say about him, really.'

'And where was he at the material time?' asked Major Enderby.

'Says he left The Dog early, at about half ten and went back to the Mess in BMH. Went to bed, knew nothing of all the drama until breakfast.'

'Can he prove that?' asked the ever-suspicious SIB man.

Steven looked at Morris. 'No one saw him at the Mess, as far as I can make out. Alf, you were called out when James was brought into Casualty, did you see any sign of him?'

'No, but there's no mystery there. All the officer's rooms are in a row down the left-hand side of the two mess buildings. They have louvred doors on each side, one facing on to the grass outside the dining room, the other outwards towards the perimeter fence. The cars are parked out that side for the night, so people can reach their rooms without coming into the mess compound.' He waved his hands to demonstrate the geography of the BMH Officers' Mess.

'But he hasn't got an alibi either?' persisted Enderby.

'I don't see that he needs one,' answered Morris obstinately.

Blackwell sighed. They were getting nowhere fast.

'Let's get away from the officers for a change,' he said resignedly. 'Here's some stuff on Les Arnold that I didn't know before.'

He pulled some Telex sheets from a large buff envelope and unfolded them. 'Police Headquarters in KL has been in touch with their Aussie counterparts in Queensland, who checked up on Arnold. It seems that he did time in the slammer some years ago.'

There was some lifting of eyebrows as Blackwell elaborated.

'In 1940, he was convicted in Cairns of causing grievous bodily harm to a guy. Got five years jail, but was let out to join the Army when the war started. Went into some tough Special Forces outfit, spent a couple of years fighting in New Guinea.'

Enderby gave a quiet whistle of surprise. 'Does it say what the GBH was all about?'

'Some trouble over a woman, it seems. The other guy assaulted him and he went after him. If there hadn't been a plea of provocation, it seems he might have been done for attempted murder.'

'Did he beat him up that badly, then?' asked the sergeant.

Steven Blackwell shook his head. 'No, he shot him – with a rifle!'

On the short drive back to the hospital, the revelation about the Australian planter was the main topic of conversation between Alf Morris and the pathologist.

'Just because he shot some chap in the shoulder fourteen years ago, doesn't make him the culprit now,' warned the major, anxious as ever never to prejudge any issue.

'No, but it can't help putting him near the top of the short-list, especially when there are no other reasonable contenders,' answered Tom. He was secretly glad that his brother officers, as he had already begun to think of them, were by implication, off the hook.

'Mustn't say a word about all this in the Mess, of course,' warned Alf, quite unnecessarily as far as Tom was concerned. He was still uneasy at having been made privy to the personal information that Steven Blackwell had produced that morning. After revealing the news about Les Arnold, the policeman had gone on to describe the background of Douglas Mackay and his wife Rosa, though there seemed little there to suggest either as suspects.

'No advantage in the manager shooting his boss,' said Tom ruminatively, as they were passing the derelict tin-dredge. 'If the plantation folds up or is sold, he may lose his job.'

'I don't envy Steven Blackwell's part in this,' said Alf. 'It must be very awkward having to interrogate and possibly suspect people you have to live with in a small place like this.'

'Yes, it would have been much easier if the Commies had shot him,' answered Tom, with unwitting cynicism. 'At least we'd not all be looking at each other as if we were afraid that one of us did it.'

As the old Hillman slowed down to turn into the gate of BMH, Alf Morris gave a sigh. 'I suppose I'd better report all this to the Old Man straight after lunch. He'll want to know what happened, word for word. Fair enough, I suppose. The chap did die in his hospital, as he calls it – and several of those in the frame are his officers.'

They passed the Blanco-belted private on guard duty, Tom sheepishly returning his salute and as they drove around the double bend on to the perimeter road to the Mess, he returned to their recent meeting.

'Talking of the colonel, I notice that his file wasn't discussed!'

Alf grinned under his moustache. 'The colonel is pretty pally with the Brigadier, they're in a bridge set over at the Garrison Mess. I can't see the OC letting the police having O'Neill's particulars in a hurry.'

As they drew up outside the Mess, the Admin Officer added a final word. 'And another person that wasn't mentioned was dear Diane herself!'

TEN

Superintendent Blackwell had not forgotten about Diane Robertson – nor had he written off Lieutenant Colonel Desmond O'Neill from his list of people to interview. He sat alone at his desk in his large, bare office, letting the air from the slowly revolving fan waft down on to his pink scalp. Even after all these years in the Far East, he still thought nostalgically of the cold, damp rain of the Manchester streets – though he knew that if transported back there tomorrow, he would be fed up with it inside a week.

He pulled his mind back to the present and with no leads whatsoever to follow on the local bank robbery, he concentrated on this morning's earlier meeting about James Robertson. The Telex from Australia was interesting, but Steven knew that some old conviction for a brawl over a woman was little use apart from suggesting a violent temper and willingness to use violence. The fact that it involved a rifle was food for thought, but since coming to Malaya, Les Arnold had not fallen foul of the law in any way, though he had been ushered out of The Dog several times for becoming too stroppy after having too much to drink.

The phrase 'brawl over a woman' stuck in Steven's mind and he wondered if history might have repeated itself, as the Australian planter had made little secret of his lustful admiration for his next-door neighbour, Diane Robertson. Yet the very openness of his libidinous admission rather defused its significance.

With a sigh, he drew a pad of lined paper towards him and began to write, cursing under his breath as the sweat from the edge of his hand dampened the lower part of the page and made the ink run when he reached it. He persevered for a quarter of an hour, then sat back and read through the notes he had made, before reaching across his desk and pinging the small brass bell that sat there. A moment later, his middle-aged Tamil clerk came in from the room next door.

'Santhanam, will you ask Inspector Tan to come up, please? And get us a couple of cold drinks from the fridge.'

His impassive assistant appeared within a few moments and sat on the other side of the desk, gratefully accepting one of the icy grapefruit sodas. Steven pushed across the notes he had made.

'I've been trying to make some sense of all this business, Tan. Let's go through each of the names and you tell me what you think.'

The inspector gravely read through what his boss had written, sucking intermittently on the straw in his bottle of 'GFS'. Eventually, he looked up and put the pad back on the desk.

'Diane Robertson, she is not a favoured candidate.' He made it a statement, rather than a question.

Blackwell shook his head. 'No, I can't see it, really. We know they had problems with their marriage, and both seem to have been routinely unfaithful, according to all the gossip. But why should she kill him?'

'Jealousy and anger at his constant affairs, perhaps,' ventured Tan. 'But separation or divorce would seem an easier solution.'

Steven mopped his neck with a handkerchief. 'Technically, she could have done it.'

'Certainly she would have been someone he knew and would have stopped for, which was what we assumed must have happened,' agreed the inspector.

Blackwell shrugged. 'Yes, but I still don't fancy her as the killer, somehow. What about Leslie Arnold?'

'He has this unfortunate past history of violence,' answered Tan. 'Though I suppose it shouldn't be held against him. He admitted to you that he had lustful feelings towards Mister Robertson's wife,' he added primly.

Steven tapped his desk with the end of his fountain pen.

'There's been a rumour for some time that Arnold would have liked to buy Gunong Besar if it came up for sale. It seems he's made a success of his own place and would like to expand. But I hardly think he would kill the owner just to get his hands on the property.'

Tan gave one of his rare smiles. 'Perhaps he thought he might get James's property and his wife with the one shot!'

The superintendent sighed again. 'He has no alibi for the time of the shooting – and he does live next door to the dead man, up a long and lonely road. But we've got not a shred of evidence against him.'

The inspector put a slim finger on the notes before him.

'The Mackays are also next door and on the same lonely road, sir.'

'Yes, I wonder about the Mackays. Upright, sober and churchgoing, not typical of most of the folks around here. Yet I sense something wrong between them, there's a tension you can almost feel when you're with them.'

Tan said nothing, as the emotions that Europeans experienced were a mystery to him. He had been brought up in a large Cantonese family in Ipoh where everyone had seemed too busy making money or working towards a career to be cursed with introspection or jealousy.

'Again the bush-telegraph around Tanah Timah whispered that Jimmy Robertson may have made a play for his manager's wife at one time, but we can't accept every bit of spiteful tittle-tattle that goes around.'

Tan was not sure what 'tittle-tattle' might be, but he got the general drift of his superior officer's remarks.

'Then there are the military people, sir. That's going to be difficult for us.'

Steven Blackwell groaned. 'Don't I just know it! They've played along so far, but a lieutenant colonel is going to be a tough nut to deal with.'

'You have no serious suspicions of the Commanding Officer, have you, sir?'

'I suspect everyone, Tan. Reluctantly and probably hopelessly! But all the people who had access or even a fragile motive have to be considered.'

'With respect, Colonel O'Neill seems a rather strange person. Several of the more junior witnesses I interviewed, claimed that he is insane.'

Blackwell nodded resignedly. 'His wife has left him, though

there was some innocent excuse put about. He seems to have
been obsessed with Mrs Robertson lately, though he has been
rumoured to have been pestering several other ladies in and
around the garrison.'

He thought back to the strange behaviour of the hospital
commandant at the funeral, when he almost hijacked Diane
and drove off with her in his car.

'What about the other medical officers from the hospital,
sir?' prompted Tan. 'Several would seem to have some sort
of a motive.'

'Motives for anger and perhaps jealousy,' agreed Blackwell.
'But sufficient for murder?'

'Captain Meredith, the anaesthetist, appeared incensed and
affronted at the fact that James Robertson stole the affections
of the nursing sister Franklin,' said Tan, using the pedantically
perfect English that he had learned in a good school and from
reading many classical novels.

'He's the one with the Olympic standard shooting skills,'
mused the superintendent. 'Though blasting a chap in the chest
at a few yards' range doesn't take much marksmanship!'

'Major Bright was also used to firearms in civilian life,'
said the inspector. 'There seems little doubt that he was
extremely keen on Mrs Robertson and wanted her to get a
divorce, according to rumours I've heard from these witnesses.'

Blackwell nodded. 'But surely, it would have made more
sense for James to have shot *him*, if Bright was trying to steal
his wife, rather than the other way around?'

It was Tan's turn to shrug now. 'If Major Bright couldn't
have a divorcee, maybe he thought he could have a widow?'

Coming from the inscrutable inspector, this almost amounted
to a witticism, thought Steven! He reached over and pulled
his pad towards him, running his finger down the list of entries.

'We're running out of suspects, Tan. Unless there's someone
out there we know nothing about.'

'You didn't specifically mention Mrs Mackay, sir. If she
had been seduced by James Robertson, perhaps she was
scorned when he turned his attentions elsewhere. Or perhaps
he had threatened to tell her husband?'

Blackwell pulled at the blackened, damp patches under his

armpits, envying his inspector, whose khaki uniform was always pristine however hot the conditions. 'Rosa Mackay? Apart from living next door and on the same bit of road where he was killed, I don't fancy that little mouse as a killer, somehow. But we must keep all our options open!'

The weekend at Pangkor was a mixed success. For some, including Tom Howden and Lynnette, it was an idyllic couple of days, but the tensions introduced by several of the couples made for some uneasy moments. Neither could the fact of James's death hanging over them be ignored and some furtive glances suggested their awareness that his killer might be amongst them.

A cavalcade of cars set off from BMH immediately after breakfast, a mixed bunch of vehicles ranging from the Matron's Typhoon to Alec's shaky Morgan. The absence of the Commanding Officer gave an almost palpable sense of relief as they loaded up their sun hats, flippers and snorkels, together with a smuggled supply of Anchor and Tiger beer, the bottles wrapped in newspaper to conceal them and reduce the rattle. It was forbidden to carry any food outside the garrison, as part of the military regime to defeat the CTs was to deprive them of all support from the civilian population. The villages near the jungle were fenced off and strict control exercised over the movement of food or any other supplies that could aid the terrorists. Though it was unlikely that a few sandwiches from BMH Tanah Timah would significantly aid the Communist campaign, the principle was firmly enforced, but a few bottles of beer at NAAFI prices was hardly likely to lead to a court martial.

The dozen or so weekenders were arrayed in their off-duty civvies, the men in shirts and shorts, the women in summer dresses or halter tops. With Albert Morris's Hillman in the lead, they set off through the gates, leaving an envious skeleton staff to deal with emergencies until the next evening. The three-hour journey took them back down to Sungei Siput, then along the main north–south road through Ipoh, the capital of Perak State. The route then wandered westward through Batu Gajah and Bruas, eventually reaching the coast

at Lumut, a small town on a wide creek coming in from the
sea. They had coffee in the nearby Rest House while waiting
for the ferry to Pangkor Island, which lay a mile or two
offshore.

Leaving the cars parked behind the Shell petrol station,
they trooped up an ominously bending plank on to a big motor
boat which smelt strongly of fish. The accommodation was
benching which ran along each side, under a wooden canopy
supported on poles. Settling themselves on the seats, clutching
their beach bags and holdalls, the party from BMH provided
a source of wonderment for several large-eyed Malay children
who stood clutching the skirts of their mother's sarongs. Forty
minutes later, they disembarked at the fish quay at Pangkor
village, on the mainland side of the island. Tom Howden,
born and bred on the banks of the Tyne, had a spasm of
nostalgia as he smelt the place, the reek reminding him of
North Shields, with its own fish quay and its herring-smoking
factory.

With Alf Morris in the lead, the party set off in a strag-
gling line along the track between the coconut trees which
lead from the village towards the opposite side of the island.
Half a mile away was Pasir Bogak Bay, an idyllic curve of
sun-bleached sand, which to Tom's eyes looked like every
tropical beach that he had seen in his childhood picture
books.

Even though most of the group had been there before, the
sight was so sublime that they all stopped at the top of the beach
where the sparse grass under the trees gave way to the glorious
sand. Opposite was the smaller island of Pangkor Laut and
farther out, some smaller islets dotted the blue waters. Smitten
by the sight, they stood and gazed until Alf Morris chivvied
them back into action.

'Right, folks, let's get settled in, then we can get ourselves
into the water or whatever else you want to do!'

They ambled behind him along the shore line to where their
accommodation lay. There was no hotel, but a line of small
chalets stood under the trees, rather like the bathing huts at
an English holiday resort. Each had a verandah with a pair of
rattan chairs and inside was a couple of beds and very little

else. On the end of the row, a larger hut acted as the Chinese manager's office, bar and cookhouse, food being eaten at wooden picnic tables under a canvas awning outside. The staple diet was *nasi goreng*, Malayan fried rice, as well as omelettes, fried chicken and a curry. When the NAAFI beer ran out, there was more Anchor and soft drinks on sale, dispensed by the manager, Lee Hong and his wife.

The party paired off in decorous fashion, the women under the watchful eye of Doris Hawkins, while the men gravitated into amiable partnerships. Tom paired up with Alec Watson and as soon as they had dumped their belongings on the narrow beds, they hauled on their swimming trunks and hurried outside, the pathologist keen to spend as much time with Lynette as possible.

'Let's get in the water before eating,' suggested Alec. 'Bad to swim on a full stomach, so they say!'

He dashed off down the beach, but Tom hung about waiting for Lynette, though he was still slightly shell-shocked at finding himself in such a beautiful place, which looked as if Man Friday's footprints would at any moment mark the virgin sand. Soon the others began emerging from their chalets and he noticed that Diane Robertson, looking extremely seductive in a one-piece swimsuit of black satin, came alone from the end chalet, apparently not wanting to share with the military.

The Matron appeared in a voluminous beach-dress, declaring that she was not going to expose herself until the sun went lower in the sky. She plumped herself down at one of the tables with a book and a large gin and tonic, and gazed benignly at her nursing officers, as they prepared to disport themselves.

As everyone gathered at the edge of the beach, various pairings became apparent, almost like blood cells aggluti-nating! Tom spotted Lynette, looking extremely pretty in a floral swimsuit and gravitated to her side, as Peter Bright marched across to Diane, a little apart from the rest. Joan Parnell made a beeline for Montmorency, but several people noticed the glare that she gave Peter as he commandeered the new widow. David Meredith somewhat hesitantly sidled up to

Lena Franklin and though they exchanged a few words, Lena broke away and ran down towards the sea.

This was the signal for everyone to jog down to the water's edge, where waves just big enough to break over the ankles washed in from the almost tideless Malacca Straits. Heedless of Percy Loosemore's pessimistic warnings abut sea snakes whose bite could kill in ten minutes, they were soon all frolicking in the warm water. The more adventurous swam out to the coral reef and, with masks and flippers, dived to look at the underwater marvels, but most stayed in the shallows, swimming, splashing and fooling about like children on holiday.

Tom tried not to make his monopolization of Lynette too obvious, but it seemed that she wanted to be monopolized. They swam and dived and splashed. At one point she ducked his head under and kept it there with a foot on his neck, but let him up before he drowned!

Diane was a powerful swimmer and no one was surprised when she and Peter Bright took themselves off further down the beach, well away from the main party. Had anyone had binoculars, they might have seen that the pair spent much of the time standing waist-high in the water, apparently in earnest discussion and sometimes apparently heated argument.

After an hour or so, the sun and the exercise began to take its toll and gradually they left the sea and flopped on to the benches and chairs under the awning, calling to Lee Hong for drinks, before deciding what to choose from the dog-eared cardboard menu pinned above the bar.

After eating, the group split up again, everyone doing their own thing. Some went back into the sea, others wandered down the beach to watch the fishermen hauling in their seine net. A dozen locals, ranging from young boys to wizened old men with sun-blackened skin, chanted rhythmically as they heaved on a great U-shaped rope which dragged a net with a few score fish up on to the beach. Tom Howden was content to lie on the sand under the shade of a coconut palm, with Lynette half asleep alongside him. The afternoon lazed away all too quickly and as the sun slid lower in the sky, they went back down the beach into the warm water for another swim. As twilight approached, Lynette decided to retreat to her chalet to put on some clothing which exposed less skin to the evening mosquitoes.

Left alone, Tom wandered along the top of the beach along the tree-line, watching with wonderment as the sun sank below the horizon in a sky which was a riot of colour, bands of peach and violet climbing up from the sea towards the zenith. After a few hundred yards, he became conscious of voices coming from within the trees and without consciously wishing to eavesdrop, he recognized the deep tones of Peter Bright.

'It's not the done thing, you know, Diane!'

'You don't damn well own me! I'll do what I like, thank you!'

Embarrassed, Tom turned and walked quickly away, his feet making no sound in the soft sand. He had no wish to listen to some lover's tiff, especially as the two people sounded very angry. Obviously the path of true love was not going smoothly. Back at the huts, people were following Lynette's example and going to get changed, long sleeves and insect repellent becoming the order of the day. The pathologist followed their example and went back to his chalet in the middle of the row, where he found Alec in a clean shirt, carefully combing his fair hair in expectations of impressing his latest target, the Junior Theatre Sister. Perhaps unwisely, given the young Scot's fondness for gossip, Tom mentioned the spat he had heard between Peter Bright and the new widow.

Alec grinned at the news. 'Join the club, lad! I was in the bog earlier on and just happened to hear voices passing outside. It was the Welsh wizard and Lena Franklin – she was giving him hell for being so jealous about Jimmy Robertson. Virtually accused him of shooting the poor bugger!'

Tom could not help being intrigued by these local dramas, in spite of his better self telling him to mind his own business.

'What did our gasman have to say to that?' he asked.

Alec shrugged forlornly. 'Dunno, they walked out of earshot straight away. Short of running after them with my pants around my ankles, I couldn't get the rest of the squabble.'

When they all met half an hour later under the awning to eat, the grouping had changed somewhat. Diane was pointedly sitting with Doris Hawkins, Lena and Alfred Morris, leaving Peter Bright with a sullen-looking David Meredith on another table. Joan Parnell grasped the opportunity to slide next to the surgeon on the picnic benches, with another of the QA captains filling the fourth place. Tom naturally shepherded Lynette to another table, where Alec and Clarence Bottomley were sitting.

The last glow of light reddened the horizon, the palms silhouetted blackly against the sky. With the gentle swish of the sea as a background, and a pretty girl at his side, Tom Howden felt as if the Malayan Emergency had been conjured up merely for his benefit. He found it hard to believe that forty thousand men were engaged in a bloody campaign up and down this lovely country, though at home this was already being called 'The Forgotten War'.

'Could have been posted to Catterick – or some gloomy dump in West Germany,' observed Alec, as if reading his friend's mind. 'Not bad this, romantic setting, good beer, plenty of grub and very convivial company!'

Tom had to agree, though his ever-present Geordie conscience nagged him later that night, as he lay in the chalet, listening to the chirp of the cicadas and the occasional screech of a monkey. This 'emergency' – for the Government stubbornly refused to call it a 'war' because of its effect on planter's insurance premiums – was no fun for a hell of a lot of people. The previous day, he had taken blood samples from three very ill soldiers, young men like himself, called up for National Service, who had come in from a week's patrol in the jungle. The lads had had to sleep in water in the swamps, contaminated by rat's urine, which had infected them with the leptospirosis germ. It could be fatal, as could the many cases of malaria which he saw on blood-slides in the laboratory every day. Amoebic dysentery, hepatitis, scrub typhus, encephalitis and a host of other tropical nasties lurked to disable or even kill the vulnerable squaddies. Though the terrorist attacks seemed to have passed their zenith, there was always the danger of a road or rail ambush and the hand-to-hand combats in the *ulu* and the deep jungle still took its toll of young lives. As he lay listening to Alec snorting in his sleep, Tom thought that only a quirk of fate prevented him from being one of those lads with Weil's disease. If he had not got his scholarship to medical school, he might well have been on that jungle patrol, instead of living well in an Officers' Mess, able to have a romantic weekend with attractive nursing officers. With this philosophical guilt revolving in his head, he soon fell asleep, to dream of drizzle-soaked pavements and the corner chip shop in a cold and miserable Gateshead.

On Sunday, they arrived back at the hospital in the early evening, before darkness fell, as part of the road back from Lumut was in a 'black area' and was under curfew outside daylight hours. Tired from too much sun and exertion, they scattered to their messes and their rooms, to get washed and dressed for dinner.

In the RAMC Mess, most gravitated to the anteroom for a beer and a nostalgic chat about the weekend, to the annoyance of those who had had to stay behind and look after the hospital.

'When's the Old Man back?' asked Percy.

Morris signed Number One's chit for his Tiger before replying.

'He's coming up on the night train, but I'll bet he'll be holding Morning Prayers as usual, so don't think of staying in bed.'

The discussion settled, as it often did, on to the colonel's strange behaviour. Major Martin, the senior physician was there, as his wife had gone off to the Cameron Highlands for a week and he came to eat in the Mess. He seemed genuinely worried about the state of Desmond O'Neill's mental health.

'Damned difficult situation, with him outranking us all and being the CO,' he said gravely. 'But I think there's something seriously amiss with him. If it was you behaving like that, Alf, I'd get the Command Psychiatrist up from Singapore and give you a going over!'

'Why don't you do a dummy run on Percy Loosemore?'

said Peter Bright acidulously, having suffered much from the dermatologist's sarcastic humour about his personal affairs.

Clarence Bottomley's languid accents cut off Percy's retort.

'Joan Parnell was telling me that Matron's concerned about the colonel's antics, too. It seems he's been lurking around their mess and the QAOR's billet at dead of night. When she tackled him about it, he claimed he was concerned about prowlers!'

'And this business of the armoury is strange,' cut in Tom Howden. 'One of my Malay technicians came to me on Friday and asked if I could do anything about the postings. I was going to see you about it, Alf.'

The Administrative Officer grunted. 'I already know the problem, Tom. What did your MOR want?'

'He said that two of his pals, who had been on a lot of night duty at the arms kote, had suddenly been posted off to BMH Kamunting, though one had only come down from there two months ago. The other has a wife and kids living in the kampong near here and it was making life very difficult for them.'

'What's going on, Alf?' asked Eddie Rosen. 'You must have authorized the moves.'

Morris sighed. 'I tried to put the colonel off, but he insisted. It was he who demanded that they went. I couldn't get any proper explanation from him, just some blather about weapons security after all the recent trouble.'

John Martin shook his head sadly. 'The man's acting very oddly, especially since his wife went away. This business with the Quartermaster is another example, he seems to be getting more and more paranoid.'

As usual, Percy Loosemore seemed to have the best information about this particular problem.

'I went down with Robbie Burns to the Gunners' Mess in the garrison the other night. After he'd filled himself up with Johnnie Walker, he started babbling and reckoned that O'Neill was threatening to have him court-martialled over him fiddling the stores. Robbie got very aggressive and began ranting that he'd swing for the bastard one of these days! I had to drag him home before he said something too outrageous.'

Alfred Morris, already with too many problems on his plate, looked even more worried at this. 'I hope to God that Robbie doesn't do anything stupid,' he muttered. 'With a grudge like that and a few whiskies inside him, he's not a chap to meet on a dark night!'

ELEVEN

Steven Blackwell was another worried man, as he sat alone in his office early on Monday morning. A Telex had come in over the weekend from the Police Headquarters in Kuala Lumpur, carrying an enquiry from the Assistant Commissioner wanting an update about progress in the Robertson investigation. Usually, the superintendent in Tanah Timah was given a fairly free hand, KL rarely breathing down his neck about cases, but it seemed that this death had come to the ears of the High Commissioner in Government House.

Though Steven had already assured his superiors that this was not a terrorist shooting, the murder of a British planter was being taken seriously by the representatives of Whitehall. The political set-up in Malaya was complicated and was likely to become more so as pressure for independence grew with the run-down of colonialism. The 'Federation of Malaya' consisted of nine separate states, though Singapore, Malacca and Penang remained British Crown Colonies. Each state had a Sultan, a nominal head, who took it in turns to be overall 'king', but the real administration and the efficient infrastructure was run by the British. Independence was being pushed hard by the Malay population, even though the numerous Chinese and Indians dominated the commercial and professional life. The problem was that many Chinese who, with British help had fought a three-year guerrilla war against the Japanese, now wanted a *Communist* state and had returned to the jungle to fight for it, with open assistance from Red China.

The superintendent sighed and mopped his sweating brow as he earnestly hoped that he could continue to convince KL that this incident was purely a local affair and not some renewed outbreak of insurgency. The best way to settle the matter would be to discover and arrest the perpetrator, but that seemed as far away as on the day of James Robertson's death.

He spent the next hour on routine matters, including a

fruitless review of the bank robbery investigation, then decided to go out. His dark blue Land Rover took him and Inspector Tan once more past 'The Dog' and up the Kerbau road to Gunong Besar estate, as he had decided that Diane Robertson had had long enough now to be ready for a formal interview. Half afraid that she might still be in her pyjamas at ten in the morning, he was relieved to see her leaning over the verandah dressed in a cream blouse and fawn slacks. For once, there was no glass in her hand, just a cigarette which she waved in welcome as they drove up the slope from the road.

'I'm afraid this has to be rather official, Diane,' said Blackwell as they entered her wide lounge. 'We've taken statements from almost everyone else, but I left you until you settled down.'

'No problem, Steven, I know you have to go through the motions!'

She said this almost gaily, as if he'd come to enquire about the theft of a bicycle, rather than the murder of her husband. Blackwell sat in one of the big rattan chairs and Tan slid unobtrusively into a corner with his notebook at the ready, as Diane went through the ritual of offering drinks and settling for fresh limes all round. After Siva had brought them and then silently vanished, the senior officer got down to business. He went yet again through the movements of Diane and her husband on that fateful night, getting a repetition of what she had said before, with no more definite timing as to when they had both left the club.

'You took a long time getting back here, Diane?' probed Steven gently. 'You said you gave an officer a lift back to the garrison, but surely that would only add another ten minutes?'

The blonde coloured slightly. 'We stopped for a chat on the way. Nothing wrong with that, is there?'

The policeman shook his head. 'None at all. We had a word with Lieutenant Crosby, he says he thinks you dropped him off at about twenty to midnight. Would that be about right?'

The widow lifted her shoulders in a gesture of indifference.

'I suppose it was, if Gerry says so. I didn't know you were going to interrogate him?' she added sharply.

'Just tying up loose ends, Diane. Quite a long chat, though?'

'For God's sake, Steven, this is the nineteen-fifties!' she snapped irritably. 'We did a bit of necking, that's all. Not much room for anything heavier in that bloody Austin of mine. The way things were between James and myself, I think I deserved a bit of fun now and then.'

Blackwell looked at her impassively. 'And how exactly were things between you and your husband?'

The blonde gave him a scornful look as she fumbled another cigarette from her packet. 'Come on, Steve! You know damn well that we couldn't stand each other. I'd even been thinking of going back to the UK.'

The police officer wondered if a certain surgeon might now figure in that scheme, but it seemed irrelevant, unless . . . ?

'We know definitely that this wasn't a terrorist shooting, so can you think of any reason why anyone would want him dead?' he asked sombrely.

Diane tapped the ash from her cigarette into a potted plant standing next to the couch. 'It's no secret that he'd been getting his leg over a few local ladies. Maybe someone took strong objection to that?'

'Are you going to tell me who they were?' ventured Blackwell.

She shrugged dismissively. 'A couple of other planter's wives, but not lately, as far as I know. Then recently there was that sister down in the hospital. She was in Pangkor this weekend, looking as if butter wouldn't melt in her bloody mouth!'

Diane paused and took a nervous drag at her Park Drive, before continuing.

'Of course, there was that holy bitch next door, though again that was some time ago.' She inclined her head towards the other bungalow lower down the slope.

This was news to Blackwell, though admittedly he wasn't as close to the social gossip as some.

'Are you saying that James had an affair with his manager's wife?'

Diane feigned indifference, but viciously stubbed out her half-smoked cigarette in the long-suffering pot plant. 'He must

have been having it off with her for years – before I even
married him, I suspect! It fizzled out some time ago, so maybe
her religious conscience got the better of her, but more likely,
Jimmy dumped her.'

'Did Douglas know about this?'

The widow shrugged. 'Hard to tell, he's never said anything
or showed any sign of knowing. James would have been very
careful, he depended totally on Douglas to run this place, he
wouldn't have wanted to lose him. Maybe that's why he gave
her up.'

Blackwell, a happily married man with no inclination to go
roving, marvelled at the risks that fellows would take in such
a tightly knit community as this. He found it hard to believe
that the news bore any relation to Robertson's death, but it
was another piece of information to add to the pitifully thin
file on the case. Looking across at Tan, he saw that the inspector
was quietly writing everything down in his notebook, so he
launched into another topic.

'Just for the record, to tidy up loose ends, it's been obvious
to everyone that Colonel O'Neill has been more than friendly
towards you recently. Is there anything you want to tell me
about that?'

He felt a little foolish asking this and Diane's reaction made
him even more embarrassed. She burst out into peals of laughter
which though nervous, sounded quite genuine.

'Poor old Desmond? Come on, Steve, where's your sense
of humour? I was just having a bit of fun, leading the poor
old devil on. Those old witches that sit around the club already
think I'm a scarlet woman, so I thought I'd give them a bit
more scandal to gossip about.'

'I'd be very careful, if I were you, Diane,' advised Blackwell.
'I think the colonel took it more seriously than you think. He
could be a difficult man, if he thought you were making a fool
of him.'

Diane Robertson waved a hand in dismissal. 'It's nothing,
he just bought me a couple of drinks in The Dog and pranced
about ushering me into his big new car. It's rather nice, having
a colonel fussing over you.'

Steven despaired of this attractive widow, who seemed to

have about as much moral sense as the monkeys in the trees outside. After a few more profitless questions, he ended by cautiously raising one last matter.

'You said that even before your husband died, you were thinking of going back to England, Diane. Would it be indelicate of me to ask if Major Bright might figure in any such future plans?'

She gave him a brittle smile. 'What you are really suggesting is an Irish divorce?'

Steven stared at her, he had no idea what she was talking about.

'An Irish divorce is with a twelve-bore, Steve, it's a joke! That policeman's mind of yours is really wondering if Peter might have shot James to make me available?' she explained cynically. 'It's an exciting idea, I suppose. A handsome young man willing to kill for me, to get the woman he desires! But I can't see Doctor Bright going to those lengths, keen as he is.'

Her head-on response to what he had hoped was an oblique question left him speechless, but Diane filled the vacuum.

'Peter's a good-looking chap, pots of money in the family. Bit of a stuffed shirt, but I suppose I could do worse. We'll see how it pans out.'

A few minutes later, the superintendent was driven back down the road where James Robertson was killed, his mind still filled with the brazen attitude of the voluptuous blonde who seemed impervious to any emotion other than her own gratification.

The eight thirty meeting with the Commanding Officer had been even more fraught than usual, with O'Neill fractious after his night on the train up from Kuala Lumpur. He found fault with everyone, starting with Eddie Rosen, who had been Orderly Medical Officer the previous night.

'Call that a satisfactory report on the SI list, lieutenant?' he ranted, after the little doctor had given the usual resume on the three men with Weil's disease. The CO carried on castigating Eddie for not delivering a blow-by-blow account of their temperature, pulse rates and blood pressures during the previous twenty-four hours, though this was a matter for the ward notes, not needed in a brief reassurance that their condition had not deteriorated.

After abusing Rosen, the colonel's cold glare went around the room, doing his best to find fault with everyone. Tom Howden sat immobile, hoping that his usual invisibility would continue. Thankfully, O'Neill almost never questioned him, as he seemed neither to know nor care what went on in the laboratory and never visited it, except for the perfunctory walk-through at Tuesday inspections.

Unsurprisingly, the focus of O'Neill's persecution fell upon the unfortunate quartermaster, Captain Burns. With a ferocity unmatched even by his previous tirades, he goaded Robbie about the state of his Stores records and demanded that a complete set of requisitions and dispensations of all drugs and medical equipment for the past three months be produced by next day. He all but accused the quartermaster of embezzlement and corruption, with veiled references to the 'medical halls' in Tanah Timah and Sungei Siput, retail pharmacies where cut-price army medicaments would be welcomed.

Robbie's normally rough and ruddy face became almost puce with suppressed anger and seemed ready to erupt under the interrogation.

Alfred Morris prodded him covertly with his elbow from the next chair, warning him against any violent reaction which the colonel would undoubtedly welcome as evidence of insubordination and mutiny under Queen's Regulations.

At the end of this blistering inquisition, the CO rapped on his desk with his cane. 'You'll see from today's Part One Orders that training will begin tomorrow for the PE tests in four weeks' time,' he snapped.

These were the annual Physical Efficiency tests that all Service personnel were supposed to pass, otherwise they could have their pay and allowances docked. Percy Loosemore had told Tom that these were something of a farce, held in the garrison athletic ground, where they had to climb a rope, jump over some boxes and perform a few other innocuous feats of strength and ability. In addition, there was a three-mile run part-way up the Kerbau road and back, that had to be completed within a certain time. Percy had alleged that last year, several of the

officers had arranged for a taxi from Tanah Timah to pick them
up as soon as they were out of sight and take them to The Dog,
where they sat drinking beer until it was time for them to jog
the few hundred yards back to the garrison. But now their
increasingly malignant colonel seemed to have other ideas.

'You may be doctors, but first and foremost, you are
soldiers!' he barked. 'You've gone soft, lolling about the Mess,
drinking and going off on pleasure weekends like a lot of
suburban bank clerks!'

Glaring around, he dropped his bombshell. 'Tomorrow
morning and on alternate mornings for a month, you will
parade at six thirty in full kit on the hospital car park. I have
arranged for a drill sergeant from the garrison to give you an
hour's exercises, which will include three full circuits of the
perimeter road.'

With his narrow jaw jutting forward, he delivered his final
broadside. 'This applies to all of you, with no exception unless
you have urgent clinical duties. I will be there personally to
make sure there are no backsliders. I'll make soldiers of you
yet, even if it kills you!'

Mutiny was in the air that day, as the medical officers digested
this latest *dictat* from their leader.

'The bugger's flipped completely,' muttered Percy Loosemore,
whose idea of exercise was walking from the car park of The
Dog as far as the bar. Appeals to the Admin Officer brought
no relief, as Alf Morris confessed that he could do nothing
with the CO when he was in this mood. After leaving O'Neill's
office, the others clustered around the notice board at the
bottom of the main corridor and read Part One Orders, a typed
sheet of paper pinned up every morning which gave details
of duty rosters and events for the day. Sure enough, there was
the command to appear fully kitted at the crack of dawn, an
order which had the Other Ranks smirking all day at the
discomfiture of their officers.

'Funny business, sir!' grinned Lewis Cropper, as he brought
Tom his pallid mug of mid-morning tea. 'If you can't find all
your kit, let me know and I'll scrounge some for you.'

The day after the pathologist's arrival at BMH, the

quartermaster sergeant had dumped a collection of pouches, green webbing and a water-bottle on Tom, together with a steel helmet. He had stuffed them into the bottom of his wardrobe and hoped that they were still there.

At the Mess before lunch, more disgruntled discussion took place, with the physician John Martin being pressured to get the Commanding Officer certified before he could wreak any more havoc. This plea fell on deaf ears, especially as the major had a cast-iron excuse to avoid the threatened parade, as he had to be in BMH Kamunting the next morning to hold a special clinic.

As it happened, the object of their disquiet was at that moment himself being interrogated. Steven Blackwell had telephoned for an appointment and Desmond O'Neill had grudgingly agreed, for the superintendent had made a point of reminding him that the garrison commander, Brigadier Forsyth, had sanctioned the questioning of all military personnel. The colonel did it with ill grace and sat stiffly behind his desk, glowering at the police officer.

'This is highly irregular, Blackwell,' he snapped. 'The civil police have no jurisdiction over Her Majesty's Forces, you know.'

Experienced copper that he was, Steven knew when to come on as a hard man and when to tread lightly.

'Indeed, sir, I'm sure that if any serviceman was charged with this offence, he would be tried and sentenced by the Army. But as this is a civilian death and your SIB are collaborating fully with us, then the actual investigation is well within the ambit of the Federation Police.'

O'Neill snorted, but he had no valid argument against something sanctioned by the Brigade Commander. 'What d'you want to know, then?' he grunted sourly.

'I have to record the movements of everyone, even those only peripherally involved, sir,' Steven began diplomatically. 'I gather that the first you knew of this death was when you arrived back here, some time after James Robertson had been certified as dead?'

'The place was like a madhouse, people milling about the front of my hospital as if it was a fairground. I soon cleared them out, they had no business bringing a civilian corpse here, anyway!'

'With respect, it wasn't known that he was dead, until your doctors had confirmed that. But what time did you arrive, sir?'

'About twenty to one, I believe – not that it can matter in the slightest! I found a messenger at my quarter, telling me what had happened, so I drove down here.'

'They failed to contact you earlier by telephone at your house, I believe. Could you tell me where you had been, colonel?'

Desmond O'Neill scowled at the superintendent. 'What the devil has that got to do with anything?'

'All part of the routine, sir. You may have seen something or someone which might complement the rest of our evidence.'

The skull-like face looked balefully at Blackwell. 'I had been to the AKC cinema in the garrison, if you must know. They were showing *The Way Ahead*, a wartime favourite of mine, if you need to check on my alibi!' he added sarcastically.

'The AKC show always finishes by ten thirty, colonel. May I ask where you were between then and the time you arrived at your quarter?'

O'Neill's sallow face developed a slight flush. 'I consider that question impertinent, Blackwell. I didn't rush off from my billet as soon as I had the message, you know.'

Steven remained polite and impassive. 'But the attempts to phone you there were not made until after midnight, sir. You couldn't have been home by that time.'

The CO jumped from his chair and stood ramrod straight, glaring at the police officer. 'Dammit, are you accusing me of anything?'

'I just want answers about timing, colonel, that's all. It's essential to know where everyone was, and at what time that night.'

O'Neill subsided into his chair. 'I drove around for a while to get some air, if you must know. The cigarette smoke in that damned cinema was so thick you could hardly see the screen. I had a headache and smarting eyes, so I went and sat in the car up on the Sungie Siput road for a while and looked at the valley in the moonlight.'

Blackwell managed to avoid raising his eyebrows at this unlikely tale. He had thought it unwise to bring his inspector on this particular interview, so he had his own notebook at the ready and as he jotted down the colonel's words, he wondered how much air O'Neill had needed to keep him out alone in his car for almost two hours in the middle of the night.

'You met no one during that time, sir?'

'Are you doubting my word, officer!' snarled O'Neill.

'All policemen have to seek corroboration for everything, colonel,' said Steven imperturbably. 'I take it the answer is "no"?'

'I saw no one and spoke to no one!' snapped the other man. 'Now if you have no more sensible questions, I would like to get on with my work. We are fighting a war here, you know!'

He spoke as if he were General Sir Gerald Templer, not the administrator of a small hospital. Considering that the police superintendent had more than once been personally involved in a shoot-out with the CTs, his remark bordered on the offensive. However, Blackwell let it pass and after a few more unprofitable questions, he left the irate colonel to become more bad-tempered as the day went on.

TWELVE

That Monday turned out to be an eventful day in BMH Tanah Timah, even apart from the colonel's worsening mania. Lunch in the Officers' Mess was brought to an abrupt end by the almost simultaneous ringing of telephones and the clatter of an approaching helicopter. Grabbing their caps and belts, the medical staff reached the landing pad just as a three-ton Bedford ambulance lumbered up the perimeter road to disgorge half a dozen medical orderlies. The RSM was with them and told the reception party of doctors and QA sisters, that the casualties were coming from an ambush and a firefight up near Grik, towards the border with Thailand. Tom recalled seeing the long convoy of vehicles leaving the garrison several days earlier and assumed that this incident was the result of the new operation to attack the CTs in that area.

As soon as the Westland Whirlwind dropped from the sky on to the whitewashed circle on the ground, the orderlies ran forward to pull out three stretchers while the rotor blades were still whirring over their heads. Peter Bright and Eddie Rosen hurried to make a quick examination of the wounded men and then motioned for them to be loaded into the first ambulance as it backed up nearer the helicopter. Three other 'walking wounded' clambered to the ground, two with arms supported in bloodstained slings, the other with a bandage around his chest. All were wearing jungle kit, with green lace-up boots and floppy wide-brimmed hats. They were helped solicitously into the large box-like ambulance, as the flight crew handed out their weapons to the RSM, who carefully checked their safety state before sending them to the arms kote. Before the senior surgeon clambered aboard the Bedford himself, he called out to the pathologist.

'Looks as if we'll need blood pretty soon, Tom. Can you get cracking on that?'

As the big ambulance lurched over the monsoon drain to get back on to the perimeter road, the pathologist hurried down to the laboratory, feeling for the first time that he really was in the army, rather than on a long tropical holiday.

As he marched off down the corridor, he could hear the whine of the helicopter rise to a higher pitch as it rose off the pad and curved away to go back to the battle area.

He could do nothing until the surgical team sent up samples for blood grouping, but he put his technicians on alert so that they could get all the kit ready. As soon as he had the groupings, he could check them against his prisoner list, then get some eager donors brought over to the transfusion basha.

The rest of the afternoon and early evening went in a flurry of activity, as the X-ray department and the operating theatre worked efficiently to deal with the wounds, dealing with fractures, digging out bullets and even screws and nails, as the terrorists, short of proper rifles and ammunition, had home-made weapons that fired these random metal fragments.

Six of Tom's prisoners came willingly from the MCE to exchange pints of their blood for about the same volume of Tiger beer. He bled them straight from arm veins into bottles as they lay on bed frames in the palm-leafed hut, red-capped MPs standing at the entrance, glowering suspiciously at their charges who they considered had found yet another way to 'swing the lead'.

By dinner time that evening, things had settled down and though Peter Bright, David Meredith and Eddie Rosen were still down in the wards checking the post-operative condition of the injured men, the rest of the residents were able to eat in comparative peace. Afterwards, over coffee in the anteroom, they had at least had something fresh to talk about, other than the murder of Jimmy Robertson.

Speculation was rife as to whether this latest operation by the Brigade had rooted out any CTs. The answer to this soon came in an unusual way, as Alf Morris was called away by Number One to answer the phone. When he came back, he dropped heavily back into his chair and turned to Tom.

'That was the CO on the phone. A nice little trip for you tomorrow, Tom!'

The pathologist's stolid face looked suspiciously at Alf.

'I thought we were all doing physical jerks on the car park at half six?' he grunted.

The Admin Officer grinned mischievously as he looked around the room. 'I've got good news for you, chaps! The colonel, in that inimitable way he has of changing his mind, has decided to call off his scheme for getting you fit! Apart from this communal run up Maxwell Hill on Friday!'

There were cries of relief all round, but Tom still waited for Alf's ominous message about the next day.

'The CO has had a request from Brigade for the services of a pathologist to carry out post-mortems on three CTs who were killed in this operation up near Grik. Your predecessor was called out a couple of times for the same thing.'

Tom stared at Alf Morris, wondering if this was a wind-up, or another delusion on the part of their commanding officer.

'What the hell for? Are they bringing the bodies down here?' he asked incredulously.

The older man shook his head. 'You're going up there, lad! Flying out at eight in the morning, so take your knives with you.'

At the crack of dawn, Tom Howden was in his laboratory, where Cropper filled a haversack with the antique dissection kit, several pairs of rubber gloves, a clipboard and paper, a couple of big sack needles and a ball of twine. Tom had his little Voigtlander 35mm camera in his pocket and his heart in his mouth as half an hour later, a Land Rover dropped him at the grass airstrip behind the garrison compound and he saw the plane that was to take him into the unknown. The little Auster looked to him like a camouflaged Austin Seven with wings and, with some trepidation, he lugged his haversack across to the aircraft, where the Army Air Corps pilot was leaning against the fabric fuselage, complete with leather flying helmet like some latter-day Biggles.

After a laconic greeting, the pilot opened a door, dumped Tom's bag into the fuselage, then squeezed the pathologist into the single backward-facing seat behind the driver's position. He strapped him in, gave him a pair of large headphones and then climbed in himself. A moment later, there was a judder as the engine started and the plane began bumping across the rough grass of the old tin tailings. Through the perspex canopy over the back of the cockpit, Tom stared out in horrified fascination at the fragile tailplane as the rudder wagged as they turned upwind. The whole contraption appeared to be made of cloth, reminding him of the balsa and tissue-paper models he made as a boy. The tail rose, the bumping suddenly stopped and Tom realized that they were already off the ground. As they climbed and banked, he looked down at the garrison, the hospital and the little town of Tanah Timah, amazed that this machine was actually flying.

Soon he began to enjoy himself, in spite of the fact that the back of his head was touching the muzzle of an automatic rifle strapped behind the pilot's seat – reminding him that this was part of a war, not a joyride.

Looking down again, he saw the road going past The Dog and within the regular pattern of rubber plantations he could make out the bungalows of the Gunong Besar estate, where James Robertson had lived. With a return of his feelings of unreality, he realized that within weeks of leaving Gateshead, he had performed an autopsy on a shot murder victim and was now on his way to repeat the performance on three communist terrorists. When he had arrived in Malaya, he was inclined to think that 'terrorists' was a pejorative imperialist title for freedom fighters, until he heard descriptions of the sadistic atrocities that Chin Peng's men had inflicted on uncooperative countrymen and women in the villages.

Alf Morris had explained the previous evening that the War Office wanted information on the killing power of the Belgian-designed FN rifle that had been adopted by NATO and detailed reports on all fatal injuries inflicted by it were to be collected wherever possible, hence his present mission.

They flew over endless rubber and oil palm estates, rice paddies and dense jungle as they went north, Tom taking some photos to amaze his folks back home in Gateshead. All too soon, the fifty-minute flight came to an end, as the Auster glided in to land on another strip of grass alongside a narrow road. On one side was yet more rubber, on the other virgin jungle. A few tents were set up as a temporary camp at one end of the airstrip, where a collection of military vehicles was standing.

An infantry captain in jungle gear came up as Tom was hauling himself out of the cramped seat and helped him with the heavy haversack.

'Just in time, doc,' he said cheerfully. 'They're about to bring the bastards out of the *ulu* down there.' As he waved a hand down the straight road, a corporal crouched over a radio pack called out to him.

'They say they can see the edge of the trees, sir. Be with us in a few minutes.'

The West Berkshires officer gave a shrill blast on a whistle and beckoned to a group of squaddies waiting around a Ferret armoured scout car, a TCV and a pair of Land Rovers. As the men jogged towards them, the captain began striding down the road. 'Come on, doc, duty calls!'

Tom slung his bag over his shoulder and sweating like a bull in the cloying heat, followed the men for a few hundred yards, until a soldier suddenly appeared through the lalang grass, holding up his rifle and pointing back into the trees.

A few moments later, a strange procession appeared out of the forest, which confirmed Tom's impression that he was in a time-warp created by Somerset Maugham or some Edwardian writing about the last days of the British Raj. Some British and Gurkha soldiers appeared, followed by two Malay Regiment men carrying a long bamboo pole on their shoulders. From this hung a corpse, suspended by ropes tied around ankles and wrists. Tom had seen old photos of tigers being retrieved like this, after being slaughtered by some pith-helmeted colonial general, but he never expected to see the method used for humans.

As the two bearers thankfully dropped their burden on the wide verge at the edge of the road, two similar convoys came out of the jungle, this time carried by a pair of West Berkshires and another two locally enlisted Malay privates.

'Right, doctor, they're all yours,' announced the cheerful

young captain, as the troops set about untying the corpses
from the poles. 'Let's know when you're through, so I can
send a few lads down with shovels.'

The men from the patrol went wearily up to the tents for
food and rest, while the fresher men from the vehicles stood
around to watch Tom do his stuff. The three bodies, dressed
in ragged bloodstained clothing, were laid out a few feet apart
and he began by taking photographs of them, which seemed
a sensible thing to do, as he had no orders as how to proceed.
Two of the corpses were men, the other a young woman,
though it was hard to tell, as her head seemed to have been
exploded from the inside.

'Were they all shot with FNs?' he asked the captain.

'Two of them, doc. The other was traversed with a Bren.'

Tom set out his meagre equipment, the old box of instruments giving rise to a chatter of interest amongst the
watchers. Pulling on a pair of gloves, he asked the officer
if someone could jot down a few notes and the captain gave
the clipboard to his sergeant. Squatting uncomfortably on
his heels, Tom began his examination by pulling aside the
soaked, tattered shirt of the first man, a young Chinese with
blood dribbling from his mouth. There were two bullet
entrance wounds on his chest and a large exit wound on his
back.

After opening the thorax with one of Cropper's ferocious
knives, Tom dictated a short account of the chaos within the
chest cavity and the destruction of the spine, rather similar to
the injury to James Robertson. However, unlike the planter,
there were no bullets inside the body, the high velocity of the
FN having whistled them right through to lie somewhere out
there in the deep jungle.

He had a cursory look at the other main organs, mainly out
of interest, in case the privations of living for years on poor
rations and with rampant infectious diseases and parasites,
might have left some mark. He found nothing significant and
went on to look at the second man.

This was a different situation altogether, as there was a
line of eight bullet entrance rounds running diagonally across
his chest and abdomen, as his life was blasted away by a

moving hail of bullets from a Bren gun. One of the bullets was still in the body, one lodged under the skin of the back where it had run out of momentum after passing through a vertebra.

'That will be a three-oh-three, doc,' commented the helpful young captain. 'We've still got some of the old Brens, before they changed the barrels to fire the NATO seven-point-sixes.'

Again, Tom was chillingly reminded of James Robertson, whose spine had arrested a similar .303 projectile.

The woman, though facially utterly unrecognizable, appeared from her shape and smooth skin to be young, perhaps even a teenager. After trying to roughly replace the exploded tissues of the head, he found that the single entrance wound appeared to be in the left ear, the projectile from the FN having gone down the canal until it struck the mass of dense bone in the base of the skull. The sudden transfer of kinetic energy had been more like a bomb than a bullet, but at least she could not have known anything about it, thought Tom, in an effort to find some consolation in the midst of this carnage. Even the soldiers standing around seemed muted, with none of the usual ribald humour that was commonly used to compensate for these grim situations.

He used the rest of his film in taking close-up pictures of all the injuries, then did his best to restore some dignity to the desecrated corpses which lay naked on the side of the road. He sewed up the fronts of the bodies, using the twine and needles that Lewis Cropper had provided. There was little he could do to restore the girl's head, but as a gesture, he bound it together in several layers of clothing ripped from the men's shirts.

A couple of West Berkshires had brought entrenching tools down from the three-tonner and set about digging a shallow grave in the soft, damp soil of the verge. The three corpses were lowered into it, side by side and as the men shovelled the red soil back into the hole, Tom could not help comparing this with the recent funeral of Jimmy Robertson, where a robed priest and floral tributes had marked his passing. He had seen pet dogs buried with more ceremony than this and realized yet again that war was a cruel, callous business.

Taking his notes from the officer, he walked in a subdued mood back to the tents for a promised cup of tea, before climbing aboard the Auster for the flight back to Tanah Timah.

Steven Blackwell was a worried man as he sat in his office in the police station. Another two days had passed without any progress in the Robertson investigation and as well as having had another nagging call from his Commissioner in Kuala Lumpur, he was concerned about a rumour that had filtered through to him from the garrison. Though he did not actually have any spies inside the military establishment, he knew so many people there that it was inevitable that gossip percolated down to him, not only at the bar of The Dog, but from Inspector Tan and other police officers, who were in daily contact with civilian servants and clerks working for the army. The current gossip concerned the Commanding Officer of the hospital there, purveying suggestions varying from the fact that the colonel had gone raving mad to the milder eccentricity of stalking the compound at night with a loaded pistol.

Steven had gone so far as to corner the hospital's Admin Officer at the club the previous evening and ask him whether there was any problem with Desmond O'Neill. Major Morris was reluctant to say much, both because of his traditional loyalty to a superior officer and the plain fact that military secrets, if this could be called one, could not be divulged to civilians, even to the police, without very good legal reasons.

'The old man is just his usual bloody-minded self, Steven,' he countered evasively, before relating the strange business of the aborted physical exercise demand. The policeman suspected that Morris was keeping something back out of loyalty and discretion and he admired him for that, but sensed that there was more going on in BMH than just their commandant's persecution of his medical officers.

'Alf, you know I can't exclude anyone from my investigations and that includes O'Neill. In fact, he's got no satisfactory explanation for where he was at the time of the shooting. If there's anything you think you should tell me that's relevant to my enquiries, I should know about it.'

The Admin Officer looked uncomfortable at this.

'Steve, it's very difficult for me to talk about this. It's an internal matter and I'm sure it has nothing to do with your investigation.'

The superintendent sighed at Morris's unconvincing tone.

'Look, I realize your problem, but if you want to keep in the clear, why not have a word with the legal bloke in Brigade and pass the buck to him?'

They were sitting at a corner table in the lounge of The Dog, almost deserted at this early part of the evening. Alf Morris gave an almost furtive look around, then leaned towards Blackwell.

'The CO is acting more oddly than usual, but maybe that's due to end-of-tour blues. He's due to go home in about seven weeks' time. The thing is, some of his dottiness seems to centre around the armoury. He's always been obsessed with security there, but recently he's suddenly posted two Malay Other Ranks out of the unit with no real reason. Both have been on night duty at the arms kote.'

Steven frowned, trying to make sense of this.

'Why should that worry you?' Then the possible relevance suddenly struck him. 'Are any weapons missing?' he hissed.

He relaxed a little when the other man shook his head.

'No, I went up there today and checked through the record book. But the odd thing is that the colonel had withdrawn a rifle a couple of weeks ago – and returned it last Friday!'

Blackwell stared intently at Morris. 'Can he do that? What the hell for?'

Morris shrugged. 'He's quite entitled to draw a weapon, if he wants. After all, he's the Commanding Officer of the unit, so who's going to query it? Maybe he wanted to practice his marksmanship on the garrison range. We are on active service, even though we're a medical unit. All the MOs have to put in target practice at the Depot when they first join, God help us for their uselessness at it!'

As a former non-medical Regimental Sergeant Major, he couldn't resist a dig at the doctors' lack of military skills.

The policeman took up his beer glass with rather nervous fingers. 'Alf, you realize that the period when he took the gun out, covers the date of Jimmy Robertson's killing.'

Morris nodded. 'It had occurred to me. But it's ridiculous to think that O'Neill could have anything to do with that. Anyway, the previous shoot-up at Gunon Besar was outside the time when he had the rifle.'

Blackwell shook his head. 'But those shots came from a different weapon. Had he taken out another gun previously?'

'No, there's nothing in the book,' replied Alf, rather abruptly. He was becoming uneasy about this line of questioning

'He could have badgered some little MOR to let him take one out without signing the book,' suggested Steven. 'Perhaps that's why he posted the fellows away, so that they couldn't be questioned.'

'Oh come on, Steve! This is verging on the fantastic. Where would he get the ammunition from? There's no record of any being issued with the rifle.'

The superintendent was unimpressed with this argument.

'There's plenty of spare clips knocking around the garrison, you know that as well as I do. And O'Neill was posted here from Korea, that place was awash with buckshee weapons and ammo.'

Alf Morris stared into his glass of Tiger, worried by the way things were going. 'What are you going to do about it? I shouldn't have told you, really, without authorization from a more senior officer – and my immediate superior is the colonel himself.'

Steven ran a hand over his tender sunburnt scalp. 'Can you identify the actual rifle that he took out?'

Morris nodded. 'The serial numbers are recorded in the armoury book.'

'Then I must have a test-fired bullet from it to send to the laboratory in KL to compare with the one Tom Howden dug out of Jimmy. Can you arrange that on the quiet? If it doesn't match, then no one will be any the wiser, but we can breath more easily again.'

Reluctantly, Morris agreed. 'It will have be done within the garrison, no way can I let a weapon go outside without the Brigadier's consent – and that would lead to a lot of awkward questions, especially as he's one of our colonel's cronies.'

Blackwell swallowed the rest of his beer and reached for his black uniform cap on the nearly chair. 'Thanks, Alf. If I don't make some progress soon, my senior officers are going to crap on me from a great height. It might come to test-firing all the weapons in the BMH arms kote, so doing one early might be a start.'

'Did you get any results from the guns the planters had?' Morris asked, as he rose to his feet with the policeman.

'Just had the results from KL. None of the rifles that came from Gunong Besar or Les Arnold's place up the road matched any of the bullets that were fired at the bungalows or the one that killed poor Jimmy.'

That rather prickly conversation had taken place the previous evening and now Steven Blackwell was in a dilemma as to how to proceed. Given the hostile attitude of Desmond O'Neill, he could hardly ask the colonel whether he had shot the Gunong Besar planter. Frustratingly, all he could do was to wait until Alf Morris had produced the promised bullet from a test-firing, presumably made by an armourer from the garrison. At least this would not give rise to any connection with the CO of the hospital, as it was common knowledge that a variety of weapons were likely to be examined for exclusion purposes.

As he had told Morris the previous evening, the barrel striations on the bullets fired through the rifles borrowed from Douglas Mackay, Les Arnold and even the one belonging to James Robertson, showed that none had been used in either incident at or near Gunong Besar.

As he sat sweating under the rotating overhead fan, Steven's mind reverted to the other suspects, if such unlikely candidates could be thought of as such. He was convinced that a woman was at the bottom of this crime, as he could not bring himself to believe that any other motive was credible. There was no possible financial reason why Jimmy should have been shot – Doug Mackay would not benefit from Robertson's death. Indeed, he stood to lose his job and bungalow if Gunong Besar was sold up. Perhaps Les Arnold might have a slight motive, if he wanted to add that estate to his own holdings up at Batu Merah, but it seemed unlikely that he would devise such an elaborate scheme just to get hold of extra land. With any terrorist involvement ruled out, as it must be given the dumping of Jimmy's body outside The Dog, then some motive related to passion, sex or jealousy must surely be the answer.

His train of thought was interrupted by one of the Indian civil employees coming in with a tray containing his eleven o'clock grapefruit soda to wash down a Paludrine tablet, his daily defence against malaria. Behind him came Inspector Tan, with some statements about a recent serious wounding in a kampong a few miles away. Steven motioned to him to sit down on the other side of the desk. He had not told him of the business with Colonel O'Neill and the armoury as, if it was a total red-herring, the fewer people who knew about it, the better.

'Tan, where do we go from here, eh?' he began, wanting to see if the highly intelligent inspector had any new thoughts to offer about the impasse in which they found themselves. 'Do you feel that it is at all possible that our culprit is from the hospital?'

The smooth-faced officer sat primly in his chair opposite his chief. 'Anything is possible, sir. Who of us can ever tell what emotions are seething beneath the surface of any of our fellow men?'

Steven had a fleeting impression that he was listening to some saying of Confucius, but Tan soon became less philosophical and more practical.

'Sir, we have the surgeon gentleman, Major Bright, who it seems is very enamoured with Mrs Diane. I came to learn that he would very much have liked her to divorce her husband so that they could marry – and time was running out, as he is soon due to return to England. That could be a motive for him to rid himself of Mr Robertson. He has no firm alibi for the time of the shooting.'

'So he's a favourite of yours for the killing?'

Tan gave a slight lift of the shoulders, his face remaining impassive. 'It seems unlikely, but it is a possibility. Perhaps a better one than for his colleague, Captain Meredith, the anaesthetist. He too had a motive in that Mr Robertson appears to have captured the affections of one of the nursing sisters, who the captain had considered his own lady friend. But that seems a much weaker motivation than the first.'

Trust his inspector to lay out the facts in such a clear, if dispassionate way, thought Blackwell.

'Any other suspects appeal to you, Tan?' he asked.

'I understand that the Commanding Officer has been acting somewhat strangely,' replied Tan, again surprising his boss with his grasp of the local gossip from BMH. 'Recently, he also seems to be unusually attentive to Mrs Robertson, though I fail to see the relevance of that.'

The Chinese officer paused for a moment. 'Those are the military candidates, sir. But of course, there are the civilians, the planters. Mr Arnold has a rather dubious past, including using a gun to wound someone in Australia, but I see little motivation for shooting Mr Robertson. I have heard that he has expressed open admiration for Mrs Diane, but I doubt that he wanted to remove her husband in order to marry her.'

'What about the Mackays?' asked Steven, curious to hear what his inspector's analytical mind felt about them.

'From my interviews with them when I took statements, I felt that there was some unhappiness between them. I heard rumours from elsewhere that it was possible that Mr Robertson had carried on some adulterous relationship with Mrs Mackay, but that seemed in the past. I cannot believe that it would be in the best interests of Mr Mackay to kill his employer, unless he was consumed by an excess of outraged jealousy.'

Steven was secretly amused by Tan's rather pedantic and prim phraseology, probably culled from classic English novels, but he appreciated his clear overview of the situation, which confirmed his own feelings.

He placed his Paludrine tablet on his tongue and washed it down with the fizzy grey juice.

'We'll just have to wait and see what happens next, I'm afraid,' he said to his inspector, reaching across for the reports on the local assault.

They had not long to wait.

THIRTEEN

The next couple of days seemed relatively placid in BMH Tanah Timah, though various things were going on under the surface. Major Morris went discreetly to the arms kote and identified the rifle that his commanding officer had taken out. Through his many contacts in the garrison, he arranged to have it test fired over there, taking it personally in his car to one of the Brigade armourers. He brought it back almost immediately, together with the spent bullet and took the latter over to Steven Blackwell, to be sent down on the night train to the forensic laboratory in KL. He knew he was taking a chance over this, as if the colonel ever learnt of it – assuming that he did not eventually turn out to be the guilty party – then he was likely to face a court martial and the end of his career and pension.

Desmond O'Neill was also unaware of another matter concerning himself, as Major Martin, the senior physician, had had a covert telephone conversation with a friend and colleague in BMH Singapore, another major who was the Command Psychiatrist. After hearing what Martin had to say, he promised to come up to Tanah Timah the following week, in the guise of one of his routine visits to the physicians in the other four military hospitals.

The more junior medical staff, including Tom Howden, knew nothing of these machinations. The pathologist was quite content to get on with running the laboratory, the novelty of having his own place for the first time keeping him as happy as a sandboy. He spent half a day writing up a full report of his examinations of the shot terrorists. The film he had exposed up near Grik was developed by the photographic unit in the garrison and he was glad to see that his amateur efforts had resulted in clear, if horrific, pictures. These were duly sent down in the official mail to GHQ in Singapore and presumably would eventually find their way to the War Office

and their gun experts in Woolwich. He carefully excluded
the aerial shots he had taken from the Auster, which he
airmailed home to his parents, to be shown around the rest
of the family and neighbours to proudly demonstrate how
their young Tommy was fighting to keep back the Communist
hordes!

On Friday, after a nine-o'clock cup of pale fluid which his
corporal alleged was Nescafé, he was at his microscope
studying the first batch of blood films, two of which his technician Embi bin Sharif said were positive for malaria. In the
middle of this peaceful exercise, he heard a sudden clatter of
ammunition boots on the concrete floor of the main laboratory
and a moment later the blond head of Sergeant Oates appeared
around his door.

'Sorry to disturb you, sir, but a guardroom runner is here
with a message for you to go down to Major Morris's office
at once. He says it's really urgent.'

The pathologist grabbed his cap and hurried after the runner,
who had no idea what the panic was about. When he reached
Alf's office, he found Steven Blackwell sitting in front of the
Admin Officer's desk, both men looking extremely grim.

'I didn't use the phone, Tom, you never know who's listening
on that switchboard. This is a very sensitive issue.'

Howden wondered if the colonel had gone completely
berserk or perhaps the Third World War had started, but Alf
rapidly explained, speaking quietly as the slatted shutters
offered little privacy on the front verandah of the hospital.

'The superintendent here has been told that two bodies have
been found up at Gunong Busar this morning. He thought it
would be as well if a doctor went up there with him and you
seem the obvious choice, as there isn't a civvy doctor nearer
than Sungei Siput.'

Tom looked at the superintendent. 'Two more dead? Who
are they?'

'I only have third-hand information, but I'm afraid it seems
likely that they are Mr and Mrs Mackay. I had a phone call
from Les Arnold, who was phoned by the Robertson's head
servant. Les was going down there straight away, but he rang
me first.'

'Better get going, Tom,' said Morris. 'The police Land Rover is waiting outside.'

'What about the colonel?' asked Tom warily. 'Has he given it the OK?' He recalled the fuss that O'Neill had made when Jimmy Robertson's body was brought in to 'his' hospital.

'He's not here, he was summoned down to Kinrara for some meeting, thank God!'

'You're not coming with us?'

Alf shook his head. 'I've got to mind the shop, when the CO's away. And anyway, it's not Army business, this. You happen to be the only doctor around here used to seeing corpses! Now be off with you.'

Tom climbed into the back of the blue police vehicle and they shot off, the Malay constable who was driving being obviously delighted to have an emergency as an excuse for putting his accelerator foot flat on the floor.

As they zoomed out into the road and accelerated past the garrison gates, Steven half turned from the front seat.

'I know no more about this than you heard from Alf. I suppose the servant in Gunong Besar rang Les Arnold as he was the nearest. All Les knew was that for a change, this time it was not a shooting.'

The Land Rover turned up past The Dog on to the laterite road to Kampong Kerbau and within a few minutes was roaring up the steep entrance drive to the Robertson's bungalow. As the driver skidded to a halt on the gravel, Steven half expected to see Diane leaning over the balcony holding a glass of gin and a cigarette. But she was gone, staying at the best hotel in Penang until the coroner's inquest was held on her late husband – and until the arrival of the next Blue Funnel ship bound for Britain.

When they clambered out, Tom saw a battered ex-US army jeep parked at the bottom of the steps. He knew this belonged to Les Arnold, but there was no sign of the Australian. The superintendent made to climb up to the verandah, but a Chinese girl appeared above him, with a Tamil woman hovering anxiously behind her. The *amah* pointed away to the other bungalow, just visible behind the trees and bushes.

'Siva took Mister Arnold down there, sir!' she cried.

Steven raised his swagger stick in acknowledgement and with Tom and the driver in tow, hurried between exotically flowered bushes to the driveway of the Mackay bungalow.

Here they found the Australian sitting on the steps up to the house, smoking a cigarette while waiting for them to arrive. He stood as they came near, dressed in khaki shirt and shorts, with a wide canvas bush hat on his head. His usual laconic, sarcastic manner was missing and his long face was solemn.

'Bad business, this. The damn place must be cursed!'

A few paces away stood Siva, the senior servant in the Robertson household and Arnold waved a hand towards him.

'The boy here phoned me less than an hour ago – just before I rang you, Steve,' he said. 'So I came down here bloody quick to see what was up.'

'And what was up, Les?' demanded Blackwell.

'Come and see for yourself – under here, first of all.'

He loped away down the slope which ran around the further side of the bungalow. The house was built up on a number of brick columns which, due to the uneven slope of the ground, were higher on the end further away from the Robertson house. Here the underside of the floor was eight feet off the ground, giving plenty of height for the two cars which were parked underneath.

Towards the back of this undercroft, a sombre sight awaited them. Hanging by the neck from a rope suspended from a beam supporting the floor above, was the body of Douglas Mackay. His feet were just touching the ground, his legs slightly bent at the knees and his head was tilted acutely sideways. Nearby was an overturned wooden crate.

'Siva says this is exactly how he found him,' said Les Arnold. 'Nothing's been touched.'

The grave-faced Indian servant nodded. 'I just went near enough to make sure Mr Mackay was dead, sir. I knew I could do nothing for him, so I phoned to Mr Arnold.'

'How did you know he was here? You live next door.'

'The sweeper found him, sir. He goes around the place every morning to clean up. He ran to tell me.'

Blackwell decided to check on the body before things got even more complicated.

'Tom, let's have a quick look here first.' The three whites advanced on the body, which hung in frozen stillness, its contact with the earthen floor preventing any swinging in the slight breeze.

The pathologist had attended three hangings dealt with by his boss during his year of pathology in the UK and as far as he could see, this one was a classical self-suspension. The thin woven rope had cut deeply into the neck, a slip knot riding high beneath the left ear. The skin above it was purple and the face was red and suffused, with small pinpricks of blood under the skin.

The eyes were half open and he could see more small bleeding points in the whites. Tom used the back of his hand to test the temperature of Mackay's bare forearm. Even given the warmth of the climate it felt cool, and when he gently tried to lift the wrist, there was firm resistance from rigor mortis.

'How long d'you reckon he's been dead?' barked the Australian, heedless of the superintendent's presence.

'God, I'm no forensic expert,' exclaimed Tom. 'And it's hard enough for them at home. Here the climate makes a nonsense of temperature calculations, but he's certainly cooled down a bit.'

'It looked as if he was in rigor mortis when you moved his arm,' said Steven, reclaiming his investigative role from Les Arnold.

Howden nodded. 'He's still very stiff. I've read that rigor comes on and goes off much quicker in hot climates, but he must have been dead for at least some hours. There's no sign of decomposition or of insects laying eggs on his eyelids, so at a wild guess, I think he must have died sometime during the night or early this morning.'

Blackwell gave him a very worried look.

'Anything about it that suggests he didn't do it himself?'

Tom shrugged, reluctant to give too many opinions about things he was not really qualified to pronounce upon.

'He's certainly died from having his neck squeezed by that noose. There's that crate that presumably he stood on to tie the rope around that beam. Then he must have stepped off it!'

'But his feet are still on the ground,' objected the planter.

Tom had read many of the forensic textbooks, partly from a morbid interest and he had an answer to that.

'No problem, the weight of the body leaning into the noose is enough. I've seen pictures of people who have hanged themselves from a door knob.'

'Could anyone else have croaked him and made it look like a suicide?' demanded the irrepressible Aussie.

Tom was getting out of his depth. 'I've no idea, Les. But I've also read that murder by hanging is very rare, unless the victim is drunk, drugged or physically restrained.'

The police officer turned to the servant from next door. 'Now, what's the situation about Mrs Mackay? Where is she?'

'Upstairs in her bedroom,' cut in Arnold, once again. 'I just had a quick look from the doorway. I didn't go in, she was on the floor, obviously dead.'

They began hurrying up the steps to the verandah, Steven Blackwell still questioning the Tamil servant.

'How did you learn about it, Siva?'

'After Mister Mackay was found, they sent to next door for me, as their houseboy is very young chap. I told the *amah* to go wake his wife. She does not get up very early these days. I thought it better that a woman broke the news first. Then the girl came screaming down to tell me what she had found.'

They marched through the open doors from the verandah into the lounge and Nadin led the way into the back corridor, from which the bedrooms opened. At the second door, he stood back to allow the others to look inside. The bare room with its wooden walls and slowly rotating fan had two single beds each with high mosquito nets. The single sheet on the further bed was undisturbed and it had not been slept in, but the one nearer the door was crumpled and the net was thrown up on one side.

'Where is she?' demanded Steven Blackwell, always hesitant to barge into what might turn out to be a crime scene. Back in Manchester, he had dealt with several cases where a husband had hanged himself after killing his wife.

'Between the beds, lying on the floor,' supplied Les Arnold, more subdued now in the presence of a dead woman.

'Tom, have a quick look first, will you,' directed Blackwell. 'I don't want us all trampling over everything until we know what's what.'

The pathologist trod delicately over to the foot of the nearest bed and peered into the space between them. Rosa Mackay was lying sprawled on the planked wooden floor, face up, arms and legs splayed out. She wore thin cotton pyjamas, the jacket stained with vomit, which was also smeared over the floor, as if she had been thrashing about. Her face was contorted and a pinkish froth was issuing from one corner of her mouth.

Tom went nearer and crouched alongside the body. As with her husband a few moments earlier, he touched the skin and tested the rigidity of both an arm and her jaw.

'Still a bit of warmth there,' he reported. 'And she's just starting to get stiff. I reckon she died quite a bit later than her husband, probably not more than a few hours ago.'

'But died of what, Tom?' asked the policeman, in a sepulchral voice.

'I suppose poisoning is the most likely cause, given the circumstances. But I don't know what poison!'

Les Arnold surprised them by giving them the answer.

'Reckon I know what it was. Can't you smell it?'

He gave some exaggerated sniffs as his eyes roamed around the room.

Tom bent nearer the body and followed his example.

'Smells like paraffin – and the vomit's a bit greenish.'

'There you are, then! Got to be paraquat, ain't it?'

Steven Blackwell cut back into the dialogue. 'Paraquat? That's that herbicide, isn't it?'

The Australian nodded. 'Yep, used by the gallon around the estates these days. A couple of years ago, one of my tappers, a young girl, topped herself with it after some broken love affair. That's how I remember the smell, she sicked up this stinking stuff as well. The chemical is dissolved in kerosene for spraying.'

Blackwell was looking around the room and walked over to a chest of drawers on which was what appeared to be an empty Coca-Cola bottle. Without touching it, he looked closely at it and then cautiously sniffed the open top.

'This smells strongly of paraffin. There's still some oily green liquid in the bottom.'

His eyes strayed to the top of the piece of furniture and he gave an exclamation. 'Hah! Is this a suicide note she's left?

Picking up a single sheet of airmail paper by a corner, he quickly scanned the message. It was a suicide note, but not Rosa's. Tom suppressed his natural curiosity, but Arnold had no such inhibitions.

'What's it say, Steve?'

The superintendent had humoured the planter so far, but now began to put on the brakes. 'Look, Les. This is police investigation – might even turn out to be another murder. I have to play it by the book from now on, but I can tell you that this appears to be a suicide note written by Douglas Mackay. I can't say more, I'm afraid.'

Rather surprisingly, Arnold accepted the mild rebuff.

'Sure thing, Steve. I'll leave you and the doc to it. I suppose you'll want some sort of statement from me?'

Blackwell nodded. 'I'll send Inspector Tan up to Batu Merah to see you. Thanks for all your help.'

Just before he left the room, the rangy Australian took a last look at the body lying pathetically between the beds.

'Poor Rosa, she was a nice woman,' he said with rare compassion. 'Reckon she couldn't carry on when she heard that she'd lost Douglas. It's a tough old world, mate!'

When he had vanished, Steven turned to Howden.

'He doesn't know the half of it, Tom! Mackay confesses in this letter to killing Jimmy Robertson – and shooting up the bungalows a few weeks back!'

The pathologist, still crouching alongside Rosa's corpse, looked up in astonishment at the police officer. 'That's extraordinary, Steve! But as you said to Les – should you be telling me this?'

Blackwell turned up his palms in almost Gallic gesture.

'You're part of the team now, Tom, whether you like it or not. You're our expert medical witness, though hopefully this will end at a coroner's inquest, not the High Court.'

His 'expert' felt rather proud at being so valued, but a little overwhelmed at all that had happened to him professionally in the last week or two.

'What are we going to do with the bodies?' he asked. 'Our colonel will go spare if we try to dump a couple more civilians in the BMH mortuary!'

Blackwell's own grapevine had told him that moves were afoot to deal with the commandant of the hospital, but this was no time to stir up more aggravation there.

'I'll check with Alf Morris, but if there's any hassle, I'll get our police van to take them down to Ipoh General Hospital.'

Tom nodded and looked down again at the body of Rosa Mackay.

'There's nothing more I can do here. There needs to be either a post-mortem or at least an analysis of the vomit and blood for paraquat, just to confirm things. I'd better have a quick look at her back, just to make sure she hasn't been shot or stabbed – it would be damned embarrassing to miss them!'

He pulled on one shoulder and the small body of the Eurasian lady lifted easily on its side so that he could see the back. There were no injuries there, but something else was immediately obvious.

'Look at this! Another note, by the looks of it.'

He picked up a pale blue sheet of flimsy Basildon Bond notepaper, similar to the one that Blackwell held in his hand.

'You'd better have this, Steven. It's none of my business.'

Letting the corpse subside to the floor again, he handed the paper up to the policeman. Once again, the superintendent rapidly scanned it to get the general sense of the message. Though not normally given to blasphemy, this was too much for his usually restrained vocabulary

'Jesus H. Christ! Come back all I said just now!'

An hour later, Tom was again sitting in the Admin Office at the front of the hospital. As before, the police superintendent was with them, as he had come to regularize the situation between the civil and military authorities.

'There's two sides to this, Alf,' he began. 'First, we don't have a government pathologist nearer than KL and it would take me a day to get him up from there. So having Tom here on the spot is a godsend, as long as we can use his expertise without your CO blowing his top.'

'He's still down at Kinrara,' replied Morris. 'So you picked a good day for your two deaths.'

'The other aspect is putting your mind at rest about any suspicion hanging over anyone at BMH,' continued Steven seriously, putting his swagger stick on the corner of the desk. 'Let's not beat about the bush, Alf. For a time, several of your officers were in the frame as suspects for Jimmy Robertson's murder. That's why I feel it right to tell you in confidence what we know.'

The RAMC major brushed up his bristly moustache with a slightly nervous gesture. 'If you think it's OK, Steve. I don't want to drop you in the mire for breaching some legal protocol.'

The police officer shook his head. 'I've been on the phone to the coroner and explained the situation. As far as he's concerned, as long as there's no likelihood of anyone being charged with murder, he's prepared to run a combined inquest on all three victims. He's also happy for me to disclose enough information to clear up any lingering suspicions that involve this hospital.'

'Thank God for that! We've already got enough problems here of our own,' murmured Morris, half to himself. 'But I'm still not clear what the hell has happened up at Gunong Besar. It's still hard to believe all that's gone on up there.'

Steven mopped his sweating brow with a large khaki handkerchief.

'If they hadn't left those notes, I wouldn't have known what the hell happened, either! I'd better not show them to you, but the gist of Douglas's letter was that he claimed to have killed James Robertson for seducing his wife, having first shot up the bungalows to lay a smokescreen for his murder plan, by suggesting that both were the work of terrorists.'

Tom Howden had already heard the content of the notes, so it was only Alf who was still in the dark.

'You said "claimed",' pointed out Morris. 'Does that mean he didn't do it?'

'Douglas certainly fired all those rounds at the two bungalows a few weeks ago. He says he also intended killing Jimmy
later, but decided he couldn't go through with it. I suspect his
strong religious conscience got the better of him.'

'But you said his suicide note indicated that he *had* shot
Robertson,' objected the Admin Officer.

'He was lying, for reasons that became clear later. Most of
his note was an explanation of how he had hated Jimmy for
years, after he discovered that he had been having it away
with Rosa for so long. He put none of the blame on her, by
the way. He claimed that the lascivious Jimmy made all the
running.'

'What about the attack on the bungalows? How did he
manage that? I understood that the bullets didn't come from
any of the rifles up at Gunong Besar – nor were they the same
as the one that killed Robertson.'

Blackwell again wiped the sweat from his face. It was time
he went back home to Britain, he thought suddenly. Even after
years in the Far East, he seemed to suffer even more from the
climate as time went by. He jerked his attention back to Alf's
question.

'Mackay said he had a couple of extra rifles hidden away,
in addition to the weapons that he and Jimmy gave us for test
firing. When he came up from Johore some years ago, he
brought them with him. There was a lot of CT trouble down
there then, and guns were easy to come by, especially by
planters intent on defending themselves.'

Tom Howden threw in another question. 'I wonder how he
managed to arrange that mock attack on his own?'

The superintendent shrugged. 'I assume he waited until
Rosa was asleep in bed, unless she was aware of what he was
up to. Then he went out, ran around firing almost at random,
until James appeared, then pretended to join him in hunting
for the non-existent attackers.'

Alf Morris frowned at a few of the words he had just heard.

'Are you suggesting that Rosa might have known what her
husband was up to?'

Steven tapped his tunic pocket where he had the two notes
from the estate bungalow. 'Her note doesn't say so, but I

suspect she knew. It was her note that upset everything that was in the one left by her husband. He must have written his the previous night, after he had decided to hang himself. Rosa then found it in the bedroom long before the *amah* came to wake her up – and then wrote her own note.'

Alf shook his head slowly in disbelief that such things could be going on in Tanah Timah.

'So you reckon she then decided to commit suicide? And it wasn't just because she'd lost her husband?'

Blackwell shook his head sadly. 'No, it was guilt and remorse for murdering James Robertson. She makes no bones about it in her letter, she says that Douglas had been acting very strangely lately and when she tackled him about it, he told her that he had intended to kill Jimmy, but couldn't go through with it.'

'So she knew that her husband was aware that she'd been unfaithful to him with his boss?' put in Tom.

'Sure, she went on about her sins and that although James had pestered her for a long time, it was her fault that she gave in to him. When Douglas confessed that he couldn't go through with it, she decided to finish the job herself. She knew all about Douglas's hidden pair of rifles and took one when he was asleep. That night, she went down the road and flagged down Jimmy when he was coming home from The Dog. He stopped on the road and she shot him when he got out. Then she drove the car back to the club and hurried home on foot.'

'Didn't her husband know?' asked Alf, incredulously.

'Not then, she says but later she broke down and told him what had happened. They agreed to sit tight, but she says that Douglas became more and more guilt-ridden and afraid that my investigation would eventually narrow down to Rosa. To save her, he wrote that false confession in his note, then hanged himself.'

Tom's brow was furrowed with doubt. 'But if she had continued to sit tight, it would be assumed that Douglas's confession was true and the matter would have been cleared up?'

Steven shrugged. 'But she didn't! She says that she herself

had been considering suicide for some time, which was why
she had taken a bottle full of paraquat from the stock in the
estate sheds. When she read Douglas's note, taking the blame
for her murderous action, she wrote her own letter, then drank
the stuff, poor woman!'

The three men sat silently for a while, each thinking what
mayhem had been caused by a randy planter.

Four weeks later, Tom Howden was lying on his stomach on
the warm sand of Batu Ferringhi beach, on the north coast of
Penang Island. Alongside him, Lynette Chambers was dozing
with a straw sun hat over her face and nearby a dozen other
members of both the RAMC and QA Messes were lounging
about, enjoying a leisurely weekend. Penang was a couple of
hours' drive from Tanah Timah, but due to the car ferry from
the mainland, it was easier to reach than Pangkor. An old-
fashioned hotel, The Lone Pine, sat amongst the palm trees
almost on the edge of the beach, and after one of its famous
Sunday curries eaten at tables under the trees, lying down was
obligatory!

Tom stared out at the blue sea under a blue sky, still
bemused that it was not the grey Tyne under rain clouds. He
mulled over all that had happened in the past few weeks, as
now life was returning to normal at BMH. The coroner's
inquest on the three victims from Gunong Besar had been
held in the Police HQ on the previous Wednesday. The lawyer-
coroner from Ipoh played down the drama as much as he
could and rapidly brought in verdicts of murder by Rosa
Mackay on James Robertson and suicide 'while the balance
of their minds was disturbed' on the two Mackays. As to the
suicide notes, he declined to make them public, but stated
that he was satisfied that their contents confirmed the conclu-
sions of the court.

Desmond O'Neill had returned two days after the dramatic
events up at Gunong Besar, but was in a silent, withdrawn
mood and Tom's involvement in the affair was never even
mentioned.

A week later, the CO vanished and belatedly, Alf Morris
was able to inform the Mess that he had been suddenly recalled

to the UK to take up a desk job at the Medical Directorate of the War Office. A new Commanding Officer was on his way out by air and until he arrived, Major Peter Bright was acting as temporary CO.

It was all rather mysterious and those few in the know, who included Morris and the physician John Martin, maintained a discreet silence, though they hinted that as O'Neill was so near the end of his tour and as his wife had refused to stay any longer in the Far East, compassionate grounds were involved. The whole of the hospital took this excuse with a large pinch of salt, but made no complaint about the marked improvement in the atmosphere that resulted. The business about the arms kote was also swept under the carpet, with vague murmurings from Alf Morris that O'Neill had been obsessed with security at the hospital.

Peter Bright was very relaxed in his new role as CO, and he used his new authority to award himself plenty of free time, shooting off to Penang in his sports car at frequent intervals. Undoubtedly, he was visiting the fair Diane in the Eastern and Oriental Hotel, Penang's equivalent of Singapore's Raffles. The efficient gossip system reported that she had passed up her intended passage on the first UK-bound ship, as she suddenly found the attractions of Penang much to her liking.

Similarly, David Meredith, the gloomy Welsh anaesthetist, was seen to smile on several occasions, obviously having been reconciled with his own lady love, Lena Franklin.

As to Gunong Besar itself, Les Arnold announced that Diane Robertson had accepted an offer he had made to buy the estate. He magnanimously offered to supervise the rubber production there until probate and other legal matters allowed him to move in. All in all, things had worked out well in the end, albeit after three tragic deaths, for which Tom suspected that James Robertson would have had some tough questions to answer from Saint Peter when he arrived at the Pearly Gates.

He rolled over on to his stomach and smiled happily at Lynette, whose pleasant face was only a few inches from his own. He had the feeling that even after only two months in

Malaya, his life had taken a turn that would last for the rest of his life.

Risking the eagle eye of the Matron, who sat in a deckchair twenty yards away, Captain Howden RAMC craned his neck towards Lieutenant Chambers, QARANC and gave her a quick peck on the cheek.